"Time travel, ancient legends, and seductive romance are seamlessly interwoven into one captivating package."
—*Publishers Weekly* on Midnight's Master

"Dark, sexy, magical. When I want to indulge in a sizzling fantasy adventure, I read Donna Grant."
—Allison Brennan, *New York Times* bestseller

**5 Stars! Top Pick!** "An absolute must read! From beginning to end, it's an incredible ride."
—*Night Owl Reviews*

"It's good vs. evil Druid in the next installment of Grant's Dark Warrior series. The stakes get higher as discerning one's true loyalties become harder. Grant's compelling characters and continued presence of previous protagonists are key reasons why these books are so gripping. Another exciting and thrilling chapter!"
—*RT Book Reviews* on Midnight's Lover

"Donna Grant has given the paranormal genre a burst of fresh air..."
—*San Francisco Book Review*

DON'T MISS THESE OTHER
SPELLBINDING NOVELS BY NYT & USA
TODAY BESTSELLING AUTHOR DONNA
GRANT

Contemporary Paranormal

## THE SKYE DRUIDS

(Spin off series from the *Reaper* series, as well as the *Dark Kings*, *Dragon Kings*, *Dark Warriors*, and *Dark Sword*)

Iron Ember

Shoulder the Sky

\* \* \*

## DRAGON KINGS

(Spin off series from *Dark Kings*)

Dragon Revealed (novella)

Dragon Mine

Dragon Unbound (novella)

Dragon Eternal

Dragon Lover (novella)

\* \* \*

## REAPER SERIES

Dark Alpha's Claim

Dark Alpha's Embrace

Dark Alpha's Demand

Dark Alpha's Lover

Tall Dark Deadly Alpha Bundle

Dark Alpha's Night

Dark Alpha's Awakening

Dark Alpha's Redemption

Dark Alpha's Temptation

Dark Alpha's Caress

Dark Alpha's Obsession

Dark Alpha's Need

Dark Alpha's Silent Night

Dark Alpha's Passion

Dark Alpha's Command

Dark Alpha's Fury

\* \* \*

**DARK KINGS**

Dark Heat (3 novella compilation)

Darkest Flame

Fire Rising

Burning Desire

Hot Blooded

Night's Blaze

\* \* \*

## DARK WARRIORS

Midnight's Master

Midnight's Lover

Midnight's Seduction

Midnight's Warrior

Midnight's Kiss

Midnight's Captive

Midnight's Temptation

Midnight's Promise

Midnight's Surrender (novella)

A Warrior for Christmas

Dark Warrior Box Set

\* \* \*

## CHIASSON SERIES

Wild Fever

Wild Dream

Wild Need

Wild Flame

Wild Rapture

\* \* \*

## LARUE SERIES

Moon Kissed

Moon Thrall

Moon Struck

Moon Bound

\* \* \*

Forbidden Highlander

Wicked Highlander

Untamed Highlander

Shadow Highlander

Darkest Highlander

Dark Sword Box Set

\* \* \*

## ROGUES OF SCOTLAND

The Craving

The Hunger

The Tempted

The Seduced

Rogues of Scotland Box Set

\* \* \*

## THE SHIELDS

A Dark Guardian

A Kind of Magic

A Dark Seduction

A Forbidden Temptation

A Warrior's Heart

Mystic Trinity (connected)

\* \* \*

## DRUIDS GLEN

Highland Mist

Highland Nights

Highland Dawn

Highland Fires

Highland Magic

Mystic Trinity (connected)

## SISTERS OF MAGIC

Shadow Magic

Echoes of Magic

Dangerous Magic

Sisters of Magic Boxed Set

## THE ROYAL CHRONICLES NOVELLA SERIES

Prince of Desire

Prince of Seduction

Prince of Love

Prince of Passion

Royal Chronicles Box Set

Mystic Trinity (connected)

* * *

Savage Moon

\* \* \*

**Dark Beginnings: A First in Series Boxset**

Contains:

Chiasson Series, Book 1: Wild Fever

LaRue Series, Book 1: Moon Kissed

The Royal Chronicles Series, Book 1: Prince of Desire

\* \* \*

# HIGHLAND NIGHTS

## A DRUIDS GLEN NOVEL

DONNA GRANT

This is a work of fiction. All of the characters, organizations, and events portrayed in this novel are either products of the author's imagination or are used fictitiously.

**HIGHLAND NIGHTS**
**© 2017 by DL Grant, LLC**
Cover Design © 2019 by Charity Hendry

**ISBN 13: 978-1-942017-27-1**
**Available in ebook and print editions**

**www.DonnaGrant.com**
**www.MotherofDragonsBooks.com**

# ACKNOWLEDGMENTS

There's no way I could do any of this without my amazing kiddos–Gillian and Connor–thanks for putting up with my hectic schedule and for knowing when it was time that I got out of the house for a spell. And special nod to the Grant pets–Sheba, Sassy, Diego, and Sisko–who love to walk on the keyboard or demand some loving regardless of what I'm doing.

Last but not least, my readers. You have my eternal gratitude for the amazing support you show me and my books. Y'all rock my world. Enjoy!

xoxox
DG

*In a time of conquering*
*There will be three*
*Who will end the MacNeil line*
*Three born of the*
*Imbolc, Beltaine, and Lughnasad Feasts*
*Who will destroy all at the*
*Samhain, the feast of the dead*

# PROLOGUE

*Sinclair Castle, Highlands*
*February 3, 1607*

"Hurry," Fiona urged her older sister, Moira.

Moira stopped and turned so fast the candle flame narrowly missed Fiona's face. "If you don't hush, I'm going to return to our chamber and leave you alone."

"All right. I promise to be quiet, but please hurry. I want to see her again."

"Her" was the newest addition to their family, a baby girl Fiona had only seen for a brief time. Now she wanted to be able to sit and stare at the tiny, beautiful babe for as long as she wanted. She wouldn't disturb her parents, for she would be quiet as a mouse.

It hadn't taken long to talk Moira into walking with her, either. She would have gone by herself, but she didn't like venturing into the dark hallways where things might jump out at her. Not that they ever had, but one never knew.

Moira stopped again and held up her hand. Fiona

brushed past her. Moira was forever acting like she knew everything, but Fiona didn't have time to find out what she was up to now. She had a baby to see.

"Fiona, stop," Moira whispered loudly.

She sighed, hoping Moira would realize she didn't want to play now. "What is it?"

"I heard something," Moira mumbled and raised the candle above her head so it would cast more glow in the hallway.

Fiona waited for her to say more, but as she turned to continue to their parent's chamber, she heard it also. The clanging of swords.

"Something is happening," Moira shouted as she grabbed Fiona's arm. "Come. We must see to our cousins."

"What about our sister?"

"Da will take care of her and Mother. Come," Moira ordered and ran back to their chamber.

Fiona quickly followed, her bare feet making nary a sound as they ran. But as they neared their chamber they heard the screams of their cousins. And the sound of men laughing.

There was no doubt in her young mind that her cousins would not live through the night. She didn't see Moira stop and hide in the shadows as she began to run to their chamber in hopes of helping her cousins, until Moira jerked her back against the wall.

"We must get to safety," Moira whispered urgently.

"We can't just leave them."

"Remember what Da said," Moira said urgently. "We must get to the woods. Now."

Fiona couldn't understand why soldiers would want to

hurt their cousins, but she didn't think on it as Moira dragged her away. Not obeying their father wasn't an option. She kept pace with her sister as they found the secret door that would lead them through the castle undetected.

Even in the passage they could hear the battle that raged in the bailey and great hall. The terrified screams reached them. When Fiona covered her ears with her hands and stopped, Moira got her moving again with a gentle yank. They didn't stop again until they reached the door that led outside the castle walls. To a place no one would find them.

Slowly, Moira opened the door and peeked out. After a few moments, she motioned to Fiona, and they quickly ran to the hiding spot their da had shown them in case something like this ever happened.

They reached the spot, but all Fiona could think of was their tiny sister. "We left her," she wailed to her older sibling.

"Nay," Moira shook her head. "I'm going back to get her."

But as she turned to leave, a shadow fell over them. They gasped and looked up to find Cormag MacDougal, their father's longtime friend and confidant.

"'Tis glad I am that I found the two of ye," he said and stuck his sword in the ground to wipe the blood off. "We must go. There's no time to waste."

"Nay," Fiona and Moira said in unison.

"I must get the babe," Moira stated. "Watch Fiona until I return," she said and slipped past Cormag.

Fiona tried to run after her older sister, but Cormag's

strong arms came around her. "Nay, lass. We'll wait for yer sister."

She buried her face in his neck and cried as they waited for Moira. The time passed when Moira should have returned.

"We must go," he said, his anxiety clear, even to a child of Fiona's age.

Then, out of the clearing, came a man Fiona had seen only once before. He was Frang, a man her parents had talked with frequently and respected mightily.

"You cannot wait," Frang said, his voice low as he glanced around them. His gaze turned to Cormag. "Take Fiona. You know what to do."

Without another word, Cormag turned and hurried to his horse. "Nay," Fiona yelled and thrashed against Cormag's barrel chest. She couldn't believe her sister had left her.

"Shh, child," Cormag said.

She ignored him and continued to struggle in his arms. To her relief, she managed to get free. She dashed toward the castle when Frang stepped in her path. He knelt down, and she ran into his arms.

"Please," she begged as he held her tight.

He put his hands on her head and said words too hushed for her to hear, but she found herself becoming sleepy. Then, Cormag pulled her into his arms and mounted his horse. He settled her against him, and Fiona found it difficult to keep her eyes open.

She gave up the struggle and shut her eyes, but she didn't sleep.

"Hurry," Frang said. "Time is running out."

"How did this happen?"

"I don't know, but the children must be kept safe. I will find Moira."

"What about Duncan and Catriona?"

A loud sigh. "They're gone. He's taken the baby."

"Saint Anthony," Cormag cursed. "You know where to find me. I will keep Fiona safe and raise her as my own."

No more words were spoken as Cormag nudged his horse. Tears coursed down Fiona's face. She had just gotten her little sister and now she was gone. Someone had taken her and killed her parents, but how was that possible?

And why hadn't Moira returned like she promised? How could Moira have forgotten about her?

## 1

*MacDougal Castle, Northwest Highlands*
*June 1625*

"Y ou must be a fool, then. 'Tis the only explanation I can come up with."

Fiona ignored Bridget, and tried not to roll her eyes as they walked amid the men of clan MacDougal. Bridget constantly fell over any man who would glance at her, and she didn't understand why Fiona didn't do the same.

But there were lots of things Bridget didn't understand.

"Besides," Bridget continued, "you aren't getting any younger. How many more men are you going to refuse?"

The day had begun gloomily, and it seemed Fiona's mood would follow the sun and stay behind the clouds. She turned and looked at Bridget. She was rather pretty with dark auburn hair and eyes the shade of amber, but the lads didn't pay her much attention.

It could be because she made a complete fool of herself anytime a man was near. It was on the tip of Fiona's tongue to tell Bridget just that, but why should she take her irritation out on Bridget? Instead, Fiona shrugged and continued her walk through the crowded bailey.

"I haven't found a man to my liking," she lied. No need to explain the true reason.

"Well, 'tis a good thing Uncle Cormag dotes on you like he does. My mother says he and Aunt Helen should have insisted you find a husband some time ago. It shouldn't matter that you aren't their real daughter," Bridget stated before waving and shouting to a lad who had smiled at her the previous week. "It must be because you are the only child they've ever known," she said over her shoulder.

The lad ducked his head and quickly walked out of sight. Fiona didn't think she could stand another "you should be married" lecture. It was the same thing every day, and she didn't know why she put herself through it. But she wasn't going to sit by and get another earful.

She turned to retrace her steps back to the castle, but was caught by a swarm of children that ran in front of her. It was just enough time for Bridget to catch her.

"If only you would try a little harder you might find someone that would accept you, despite your old age and that wicked tongue of yours."

"Bridget," Fiona began before her eyes landed on a newcomer that had ridden through the castle gates.

In all her years watching the men of her clan, she had never seen one sit so comfortably on a horse, and with such control. He pulled up slightly on the reins and the horse instantly halted.

He looked casually around the bailey until his eyes roamed her way. Her breath caught in her chest, and the disappointment that filled her because he hadn't noticed her disturbed her more than Bridget and her lectures. Then his gaze jerked back to her and she stood rooted to the spot.

For a second, he stared at her before continuing his perusal of the bailey and its occupants. She had the odd sense he was looking for something, or someone, but also studying the people.

Seemingly satisfied, the man clicked to his horse and rode toward the castle. He didn't wear a kilt so she didn't know of which clan he held from, but she would wager her finest gown he was a Highlander, kilt or no.

With Bridget still on her tirade, Fiona left her and followed the man. He intrigued her, and she certainly wanted to meet a man who could quiet the bailey so quickly with his mere presence. Even the guards were craning their necks to get a better look at the man who emanated such power.

Her pace quickened when the stranger stopped his horse before the castle steps and her foster father emerged from the castle. She reached the steps as the stranger and her father clasped forearms.

Their words were spoken in a hushed tone and she couldn't make any of them out. She was about to walk closer when her foster mother put a hand on her arm.

"Nay, child. Let them have a moment," she said quietly, and almost dejectedly. Her usually bright gray eyes held such sadness that it surprised Fiona.

Helen and Cormag had raised her as their own, and as far as they knew she remembered nothing of the night her parents were killed and Moira had abandoned her.

And she hadn't told them differently.

"Come into the hall," Cormag said loud enough to reach her ears. Fiona turned toward him, and his usually jovial face was lined with worry.

Her eyes moved to the stranger who had caused such distress to her foster parents and stared dumbfounded at the man before her. Her mouth almost dropped open. She had never seen anyone so handsome.

His blonde hair hung loose and wavy to just past his shoulders except for two braids that ran from his temples to meet in the back. Blonde brows ran straight above eyes as black as a raven's wing. His jaw was hidden by a shadow of a beard, but Fiona could see his wide, full mouth through the mustache.

She wasn't usually partial to facial hair, although most men sported it, but on this stranger it was devastating. It might also be his leather–encased legs that bulged with muscles. The leather jerkin and tunic he wore allowed her to see his broad shoulders and arms bursting with muscle and power from years of training.

He raised a blonde brow at her inspection and held the door for her to enter. Fiona let her eyes pass once more over him and noted the sword slung across his back and the hilt of a dagger out of the top of his boots.

"Sit, Fiona," Cormag said. Her foster father had never spoken to her so gruffly before, and she hurried to take a seat at the table in the main hall.

Whoever the stranger was, he had caused Cormag's iron calm to crack, and in Fiona's world that was enough to put her on edge.

To her relief, Helen sat beside her, but it was the

absence of any servants that alerted her that something was about to happen that she probably wouldn't like.

"Fiona," Cormag started after he cleared his throat. "This is Gregor. He's come to take you to your rightful place."

Her stomach plummeted to her feet. "What?"

"We should have told you long ago," Helen said as the tears rolled freely down her face.

Cormag raised sad brown eyes to her. "Fiona, we aren't your parents."

Is that all that was the matter? "I know. I have always known."

"You have?" Helen and Cormag asked in unison.

Helen's brows furrowed. "You never said anything."

"I know," Fiona said. "You made such an effort to make it seem like I was your child, and I didn't wish to talk about what happened, so I kept silent."

"Oh, you poor child," Helen cried and buried her face in her hands.

"Regardless," Fiona continued and looked Gregor straight in the eyes, "I'm not going anywhere. I'm happy here, and I want to stay."

To her amazement, Gregor didn't say a word. Instead, he looked to Cormag who seemed to be stunned by her words.

"Fiona, lass, I know we have indulged you. Since we were not blessed with children of our own, we thought of you as our child."

"I know that," she told him. "And for that I will be eternally grateful. I don't know what would have happened to me that night had you not come along."

"You were so young," Helen murmured. "We never expected you to remember that night. I was afraid of the pain it would cause you to speak of it."

Fiona reached for Helen's hand. "Don't worry about it. I've been very happy here. So, I'm not leaving."

"You were always a good child. We never had any problems with you. I'm surprised you are giving us one now." Cormag stopped and ran a hand down his face. "Still, you must go with Gregor."

"Nay," she stated softly and gained her feet.

Gregor leaned back and crossed his arms over his chest. He hadn't known what he had expected when he had finally reached the MacDougal's gate, but it wasn't this feisty brunette with blazing green eyes. She had first caught his gaze as he surveyed the bailey. Caught and held it.

It had been the green gown she wore. He'd always been partial to green, and he had wanted a closer look at her. He had gotten it when she had practically run to the castle steps. Her dark hair hung down to the middle of her back in a thick braid, but it had been her woodland green eyes that held him captive.

When he had finally torn his gaze from her eyes, he found a pert little nose, stubborn chin, and lush pink lips. His eyes had also noted her abundant curves that her gown accentuated perfectly. He had never cared for skinny women. He liked his women to have curves, and this one certainly did.

Now, as he sat and watched the flurry of emotions that crossed her face at the news that she had to leave with him, he imagined she would be quite the temptress for any man. Of course, judging by her age, she was most likely married, and he refused to think about the disappointment that caused.

"Aye, you will," Cormag ordered. "You don't have a choice, lass. I'm ordering you to go with Gregor. It was the promise I made when I took you."

The fire that sparked in her green eyes almost brought a smile to Gregor's lips. The MacDougal's might have coddled her, but that spirit was inbred in her, just as it was in her sisters.

"And just where is he," she said with the slightest glance toward Gregor, "supposed to take me? Back to my home?"

Gregor sat up and spoke to her for the first time. "To MacInnes Castle."

"Why?" she asked Cormag, ignoring Gregor all together. "I won't marry this laird Gregor is taking me to, whoever he is. I told you I don't want to marry. I've no need of a man."

Cormag coughed and gave Gregor an embarrassed look. Gregor cocked his head to the side. "That might be hard considering Laird Conall has recently married."

"Oh," she said softly and slowly sank into her chair. "Tell me why I must leave," she begged Helen.

Helen glanced at her husband. "We knew this day would come. I've been preparing you for it."

"Lass, 'tis your destiny," Cormag said, his eyes mysteriously misty. "You have to go."

Gregor felt as though he had intruded on a private family discussion and wished he could leave, but Cormag had stated he wanted him there. One did not simply disobey a powerful laird like Cormag, but Gregor did things his own way.

"I will leave you three alone to talk," he said and began to rise to his feet, but Cormag placed a hand on his shoulder.

"You need to be here," he told Gregor. "I think it best that you leave with Fiona immediately. The threat has been growing. I've no wish to chance an encounter."

"Are you so eager to be rid of me?" Fiona asked, her voice trembling with rage and fear.

Gregor wanted to explain the need for them to hasten away, but she wasn't his foster daughter. That job fell to Helen and Cormag. But what would one more night matter? He had ridden fast and hard to get here, back–tracked to make sure he wasn't being followed, and ridden in several different routes to confuse anyone to his destination. Although he didn't need the rest, he would stay one night for Fiona's sake.

By the saints, he would have to do something about this sudden generosity that had sprung into his life. He had been just fine until Conall had offered him friendship, and Glenna had reminded him of his dead sister.

By this time, Fiona was arguing with Helen and Cormag, and Gregor knew it was time to step in. "We will leave at dawn. You have today and the night to ready yourself," he told Fiona and quickly walked outside to see to his horse.

He had to leave the castle and breathe some fresh air to clear his head. Who knew what he would end up saying if he stayed another moment. He scratched the whiskers on his face. He needed a bath and a shave.

He found his horse right where he had left her. Morgane, a white mare he had found as a filly and trained himself, had originally been a present for his sister, but after her death he had kept the mare.

With a soft whistle he called to Morgane. She trotted to him and followed him into the barn. He found an empty stall toward the back and unsaddled her. After feeding her grain, he gave her a good rubdown.

He thought of Conall and Glenna and their newfound love. Gregor had learned more about the Druids, the Fae, and even himself than he ever thought possible while at MacInnes Castle and the Druid's Glen.

Who would have guessed he would have found himself in a position to choose between good and evil, and that he would actually have chosen the side of right. He had been gone from MacInnes Castle for a fortnight, and already he missed the magic that surrounded it. And, if he were truthful with himself, he would admit to yearning to have a family of his own after being around Conall and Glenna.

Maybe he would even venture toward his home again. Maybe his family would welcome him, and maybe his father would forgive him.

"Who am I kidding? I'm still a monster, and choosing the side of good one time doesn't change what I am," he said as he leaned his head against Morgane's neck. "I'm just what my father said I was. Wicked to the core."

## 2

Gregor wondered what his host would think if he stuffed a gag into his niece's mouth. The lass hadn't stopped talking from the moment he had sat down beside her, and by the little grin on Fiona's face he knew she was responsible for his placement.

He suppressed a groan when Bridget's hand touched his arm and she let out a shrill giggle.

"Oh," she cried. "You have such big arms. I bet you are really strong."

*Apparently very strong. I'm not wringing your neck.*

"I have never seen anyone so handsome before. What does a woman need to do to get your attention?"

*You mean besides keeping her mouth shut?*

Another giggle. "Fiona is watching us, but you don't need to worry about her. Many men have asked for her hand, but she has refused them all. Obviously there is something wrong with her," she said in a whisper.

Gregor glanced at the ceiling. *Someone save me.*

"I have often wondered about Fiona. She keeps to herself."

*I wish you would do the same.*

"Where are you taking her? No one will tell me. I bet 'tis a convent, 'tis it not?"

*Maybe that is where you should go to take a vow of silence.*

Keeping his mouth shut had been the wrong thing to do.

"It is," she said, her eyes huge. "I think 'tis for the best. She is becoming an embarrassment to the MacDougal's. I cannot imagine someone her age not marrying. 'Tis not normal."

*What's not normal is the rate at which your mouth moves. Don't you ever shut up?*

Bridget was about to launch into another round of talking when Cormag interrupted her.

"Enough, Bridget. I think you have talked Gregor's ears off."

"But, Uncle, he's so interesting," she exclaimed and fluttered her lashes at him.

"Do you have something in your eyes, Bridget?" Fiona asked, a very innocent expression on her face.

Gregor coughed to hide his laughter and turned his face from Bridget.

"Of course not," Bridget answered. "Maybe if you actually talked to men you might find someone that interested you."

"Enough," Cormag said a little louder. "Off to your chamber, Bridget. We must talk."

"I will talk to you later," Bridget whispered in Gregor's ear as she rose from her seat.

He couldn't hide his sigh as Bridget left. Her not so obvious attempt to gain his attention annoyed him like nothing else could. Finally, he would be able to eat in peace. His gaze found Fiona and instead of the smirk he thought she would be wearing, she looked thoughtful and a wee worried.

And it wasn't until he looked toward Cormag and Helen that he understood. Helen had barely touched her food, and Cormag only moved his around the trencher.

Cormag sat his goblet down slowly. "Bridget has been with us for almost a year now. My sister and her husband had hoped she might find a marriage here."

Gregor nodded, but knew Cormag didn't really wish to discuss Bridget. He was putting off the task of speaking to Fiona as long as he could.

For several long moments the hall remained quiet. Gregor's ears still rang from Bridget's constant babbling, but his eyes roamed over the table's occupants.

"Fiona, what do you remember of the night your parents died?" Cormag finally asked.

Her green eyes lowered. "Moira and I left the castle and hid where Da had shown us. Moira went back for our baby sister. You came and we waited for her to return, but she never did."

"You never asked about either of your sisters," Helen said.

But Fiona went on as if she hadn't heard her. "Moira never returned, and you took me away."

"Is that all you remember?" Cormag asked expectantly.

"I recall Frang telling you to take me."

"And when he did, I promised him I would keep you safe and return you when the time came."

Gregor sat back, intrigued by the story. He had heard Glenna's side, but he had never imagined anything like this.

"That time has come," Helen said, her voice barely above a whisper. "I have taught you everything I know of the Druid's and the prophecy. You will be ready."

"So she knows," said Gregor before he thought about it.

Fiona's green eyes blazed with fury. "I know I'm a Druid. I know I have a role in the prophecy. Why would they keep it from me?"

He shrugged and crossed his arms over his chest.

"What will I be ready for?" she asked Helen.

"MacNeil," Cormag nearly spat the name. "He's the man who killed your parents. He's part of the prophecy."

Gregor had to give Fiona credit. She was holding up well under the circumstances, and he was very thankful she hadn't burst into tears or thrown a tantrum.

"MacNeil," she repeated, her eyes on the table. "He took my baby sister. I recall Frang telling you that. The prophecy doesn't say anything about my parents. Why kill them?"

Gregor waited for Helen or Cormag to answer her, but they were busy comforting each other. "MacNeil came to kill you and your sisters that night."

"He succeeded in killing one of us." Her green eyes rose to meet his.

Her distress was palpable.

"Actually, he didn't. The two girls that slept in your chamber were killed, and he thought they were you and Moira. He has only recently discovered the truth."

"Are you telling me my baby sister survived?" she asked, her voice now raised a pitch higher.

"Aye."

Her chest rose and fell rapidly as his reply sank in. "And where has she been all this time?"

Gregor leaned forward to put his elbows on the table as he studied her more closely. He hated to tell her the next part. "With MacNeil."

"By the saints," Cormag hissed as Helen cried harder.

Fiona's hands shook as she reached for her goblet and Gregor couldn't blame her. If Helen and Cormag had told her half the evil that resided in MacNeil, then she had every right to be worried.

"Her name," she said after she drank from the goblet. "What is it?"

Gregor's eyes jerked to Fiona's. "Glenna. Her name is Glenna."

"She married the man who is laird of the castle you want to take me to?"

"Aye." He didn't question how she knew. She was a Druid after all.

She started plucking at her gown, her eyes lowered. "Is... is she... happy?"

"Very."

Slowly her eyes rose to his. "Not a day has passed that I hadn't thought of her and what happened. I have always assumed she suffered the same fate as our parents."

"I cannot believe you didn't know," he said. "Didn't Moira tell you?"

She stood and glared down at him, her entire body shaking with pent up rage. "Don't say that name in my presence again."

He stood and faced her. "That is going to be rather difficult since 'twas she who sent me to retrieve you."

"What?" Her eyes swiveled to Cormag. "How did she know where I was?"

Cormag continued to hold Helen. "They have always known. We corresponded many times over the years."

The anger went right out of her at hearing this. She blinked hastily as she slowly nodded her head. After a few moments, she turned and walked from the hall.

Gregor watched her depart. Cormag's statement had affected her greatly, and he could only guess how he would feel knowing an older sibling had known where he was at all times, but had never visited. It must be a fatal blow to one's heart.

Could that be why Fiona held such hatred for Moira?

\* \* \*

Fiona walked into her chamber and could only stare at the walls that had been hers for a score of years. While most women yearned to leave their homes and make one of their own, she had gloried in the safety of the MacDougal's love. She had known they couldn't leave her because they ruled the clan.

Her gaze drifted to the floral tapestry that hung on the wall beside her bed. She and Helen had made that tapestry together, and she found she had a knack for it. She walked to the chair and table before the hearth. She often sat here and thought back to how her life might have been had her parents not been murdered. Her mind had also thought many times of her infant sister and what had become of her. Had she the same fate as their parents, or had she survived somehow?

At least now she knew.

With a sigh, she turned toward the bed. Blood red drapes hung around the bed. She loved everything about this chamber and wished with all her heart she didn't have to leave. Tears stung the back of her eyes, but she didn't hold them back any longer.

Cormag had made it clear she had to leave with Gregor, even if he had to tie her to a horse. Helen had tried to tell her about it being her destiny, but Fiona had shut her out, refusing to listen.

All those years she had thought she was safe, that her foster parents could not desert her, but what she had not thought about was them making her leave.

For years, she fooled herself into thinking her fear of abandonment had lessened, but she had discovered today that that wasn't the case. The fear of the unknown scared her, but worse than that was the prospect that she might come across Moira.

They had told her to pack, but she didn't think Gregor would find anything humorous in discovering she had taken her entire chamber with her. She would settle for a few gowns and the tapestry, but she didn't want to think about that right now. There was too much pain inside her to do anything other than fret.

She pushed aside the drapes and climbed onto bed. 'Twas her last night here, and she wouldn't ruin it with hurtful words to the people who had raised her as their own. Because of her love for them she would obey, but she would return. No tears, she thought as the sound of a heartrending melody from bagpipes reached her.

*No tears.*

Yet a steady stream of wetness trailed down her checks and neck.

* * *

"Are you sure you know where Gregor is headed?"

The Shadow growled and turned toward MacNeil. "Of course. I haven't led you wrong."

"With every trail of Gregor's that we pick up it leads to a dead end. I would say you have led us wrong plenty of times."

The Shadow laughed. "Oh, you have much to learn. I knew what Gregor was doing. I simply followed to make him think he had fooled us."

"Hmm," MacNeil said and rubbed his whiskered chin. "Why didn't you confide this to me?"

"There wasn't a need. Not until I found out his true destination."

"And how did you accomplish that after all these weeks?"

The Shadow laughed again. "He slept. I simply visited his dreams."

"How do I know you aren't lying again?"

"I would never lie to you," The Shadow said, not bothering to hide the sarcasm from his voice.

MacNeil jerked hard on his horse's reins, the bit tearing into the delicate tissue of the horse's mouth. "You tried to kill Glenna when you knew I still had need of her. You promised you wouldn't harm her."

"This isn't about Glenna, and you had best realize that. If you want to survive the prophecy, one of them must die," he lied easily. MacNeil would never survive the prophecy.

It had been laughable at how effortless it was to lead MacNeil toward a lie. The Shadow's hands itched to wring MacNeil's incompetent, skinny neck. Too bad he had need of the idiot to fulfill his destiny.

"If you had killed the girls when you killed the parents this wouldn't be an issue," he continued to bait MacNeil.

*And my plans to release the magic and rule Scotland wouldn't be in jeopardy.*

MacNeil again jerked on the reins sending his horse rearing and pawing the air with his front hooves. "You say 'tis my fault Conall's castle didn't fall, but you failed to kill Glenna. Not to mention the countless times you have been able to slay Moira, but haven't. Now, we are traipsing all over Scotland to kill the other one."

In a blur of speed, the Shadow flew over his horse and pinned MacNeil to the ground with a hand around his neck. MacNeil's eyes bulged as he clawed at the hand around his throat.

"Don't tempt me," The Shadow sneered as he released his hold. "Your men's courage hangs by a thread. I could easily take control."

MacNeil shoved him off. "You need me. If I die, so do

you." He rose and dusted himself off. "And as much as you might be tempted to kill me, you won't."

"Don't be so sure," The Shadow hissed and pushed aside his long black cloak to mount his horse. "You think you know much, MacNeil, but you know less than nothing. Now, hurry! I want to be at MacDougal's castle at dawn."

## 3

G regor stood in the middle of the chamber, leaned his head to the side and cracked his neck. He had finally risen before the sun peaked over the horizon, and he wasn't in the best of moods.

Once again sleep had not claimed him and all because the music of the bagpipes had lured him out of the castle last eve and evoked memories of his clan. He walked from the castle toward the barn to see Morgane. The mare always calmed him. With his thoughts in turmoil of his family and the heavy burden of returning Fiona to the Druid's Glen, he needed a moment's peace.

While he spoke to the mare, he pictured Fiona's green eyes flashing in anger. The journey back to Conall's wouldn't be easy, and if Fiona was anything like Glenna— and from what he had seen she was—then he would have his hands full.

The quietness of the bailey settled around him like a thick mist as he led Morgane from the barn. It had been the same stillness when he had been banished from his clan, and that memory was like a stone in the pit of his stomach.

He raised his eyes and scanned the many faces of the people gathered in the bailey. They had come to bid farewell to Fiona, and their devotion was evident by their numbers and sad eyes.

"Take care of her."

Gregor turned to find Cormag beside him. "I will. Moira will have my head if anything happens to her."

"Aye. You must be very capable for Moira to send you."

Gregor didn't bother to tell Cormag he had been the only one available. Instead, he nodded and waited for Helen and Fiona to reach him.

Fiona didn't spare him a glance as she stood before her foster parents. Cormag opened his arms and she rushed into them. "Take care of yourself, lass. You'll always be welcome here."

"Don't make me go," she begged once more.

"You must. You will be back to visit before you know it," he added with a smile as he pulled her out of his arms.

She turned to Helen and the older woman broke into tears as they shared a hug. "Open your heart and glory in this, Fiona," she said and wiped the tears from her face. "Remember, you are blessed with powers for a reason."

Without another word, Fiona mounted her horse and silently waited for him. Gregor nodded to Helen and Cormag before he, too, mounted. They had just turned their horses toward the gate when a high–pitched shriek reached his ears.

"Goodbye," Bridget waved from the castle doors. "I look forward to seeing you again, Gregor."

*Not if I can help it.*

Fiona laughed deep in her throat. "I think you have found yourself an admirer."

Gregor tapped Morgane with his heels and trotted ahead of Fiona. "I would rather eat dirt."

This time her laugh washed over him like warm sunshine on a cold winter's day. Frankly, he didn't like that feeling. It only reinforced his fear that he was beginning to care again.

And that couldn't happen.

He settled himself into the saddle and concentrated on the long road ahead of them. The one thing he refused to think about was the fact they were very near to his family's land. It was too painful and brought up long buried memories he was better off forgetting.

He glanced over his shoulder and saw that Fiona lagged behind. Then that eerie sense he had when something was about to happen assaulted him. And he knew.

Despite his attempts to dissuade any followers to his destination, MacNeil had found them. The journey to the Druid's Glen might very well claim their lives.

"We must get to Conall's home soon," he said and tried to make his voice as casual as possible. "We mustn't dawdle."

"Dawdle?" she spat. "Excuse me if I'm dawdling, but I am leaving my home that I may never see again. I think you could show me a little more compassion. Look," she said as she stopped her mare. "Isn't it a beautiful place?" she asked and looked back at the place that had been her home.

Gregor squeezed his eyes closed and pulled up on the reins. Morgane came to a halt and tossed her head in agitation. The mare felt his urgency and didn't understand why they had stopped. He waited until Fiona was even with him before he reached over and grasped her reins.

"I'm sorry you were made to leave the MacDougal's. I can understand what you are feeling, but your sisters need you."

She snorted very unladylike. "I don't believe that for a moment. Moira has never needed anyone but herself. If she could do this herself she would."

The loathing that laced her words surprised him, but it wasn't the time to ask about Moira. Instead he patted her mare's neck. "I do understand."

Her green eyes swiveled to his. "Really? Why is it that I don't believe you? How could you possibly know what it feels like to have your family make you leave your home?" she asked and nudged her horse forward.

"You'd be surprised," he said under his breath. It was going to be a very, *very* long journey. He didn't fault her for being testy. Hell, he would do a lot more if someone were making him leave his home.

He caught up with her as they reached a fork in the road. Without hesitation, he veered left toward the mountains. He smothered a chuckle when he heard her sigh and just knew she had rolled her eyes as well.

"What are you doing?" she asked. "Cormag told me Laird Conall's home was to the east. Wouldn't it be easier to take the road to the right and venture through MacAllister and MacLachlan land?"

"Nay."

"Nay?" she repeated. "Is that the only answer you are going to give me?"

He blew air out of his mouth as she neared. They hadn't been gone but a short while, and already he wanted to pull his hair out. "That's the only answer you'll be getting," he said over his shoulder.

"Well, I demand more. You are taking us into the mountains, the long way around, and I think I should be given a reason. Especially after informing Helen and Cormag of the urgency."

He'd had enough. With one tug of his finger he wheeled Morgane around to face Fiona. "We're going this way because 'tis the way I'm going. That's the only reason you need."

Fiona glared at Gregor. She knew he was deliberately avoiding telling her why he had chosen this route, and she didn't know what agitated her more. The fact that he refused to tell her or that she was going to have to travel through the rough, dangerous mountains.

One look at his black eyes and she knew she wasn't going to get any more out of him. While still at the MacDougal's he had shown the patience of Job, but she had seen the deep-rooted despair in his mysterious eyes.

But that sadness wasn't what she glimpsed just a moment ago. Instead, there had been the tiniest hint of anger in what otherwise would have been a flat stare. Gregor might be able to fool others but she was a Druid and could see things others missed.

She clicked to her mare and sent her trotting after the infuriating man. Already they had begun the assent onto the mountains. She gripped her mare tightly and refused to look down when she heard the sprinkle of rocks as they fell.

They traveled in silence for a while. She didn't have

anything to say, and begging him to take her home would fall on deaf ears. She began to wonder if he realized she was still following him.

They crested a hill and she turned for one last look at her home when she spotted the smoke. "Gregor," she called.

In a heartbeat he was beside her. "'Tis the MacDougal's."

"I must help them."

His hand gripped her arm painfully. "Trust me, Fiona. You don't want to see what's down there and this only hastens our need to reach Conall's."

She wrenched her arm free. "I refuse to sit by while my clan is in need. Stay here if you must, but I won't." She kicked her mare, and it sent her running down the path.

Gone were her earlier worries of plummeting to her death on the jagged rocks as she raced her mare down the steep slope. All she cared about was reaching the only family she knew. Her mare stumbled, but quickly righted herself and continued their headlong dash toward the castle.

Much to her delight she reached the bottom of the crag faster than when she had climbed it. Once her mare's feet touched the flat ground, she lowered herself across the horse's back and kicked her into a run.

The castle came into view and she gasped at the many men that swarmed her clan. She swerved to go through the gates when a hand reached out and snatched the reins from her hands. She shouldn't have been surprised to find Gregor beside her.

"Do you want to get yourself killed?" he spat through clenched teeth.

"I want to help."

"How do you think you'll help? Take a look around. There isn't much you can do."

"I'm not afraid to die," she cried and slid from the mare.

She heard his footfalls behind her. She picked up her skirts and dashed to the postern door in the curtain wall. She had just opened the door when he stopped her.

"You are going to get yourself killed."

"Maybe, but I must see if I can do something."

She watched as he struggled with something before finally giving in. "All right. But when I say we need to leave, we leave."

She gave him a smile and rushed through the door. With his help, they managed to make it into the castle without being discovered. Quickly, she led him into the castle through the kitchen.

They reached the main hall and had Gregor not pulled her back she would have ran into an enemy soldier. "What clan are they?" she whispered.

"MacNeil," he whispered into her ear.

"Why?"

"It doesn't matter," he said.

"I demand you tell me."

"Well, since you *demand* it, I will import a wee bit of knowledge to you. MacNeil is here for you. To kill you."

Her mind refused to believe he had managed to find her so quickly after all these years. "Did you lead them here?"

He spun her around to face him. "Never. 'Tis my duty

to make sure he fails. I should never have let you come this far. We must return to the horses now. I cannot let anything happen."

She was about to go with him when she heard a loud crash and jeers coming from the hall. She jerked out of Gregor's hands and peered around the corner.

"Nay," came a whisper in her ear before large hands covered her eyes. "You don't want to see this."

But she already had. Blood. So much blood flowed on the hall floor that Helen had always kept immaculate.

"Come," Gregor murmured urgently.

When they turned to retrace their steps they found the way blocked by four MacNeil soldiers. "Is there another way?"

She nodded and ran down a hallway. Gregor stayed close behind her, and although she wouldn't have admitted it to him, she was glad he was with her. They reached the side of the hall, hidden from view by a tapestry, when she heard the bellow of pain.

"'Tis Cormag," she said. She turned and looked beseechingly at Gregor.

He closed his eyes and mumbled something under his breath about Moira and his hide before he nodded. She ran toward the sound of his cry of pain and came into contact with one MacNeil soldier. Before the soldier could alert anyone to their presence Gregor had already slit his throat.

She watched the dead soldier fall to the ground when Cormag groaned again. "He's in the solar. I know a way in where they'll never see us."

Gregor gave a quick nod and followed. She hurried through the maze of hallways until she came to the spot.

She turned and looked at Gregor before she leaned against the wall.

"Come," she said before the wall turned.

Had the situation not been so dire she might have laughed at his incredulous expression. Instead, she had only to wait a moment before he followed her example and stood beside her in the dark passage.

The passageway was very narrow and with him beside her, Fiona couldn't help but notice the hard maleness of his body. He radiated power and authority with little more than a look or touch. Her skin heated when his hand touched her face, then her neck.

"Where are we?" he whispered as his hand grabbed her shoulder.

She was thankful for the diversion of her mind from his body. "Cormag's ancestors liked to build these secret passages throughout the castle. I've found many of them, but I'm sure there are many more I haven't come across."

He grunted in response, which caused her to grin. "Stay next to me. I have to feel my way through these passages, and I don't want you to become lost."

When she had told him to stay close she hadn't expected him to mold himself along the backside of her, nor put his hand around her waist. Never had a man been this close to her, and the fact that she enjoyed it bothered her immensely.

She concentrated on feeling her way through the passage as quickly as possible. She found the spot where the passage wall turned suddenly to the right, and where she needed to continue forward. She was surprised that

Gregor never questioned her. Thankfully, they came to the end.

As silent as ever the wooden door swung toward them to reveal another of Helen's massive tapestries.

"This is one of the first passages I found, and Helen admitted to hiding the door with this tapestry."

"I'm glad she did," Gregor said and pushed her behind him.

She allowed him the first look.

"'Tis clear for the moment. Cormag is in there, but..."

"I know," she said and swallowed hard. She didn't know what she expected to find, but when she looked around the tapestry it wasn't to find Cormag strung on a rack that had wrenched his shoulders out of socket.

Blood stained his shirt at his shoulders, and it was all she could do not to run to him. Gregor must have known what she might try because his hands came around her waist.

"Cormag," she whispered.

His bruised and bloodied face turned toward her. He opened one eye, barely a crack because of the bruises. His other eye was sealed shut with blood and puss. "Lass? Is that you? What are you doing here?" he asked before coughing blood.

"I came to help."

"You must leave. All of Scotland depends on you. Where's Gregor?"

She was shoved aside as Gregor moved around her. "Here."

"You fool man. Get her out. He's come for her."

"I know. We're leaving now."

But Fiona wasn't finished. She pushed Gregor away and ran to Cormag's dying body. Tears she couldn't control ran down her face. "Don't leave," she begged.

"Ah, lass," he said. "I will always be with you. Now, go so you can save other clans from this destruction."

"Nay," she cried and tried to hold onto him, but Gregor's arms encircled her.

"Get her out, lad," Cormag ordered.

She was no match for Gregor's strength when he picked her up and carried her back to the passage. Cormag was right. She needed to get away and quickly. Without any urging from Gregor she swiftly retraced their steps, but she misjudged.

When they opened the door they were no longer inside the hall, they were now in the kitchen.

"This way," Gregor said and pulled her after him into the bailey.

She stayed at his back as he dispatched any enemy that came in their path. They were passing the blacksmith's hut when she heard the scream. Gregor was busy fighting a MacNeil soldier, and she looked into the doorway to find another MacNeil raping one of her clanswomen.

She saw the long metal rod by the door and picked it up as she walked toward the man. She raised the rod above her head and sent it down upon his back with all the strength she could muster. The soldier stopped his rutting movements and turned on her.

"Ah, ye want a piece of me, do ye?" he snarled. "Come on then, lass."

He was a great bear of a man and before Fiona could muster a scream in her throat, he was on her, jerking up the hem of her gown. She struggled, but it seemed as if he had the strength of twenty men.

All of a sudden, he let out a roar and rolled away from her. She watched in amazement as he clawed at his back, and it was only then she saw the dagger sticking out of him.

Her eyes went to the doorway to find Gregor standing there. He gave her a little nod, and she got to her feet as he walked out of the cottage.

"Fight me like a man," the soldier bellowed at Gregor.

A shiver went down Fiona's spine at the feral look that came into Gregor's black eyes. He twisted his wrist, sending his sword dancing around him. With the other hand he motioned for the soldier to come at him.

Fiona barely had time to blink before Gregor smashed the hilt of his sword into the soldier's face, sending him to his knees. He then put the end of his sword on the soldier's neck and sliced.

She opened her mouth in shock, but Gregor had already pulled her behind him as he raced from the small cottage.

"Do you understand now?" he asked. "We must get you to Conall's posthaste."

* * *

"Where the hell is she?" MacNeil demanded of Cormag. "Tell me, and I will give you an easy passing."

Blood bubbled from the corner of Cormag's mouth as he laughed. "She's gone and you'll never find her. The prophecy will come to pass, and you'll be sent to Hell where you belong."

This couldn't be happening, MacNeil thought to himself. How had they missed the bitch? How hard could it be to kill these Druids? The parents had died easily enough.

*He* would be here soon, wanting to know where Fiona was, and still Cormag had told him nothing. If only Glenna wouldn't have left him, he would have no need of the man, but now MacNeil needed him more than ever.

With one last effort, MacNeil grabbed Cormag by his shirt. "Tell me, and I will cut you loose. Tell me," he ordered.

"Roast in Hell," Cormag uttered as the life drained from his body.

"So," said the voice that sent chills down MacNeil's back, "I see you have failed once again."

MacNeil turned toward the doorway to see the cloaked figure. Even after all these months he still hadn't gotten a name out of the man. Most people called him The Shadow, which is exactly what he was.

"I know she left here recently," MacNeil answered and shifted his feet nervously.

"Hmmm," The Shadow said as he walked into the chamber. "Gregor traveled faster than I anticipated. I could have been here sooner had there been no need to retrieve you."

MacNeil refused to show The Shadow how much his tone terrified him. After all, MacNeil was the one known in Scotland as the Butcher. This *Shadow* should fear him. This thing that wore the black cloak that shielded his face at all time.

"Then we ride to MacInnes Castle. Again."

"Nay."

MacNeil heard the violent note in The Shadow's voice. "Gregor takes her to the Druid's Glen. We must get to them before they reach that haven."

The Shadow's laughter resounded in the chamber. "They won't be headed to the glen and MacInnes Castle. Yet. I have something planned for them."

MacNeil rubbed his hands together. Whatever The Shadow had planned for Gregor and Fiona would most definitely be gruesome.

"About time," he muttered and looked down at the dead form of Cormag MacDougal.

"Cut off his head," he told his soldiers. "Place it on a pike at the gatehouse. I want all to see what happens to any who opposes me."

4

F iona didn't need to see the storm clouds to know they were about to burst. For hours her soul screamed her sorrow as they rode farther and farther away from her home, but she kept silent as she always had when in pain.

She kept her gaze to the ground, but she could feel Gregor's eyes on her. The dam of tears was about to rupture and she refused to allow him to see them.

A fat raindrop landed on her hand, and she pulled her mare back to let Gregor lead the way. When he was far enough ahead, she raised her face to the clouds and called for the rain.

Gregor cursed when the sky opened and let the rain fall. This would slow their progress, but it would also slow MacNeil. He turned and saw Fiona lower her face. She had been silent and withdrawn since their departure from the MacDougall's, but he couldn't blame her.

She had seen her clansmen murdered and her foster father dying. He didn't want to think about what happened to Helen or Bridget, and he prayed Fiona never asked. He expected her to shed tears and had been rather surprised when she had remained quiet.

He slowed Morgane's pace until Fiona caught up with him. She said not a word, but he could have sworn it was tears he saw through the rain.

"Fiona?" he asked, wondering if he should comfort her. He recalled the many times his sister, Anne, had told him how he should console a woman in distress. Now was obviously one of those times, but Fiona was anything but what one would classify as a normal lass.

"I'm all right," he heard above the drone of the rain.

He snorted. She was anything but all right, but he wasn't about to argue with her. At least she was smart enough to wrap her plaid around her to help her stay dry. They forged on until his stomach began to rumble. All this time and Fiona had not complained about anything. His respect for her grew, much to his vexation. She was one woman he had to—at all costs—stay away from.

And yet he was extremely attracted to her.

At least he needn't worry about her wanting him. She had made it painfully clear she couldn't stand him. He put her from his thoughts and concentrated on finding the old cave. It had been many years and as far as he knew it could have new occupants.

He squinted through the rain and pulled up on Morgane's reins. This was it. He dismounted and crept toward the cave entrance. He palmed the dirk from his boot and stepped into the darkness.

It didn't take long to find that the only inhabitants were a few bats toward the back. He whistled to Morgane as he emerged and motioned to Fiona.

"We'll be dry in here for the night," he said as he helped her dismount. "I will get a fire started while you get out of those wet clothes."

She nodded and walked into the cave. "I didn't realize it was so big."

"There's enough room for us to make camp on the right while I tie the horses on the left."

He led the horses into the cave and began to unsaddle them. "Just stay away from the very back. There are bats."

She chuckled behind him and it sent a tingling up his spine. "I'm not afraid of bats."

"Good," he said and tossed her a plaid from her bag. He quickly gathered what wood he could find in the cave and set about making a fire.

Before long he had a good blaze going, and Fiona had taken off her wet garments. She hung them on a boulder to dry and sat watching him. He rubbed the back of his neck.

"You do that a lot."

"Do what?" he asked.

"You either rub your neck or pop it. Why?"

He shrugged. "Habit, I guess. Are you hungry?"

"Do you have any other habits?" she asked, ignoring his question.

"Not that I know of. Are you hungry? I've a few things Helen packed for us."

She waved away the food and huddled closer to the fire. He put away the food. As he began to take off his shirt and vest so they could dry, he noticed her eyes on him.

A faint smile curved his lips. *Maybe she doesn't find me as repulsive as she puts on.*

It was as if she read his thoughts because her eyes

jerked to his before turning away. Gregor wouldn't be a cad and rub it in. He probably should, but he didn't feel up to it. He was soaked from the drenching rain, angry that MacNeil had attacked the MacDougal's, and heartsick because he was so close to home.

The savage his father claimed him to be was at rest this night, and frankly, Gregor wasn't upset about it. He wasn't up to trading barbs with Fiona, and he knew too well her tongue could cut deep, especially after the day she'd had.

The popping of the fire filled the quiet cave as the rain continued to pour. It was going to be a very long night at this rate. At least they made it farther than he had expected. Fiona hadn't slowed him down as he anticipated after seeing the MacDougal's attacked. He wondered when she would grieve for them.

He raised his eyes and instantly regretted it. The plaid she had draped around her had fallen to reveal the creamy expanse of her shoulder. He swallowed and tried to look away when she rose to her feet.

Her long shapely legs peeked from the plaid as she checked her clothes, and it was all Gregor could do to stay seated. He cursed silently and fought to bring his body under control.

His control was legendary, and he would be damned if one woman would break it. All thoughts of control evaporated when she squatted down and the plaid parted to expose her thigh.

Fiona was tired of sitting in the plaid. She wanted her clothes on, but didn't want to risk illness just because Gregor made her uncomfortable. A sound, like a grunt, came from his direction, and when she turned to look at him, she was surprised to find his eyes on her. She had seen that look before in a man's eyes and knew what it meant. Although she found him pleasing to look upon, he did not attempt to gain her notice like the other men of her clan. She took that to mean he wasn't interested, but Gregor wasn't from her clan.

That turned her thoughts to Cormag and Helen. She had resolved to stay alone and never give anyone the pleasure of leaving her again. Nonetheless, that is exactly what happened today. She pushed away the tears, not yet ready to face her feelings.

"Are they dry?" His voice was rough, as if he were having trouble speaking.

"Not yet," she answered.

Silence filled the cave again, and after being woken by that horrible dream the night before, she decided to get some rest. Her dreams were prophetic but it hadn't been her clan she had seen destroyed.

It had been another.

\* \* \*

Moira waited patiently beside Frang, the Druid high priest, outside their sacred stone circle as Aimery walked toward them. Aimery wasn't from this world. He was a Fae who lived where magic ruled.

She had been waiting for word from him for days now, and her patience was nearing its end. She shifted from one foot to the other while he stopped and conversed with another Druid.

"Patience is a virtue," Frang whispered and stroked his long white beard.

"Not today it isn't. I have waited years to have my sisters united." She turned toward the man who had raised her as a daughter and looked into his light blue eyes. "I fear I cannot wait a moment longer."

"But longer you must wait," Aimery stated as he joined them.

Her head swiveled to him and her eyes narrowed. "What do you know?"

Aimery's unusually bright blue eyes, eyes of the Fae, dimmed. "'Tis much worse than we originally thought. Whoever is aiding MacNeil is using a spell known only to the Fae to hide himself."

Frang cursed and leaned upon his tall staff.

She looked from Frang to Aimery. "Tell me what has happened."

"MacNeil has attacked the MacDougal's," Aimery answered.

"Did she... did she..." Moira couldn't bring herself to ask the question. If MacNeil had captured Fiona then all was lost.

"My envoy spotted Gregor and Fiona riding away."

"Thank the saints," she said as relief rushed through her. "I had no wish to tell Glenna that Fiona had been captured or killed."

"Glenna is enjoying her new marriage. Leave her be with this," Frang said, but he had a knowing smile on his face.

Moira watched as Frang and Aimery conversed privately,

and she couldn't help but compare the two. Frang looked old with his white hair and beard, and when you looked into his eyes he seemed even more ancient. Yet, to look at his face, it was hard to guess his age. At times he looked as young as a youth.

Aimery, on the other hand, had to be one of the most handsome creatures she had ever laid eyes on. It was the Fae in him, with his glowing blue eyes and long, flaxen hair. His body was perfect, down to the last detail. Though many of the Druid women wanted him, Moira did not.

There had been one man who had always captured her attention. She turned and found him standing behind her like a statue just as she knew he would be. Far enough away not to hear her words, but close enough to reach her if need be.

Dartayous. He was a Druid Warrior, one who watched over the Druids, and for as long as she could remember he had been among them.

She tried once to get close to him, but that had ended badly, and she had learned her lesson. He had been her first infatuation, her first and only if she were honest with herself.

Moira had given up on ever thinking she would have a husband and children. Her life was centered on the prophecy. Besides, she was too old for a husband now.

## 5

Gregor groaned as more of Fiona's leg appeared outside the plaid. From the tips of her toes to her thigh, her flesh glowed and beckoned in the firelight. It was one of those rare moments he wished he had powers of his own to move the plaid and gain a look at her naked body.

His body throbbed with a need so strong he nearly shook with it. If she could do this to him just by looking at her, what could she do if their lips ever met? He really didn't need to worry over that point, because he knew she wouldn't let him near her.

He put his head in his hands. He had a strong willpower and exerted that over his fast growing desire. Fiona would never know how much she affected him. His head jerked up when he heard her moan. By the way she tossed and turned she was about to come out of the carefully wrapped plaid.

And that would tempt a saint.

"Ah, hell," he muttered and rose to wake her. His new conscious was making his life pure torture.

He got within a few paces of her when she suddenly jerked upright. His worry grew when he saw the fine sheen of sweat covering her forehead. It wouldn't do to have her come down with a fever.

After kneeling in front of her, he reached out his hand to feel her head, but she slapped it away.

"What are you doing?" she snapped

"Making sure you aren't ill. You were in wet clothes," he reminded her.

She rose to her feet with as much dignity as one could have while barely covered in a plaid. "I'm not ill. I just had a...dream."

"Do you have them often?" He wasn't sure what made him ask.

She slowly raised her eyes to his. "A handful over the years. Until recently..."

He watched as she thought about her comment, seemingly transfixed about something.

Then, she whirled around. "Turn your back while I dress," she said.

"Of course."

He walked to the horses. Morgane nickered softly and pushed her muzzle at him. He laughed and patted her on the withers.

"Why don't you tie her?"

He looked toward the fire and found Fiona dressed. He shrugged at her question. "There's no need."

"She will leave you the first chance she gets."

"I have had her since she was a foal. She hasn't left me yet and I seriously doubt that she will."

"You will be the one walking, not me," Fiona said with a toss of her brown mane.

He chuckled and gave Morgane another pat before he returned to the fire. "You don't know that horse or the relationship we have. Morgane isn't going anywhere."

"Morgane? You used a Celtic name for your horse?"

Gregor rubbed the back of his neck. "Aye." She didn't need to know that he'd picked the name because his sister, Anne, liked it.

Fiona could only stare at him. Was it just coincidence that he picked a Celtic name for dweller of the sea and her power was over water?

How many times had Helen told her she would know when she found her mate? How many times had Helen said it would be so obvious to her that she wouldn't question it?

She put a hand to her forehead. Helen had taught her about the ancient Celts and their way of life as well as the Christianity that now ruled the land. Not many people knew of the Celtic gods anymore.

Her gaze found Gregor. He was handsome. Very handsome, in fact. The power that radiated from him sent chills down her body. He had been the one man in many years that had made her stop and take notice. She hadn't liked being interested in him, but she couldn't help how she felt.

*No one said you had to marry him. Take what pleasure he can give you, and then leave him before he gets the chance to leave you.*

Now that had merit. Helen had constantly talked about

the relationship between a man and a woman and how fulfilling it could be.

*Everyone deserves some pleasure. Isn't that what Helen told me?*

Her gaze followed Gregor as he rose and walked to the cave entrance. She liked the way his leather pants hugged his legs, and when he bent over she bit her lip at the view she received. Although she wasn't a beauty, she wasn't homely either. Surely he would take her up on an offer. He was a man, after all, and all men loved what happened between a man and a woman in bed.

He had looked at her when the plaid had nearly fallen from her body. And, if she had learned anything from Bridget, it was how to entice a man. Surely she would be able to pull it off.

"The rain has stopped. I think we should go."

Gregor's words startled her she was so deep in thought. She looked outside and saw the sun setting behind the clouds. "All right."

"Are you rested?"

"Aye. Don't worry, I will keep up," she said and began to gather her things.

"I wasn't worried. You have held up better than any lass I've known. We must travel fast and I don't want to tire you."

She smiled to herself at his compliment. It wouldn't be hard at all to entice him.

\* \* \*

Fiona began to think of the many ways she could seduce Gregor as they rode through the mountains. She had to have something to think about instead of sliding off the side of the mountain.

When Gregor pulled up and handed her a piece of bread, she accepted it with a smile. His startled look almost sent her into a fit of laughing. He hadn't expected that, nor would he expect what she had planned next.

She hummed softly as she ate. Thoughts of exactly how she was going to seduce him filled her mind.

\* \* \*

Gregor shifted in the saddle. Fiona's smile had unsettled him. Why, all of a sudden, had she sent him such a dazzling smile that had lit up her whole face? He thought her pretty, but when he had seen that smile it had transformed her into something so beautiful it hurt his eyes to look upon her.

Now, every time he turned around to check on her she sent him a smile. What was her plan? And why? He knew women well enough to know she was up to something. Did she think to distract him with her smiles?

If so, he had to admit, it was working. Already he had passed a resting spot he had wanted to stop at. He didn't want to turn around and admit just how she affected him. Instead, they would travel until they next meet the river.

Hopefully by then he would have more control over himself. Even if it meant he didn't look at her.

\* \* \*

Aimery sighed and rubbed his temples. The fact that someone was using Faerie magic to hide themselves from the Fae wasn't good. In fact, it was downright dreadful. How was he going to tell his king and queen? He recalled his teaching of the prophecy and all that would occur. Never in all his readings had there been a mention of a rogue Fae.

Unless it was in a hidden text.

That gave him a thought, but he pushed it aside for the moment. He concentrated on Fiona and Gregor. They were traveling and headed away from MacNeil.

Aimery laughed when he realized where they were. "So very close, Gregor. Will you resist the urge to see your clan?"

He knew Gregor would. Gregor was predictable when it came to his family but would Fiona allow him to continue on? Now that was something he would love to see. Maybe a visit to them was in order.

They were so close to fulfilling the prophecy that he could taste it and MacNeil knew it. Just a few more things to put in order and his race and the Druid's would be safe once again.

And Duncan and Catriona Sinclair's children would be together and happy as they always should have been.

After he had been fooled and missed the signs about Duncan and Catriona's murder he needed to make it up to them. He mourned the loss of his dear friends, and he would see the wrong put right any way he had to.

Even if it meant sacrificing himself.

* * *

Gregor spotted the cottage as they crested a hill. The moon, bright and full in the night sky, gave him a clear view of the area. The cool summer night breeze brought the smell of fresh cooked bread their way. Before he nudged Morgane forward, he searched the area. As usual in this remote corner, there was nothing but rolling hills and the occasional herd of cattle or sheep.

The jostling of Fiona's bridle reminded him of her presence and the need to reach safety. He clicked to Morgane and quietly made his way to the cottage.

Instead of the usual greeting he received upon reaching the cottage, an eerie silence filled the air. He held up his hand for Fiona to stop, and he was grateful she did as he asked without question.

As he dismounted, the hairs on the back of his neck began to tingle, signaling that an attack was imminent. He unsheathed his sword and whirled around, ready for the ambush.

He spotted the crouched figure in the shadows by the door, and lowered his sword. "You can come out now."

The shadowy figure rose slowly to his feet. "Gregor? Is that ye, lad?"

"Aye, 'tis me, Allen."

"Ye always come alone," Allen said and step from the shadows. "I didn't think it was ye."

Gregor smiled at his old friend. Allen had been around for as long as Gregor could remember, always there when he needed something or someone. Allen's hair was white, or at least what was left of it was white. Old age had stooped his once proud frame, but Gregor could tell Allen could still hold his own if need be.

"I've brought a woman with me," Gregor began.

Allen laughed. "About time ye settled down."

"My job is to bring her to her sisters. She's not for me."

"That's too bad," Allen said with a loud sigh. "I was hoping ye'd put the past behind ye."

Gregor had to keep himself from sighing. "She doesn't know who I am and I want to keep it that way."

"All right, all right. Bring her in. I will make up some tea," Allen said over his shoulder as he shuffled into the house.

Gregor raised his hand and motioned for Fiona to come. He stood by the door waiting for her, but she stayed atop the horse. "What is it?"

"I need you to help me dismount."

He took a deep breath and slowly exhaled. This was the first time she had asked for his help, and he knew she really didn't need it. She was up to something, that was for sure.

With heavy feet, he took the few steps toward her. He raised his arms, and she slid into them and onto his chest. And much to his chagrin found her mouth inches from his. Her lithe body settled along his with the fit of well–worn boots. And his body reacted instantly to her lush curves.

"Oh," she huffed and put her hands on his shoulders. "How clumsy of me. I suppose 'tis been the long ride. I didn't realize how tired I am."

He knew she lied, but it was difficult for him to think with her hands on him. He nodded and set her down, as far away from him as his arms could reach.

"If I didn't know better, I would say you couldn't stand to be near me," she purred.

He shook himself and stepped away. He didn't know what her game was, but he was going to find out and soon. "Fiona—"

"Are you going to bring the lass in or stay out there?" Allen's voice barked from inside the cottage.

"We'll talk later," he warned before ushering her into the small cottage.

Fiona couldn't keep the smile from her face. Her attempts were working. She was keeping Gregor off balance, just where she wanted him. It wouldn't take long to make him want her.

"Come in, come in," said an elderly man. His sun–weathered face was creased with deep lines, but his hazel eyes sparkled with mischief.

Fiona liked him instantly. "Hello. I'm Fiona MacDougal," she said.

"Always a pleasure to have a lady grace my home," he said and lifted her hand to his lips. "Call me Allen."

She gave him a bright smile. "Thank you, Allen. We appreciate you sharing your home with us."

"Anytime," Allen said and went back to the hearth. "There's fresh bread on the table. Help yerselves while I get the tea."

Fiona turned toward the table and found Gregor's black eyes intent upon her. She flashed him a smile and a wink, and was pleased to see his forehead crease in confusion.

She began to cut the bread and offered Gregor a piece. "'Tis still warm," she said.

He took the bread, and she couldn't help the laugh that

escaped when he went to great lengths not to touch her. "I won't bite, you know."

"I know no such thing," he said, his surly tone lowered for her ears only.

She wasn't able to reply as Allen arrived with the tea. While Allen poured she kept her gaze locked with Gregor's. She wasn't about to give in.

"Sit, lad," he ordered Gregor. "I'm too old to be looking up all the time." He laughed as though that were funny. "Now, what brings a young couple like ye out in the wilderness?"

"Nothing," Gregor answered quickly.

Fiona narrowed her eyes at him, and turned to Allen. "Actually, we are traveling. Whose land are we on?"

"Mac—"

"It doesn't matter," Gregor nearly yelled over Allen. "Leave it be, Fiona."

She took his warning to heart and turned to her tea. She didn't want to admit that his tone had hurt her feelings.

"Ye must be newly married," Allen stated.

Fiona jerked her eyes to Gregor to find him giving Allen a murderous look. "What makes you say that?" she asked.

"The looks ye've been giving him," he pointed to Gregor. "And the annoyed looks he keeps sending ye. Ye make a handsome couple."

"You think so?" Fiona refused to look at Gregor for she was sure his hands itched to wring her neck.

"Oh, aye, lass."

"Fiona," Gregor's voice warned.

She ignored him and faced Allen. "Why do you think so?"

"With a stunning lady like yerself and a good–looking, strong man like the lad here, ye can't go wrong. Ye two were made for each other."

Fiona thought over his words, and wondered if he knew how true they might be.

"I wager yer children will be beautiful," Allen continued.

She raised her eyes to see Allen and Gregor exchange a look. "Allen, do you know Gregor?"

Allen refused to meet her gaze and drank his tea instead.

It was Gregor that answered. "Nay, he doesn't."

"I asked Allen," she said. Something was going on. 'Twas almost as if Gregor didn't want her to know where they were. She knew they were either on MacLachlan or MacAllister land, so what difference did it make?

"Allen," she urged. "Do you know Gregor?"

Allen shrugged. "Me mind is old, lass."

"You can't fool me with that excuse," she said and waited for him to tell her the truth.

Allen laughed and slapped his knee. "Ye've got yerself a smart one here, Gregor. I would watch yerself around her."

"You have no idea," she heard Gregor grumble.

"So, you do know him?"

"Aye, lass," Allen admitted. "Gregor comes through here every couple of years."

"And where is here?"

Allen once again looked to Gregor, who shook his head.

Allen sighed. "I'm not sure, lass. 'Tis late, and me old bones tire easily. Lass, ye can have my bed."

Fiona rose and put a hand to stop him. "I would never dream of taking your bed. I can make do anywhere. Don't worry about me."

Allen stared at her a long moment before he turned to Gregor and said, "Ye better not let this one go, lad. She's a keeper for sure."

## 6

Gregor came awake instantly. He lay quiet, waiting to hear the sound that had woken him. In the other room, Allen snored away. With the smallest of movements, Gregor turned his head until he found Fiona.

It was then he heard the soft moan. He rose and walked toward her. It was another dream. It would be strange except for the fact that she was a Druid, and if Gregor had learned anything while at Conall's 'twas that you never learned all there was about Druids.

He knelt and touched her shoulder. "Fiona," he whispered.

Her eyes flew open, but her breathing was labored, making her chest rise and fall quickly. Gregor turned his thoughts away from her plump breasts to the matter at hand.

"Fiona," he said again. "You were having another dream."

"Blood. So much blood," she whispered.

He sighed. "I was afraid seeing what MacNeil did to your clan would have this affect."

She sat up and shook her head. "You don't understand. It wasn't the MacDougal's."

"Then who was it?"

"I don't know," she said and rubbed her temples. "With each time I think I will catch a glimpse of a plaid or something but it fades before I'm able."

"A prophetic dream?"

She turned troubled green eyes to him. "I feel their pain, their terror. 'Tis so real."

"Was this one worse than your last?"

"Aye. They seem to be getting more terrible with each one."

He watched as she hugged her legs and laid her head on her knees. She seemed so fragile that he almost took her in his arms to comfort her.

Almost.

Until he realized this was the first time she hadn't been smiling at him or trying to touch him. This was the true Fiona, the one she rarely let anyone see, and he would bet his best dagger it was about to disappear beneath that cool surface of hers.

She raised her eyes and gave him a smile. "Since you are here, do you want to share the blanket with me?"

He fought to keep from rolling his eyes. "I'm fine. Go back to sleep."

Her laughter followed him back to his pallet by the door.

* * *

Gregor popped his neck and ran a hand down Morgane's muzzle. He had slept little after Fiona's dream and knew she hadn't got much more than he. He had planned to let her rest as long as she wanted. He needed to get to the Druid's Glen quickly, but he couldn't have her overtaxed in the meantime.

When she rose with the sun and asked when they would be heading out, he had been more than a bit surprised. After they ate a quick meal with Allen, Gregor readied the horses. He turned and found Fiona and Allen embracing. They said their farewells, and Gregor waited for Allen.

"Thank you," Gregor said.

"Any time, lad. Ye know that."

"I don't know when I will return."

"I ken. Ye be careful, and take good care of the lass. I wasn't lying last night. Ye are right for each other. Only a fool would let her go."

"She's something I could never have. Not after—"

"Ye need to bury the past, lad. Visit that family of yers. Time heals all wounds," he said, an earnest expression on his wrinkled face.

"Not these wounds. They run too deep and well, you know it." He slapped him on the back. "Take care of yourself. I will be back when I can. Do you need me to bring anything?"

"Just the lass. She did these old bones good. 'Tis been awhile since I've seen one as bonny as her."

Gregor smiled and went to mount Morgane when he spotted Fiona by her mare. "What's wrong?"

"Could you assist me?" she asked coyly.

Once again Allen's laughter reached him. He sighed and walked to Fiona. She gave him a smile as his hands spanned her waist. He had known she was curvaceous, but the feel of her small waist beneath his hands made his heart pound. He stood looking down at her before he realized he hadn't moved and her smile let him know she knew it as well.

Quickly as he could, he lifted her atop the mare. Once he mounted Morgane, they waved their last farewell to Allen and set out.

"Are you going to tell me where we are?" she asked after a few moments.

"Nay."

"I know 'tis either the MacAllister's or the MacLachlan's."

He kept silent, hoping she got the message and stopped asking questions.

"Do you know anyone else around here?"

He should have known better than to want the impossible.

Fiona refused to tell Gregor how exhausted she was. They had traveled all day, and it was all she could do to keep her eyes open thanks to her lack of sleep. She had managed to notice they entered a small forest.

He asked many times if she needed to rest. How she regretted trying to act as though she was well. She should have told him she needed a brief rest, but she had wanted to impress him.

*You better come to your senses soon.*

Quickly, she gave him a smile when he turned and looked over his shoulder at her. When he turned his horse around she knew she had failed miserably.

"Something the matter?" she asked in her most cheerful voice.

"You tell me."

"I don't know what you are speaking of."

He cursed long and low, and then shook his head. "Don't do this again, Fiona. We have a long road ahead of us."

She couldn't meet his eyes, because she knew he was right. She had acted foolish for the first time since she was a young lass and she was ashamed of it.

"We rest here tonight." To her surprise, he dismounted and reached to aid her.

"Thank you," she said and slid into his awaiting arms.

Her arms buckled when she tried to hold onto to him, and she ended up falling onto his chest. It was the perfect time to try and seduce him, but she just wasn't up to it. She pulled back to apologize and saw the fire in his eyes. He held her firmly against him.

Her hands were flat against his chest, the feel of his leather vest beneath her hands made her itch to touch his skin. It would be so easy to entwine them around his neck and feel the texture of his hair.

His fervent gaze made her heart skip a beat. His eyes dropped to her lips, and she licked them. He groaned and her breath caught in her chest. He was holding back, she realized. Even when she lifted her head for his kiss he didn't move.

"You need to rest."

His voice penetrated her mind and she pursed her lips together. "Aye, I do."

Gently, he set her away from him. "Rest while I take care of the horses."

She sat on a fallen log and watched as Gregor swiftly and efficiently took care of both horses. He reached into a bag and withdrew a loaf of Allen's bread.

"Eat," he commanded as he handed her a piece of the bread and some oatcakes.

Thankfully, Allen had given them some wine and she greedily drank from the skin, hoping it would numb her aching body. She looked up at the sky and saw it streaked with bright orange and pink.

"I've always loved sunsets." Nothing had been said while they ate and the silence bothered her.

He turned his gaze to the sky. "They are beautiful."

"How far do you think we have come this day?"

"Further than I had thought, but not as far as I had hoped."

She rolled her eyes and laughed. "Can you give a direct answer?"

One blonde eyebrow cocked up. "I did, lass."

"Will you tell me whose land we are on now?"

"Why do you wish to know?"

"Why won't you tell me?"

"Why is it so important?"

She laughed. She couldn't help it. It was either laugh or cry. Oh, the man was infuriating. "I'm too tired to continue this."

"Good night then," he said.

She lowered herself to the ground and turned on her side, using her arm as a pillow. She took one last look at Gregor as he stood and watched the sunset, his blonde hair lifting off his neck in the breeze.

It was that image and the fire in his eyes that she hoped she would see more of in her dreams.

The last sound she heard was an owl nearby.

* * *

Gregor placed the plaid over Fiona in case she became chilled during the night. He couldn't chance a fire, but he had known she would have liked one.

He should have paid closer attention to her to notice she lied about feeling all right.

His mind had been on his family. He rode hard because he wanted off their land before someone realized he was there. Many times he had ridden through here and he had been able to stay unnoticed. Now, he had Fiona with him and couldn't ride like he usually did.

He stretched his neck and prayed they would make it through without being seen, but he had a feeling that wouldn't happen. The sound of a stick breaking caught his attention. He listened intently, but didn't move.

His gaze flew to Fiona. He would have to take care of who ever tried to sneak up on him before she woke. By this time he could hear their breathing. They were just a few paces behind him.

A slow smile of anticipation split his face. If there was one thing he was good at, it was battle, and he always looked forward to one.

In one quick movement, he unsheathed his sword and whirled around to face his opponents. To his surprise, it was two of his clansmen.

"We found you."

Gregor turned his eyes to Malcolm. They had grown up together and had trained together, and it had been Malcolm who had made sure Gregor left the MacLachlan land. Malcolm had been like a brother to him and a son to his father. That day had been all the more painful because it had been Malcolm that had turned his back on him.

"Has he lost his tongue?" asked the lad beside Malcolm.

"Cease your prattling, Dugus," Malcolm hissed. He turned his head toward Gregor. "I never thought to see you again. You must come to the castle."

"Why?" Gregor asked. "To be killed in front of the entire clan? I think not. If you want me to go, then you will have to best me first."

"Then what are we waiting for?" Malcolm asked as he unsheathed his sword.

Gregor gave him a grin and motioned for him to attack. Malcolm brought his sword up and slammed it down on Gregor's. He pushed Malcolm away and shook out his arms. Malcolm had never been as good with his sword as Gregor. He took advantage of Malcolm's clumsy attack.

When he lunged, Gregor ducked the swing and stuck his foot behind Malcolm's, sending him to the ground. Malcolm's sword went flying, and Gregor put his foot on his chest to keep him down. Gregor raised his sword and pointed it at Dugus' throat.

"Don't even try it, lad. You will end up next to Malcolm."

"What do you want me to do?" Fiona asked as she came to stand beside him.

He didn't know what to tell her. He couldn't allow Malcolm and Dugus to return to the clan with news that he was here, but he couldn't stand the thought of killing them either, regardless that they were here to do the same to him.

"I will take care of them," said a man as he walked from behind a tree.

## 7

Gregor and Fiona turned to see a man standing behind him. Gregor recognized him as Fae instantly. Just what he was doing there was another thing.

"I will answer your questions in a moment, Gregor," he said before he put his hand over Dugus' eyes. After a few murmured words from the man, Dugus turned and walked away. He repeated the process with Malcolm.

"Now," he said and dusted off his hands. "I am Aimery. I came to check on the two of you."

Gregor groaned and resumed his seat on the tree stump. "Did Moira send you? Did she have so little faith in me?"

"Moira doesn't even know I'm here," Aimery answered. "And no one sent me. I came on my own."

Fiona couldn't take her eyes off the man as he and Gregor talked. He was beautiful. His flaxen hair hung nearly to his waist and seemed to glimmer, and his eyes glowed the most unusual blue. "What are you?"

He turned toward her and gave her a kind smile. "I am

pleased to finally meet you, Fiona. I'm not of this world, as you have already guessed."

"He's Fae," Gregor said and rose to his feet.

"Truly?" she asked. "I didn't think Faeries were real."

"We are real," Aimery said. "Let us sit for a while."

"What did you do to those men?"

"Don't worry about them," Aimery said as he patted the spot beside him on the fallen tree. "They won't even remember seeing either of you."

Fiona sat beside him and looked to Gregor, who had been rubbing his neck since Aimery had shown himself.

"Don't be concerned about Gregor," Aimery whispered. "He's not upset about me being here, he's upset about those men."

She would have to talk to Gregor about that later. Right now, she was curious about the Fae beside her, but did one just come out and ask questions?

The Fae's laugh sounded beside her. "You can ask me anything you like."

"You read minds?"

"'Tis one of the many things I do."

"Can you teach me?"

Aimery's smile disappeared. "Maybe one day. Right now, you need to concentrate on what is to come."

"The prophecy."

"'Tis more important than you realize, and it will touch every person in Scotland whether they know it or not."

*But I'll have to see Moira.*

"Moira is part of the prophecy, Fiona. You cannot get around that."

She hated that he could read her mind. If only she

knew some way to block him. She sighed when she saw his eyebrow rise. He had read her mind once again.

"Why didn't anyone come for me before now? Why am I just learning of you?" she asked and hated herself for the yearning that was in her voice.

"Moira wanted you to be happy."

Anger consumed Fiona. She stood and began to pace, not paying attention to the fact Gregor and Aimery were staring intently at her.

"Moira? If she had any thought of my happiness she wouldn't have abandoned me to begin with. How dare her say it was for my happiness. She doesn't give a pig's arse about my happiness."

"Fiona—" Gregor began.

She whirled around to face him. "Don't you dare speak for her! Do you hear me? You have no idea what she did."

Gregor held up his hands. "I wasn't."

She blinked away tears she hadn't shed in years. The fury was replaced by old demons that had never died, and the fact that she would have to face Moira soon compounded those fears.

Without a word to Gregor or Aimery she turned and walked away.

"Let her go," Aimery told Gregor when he began to follow her. "There is much anger in her heart, and I fear she will not put it aside. You must help her do this."

Gregor continued to look in the direction that Fiona took.

"Maybe then she can help you get past the fears that haunt you."

Gregor turned and looked at Aimery. "Stay out of my affairs. They don't concern you."

"Really?" Aimery asked and gained his feet. "Tell me. Do you know what Fiona's power is?"

"Aye. Water."

Aimery smiled. "Have you heard the prophecy, Gregor? The *entire* prophecy?"

"Nay."

"Then I think 'tis time you realize just how important everything is. Including your role in it."

Gregor turned his head and stared at the Fae. "What?"

"Listen...

*In a time of conquering*
*There will be three*
*Who end the MacNeil line.*
*Three born of the*
*Imbolc, Beltaine and Lughnasad Feasts*
*Who will destroy all at the*
*Samhain, the Feast of the Dead.*
*One who refuses the Druid way*
*Inherits the winter and in doing*
*So marks the beginning of the end.*
*For the worthy to prevail, the fire*
*Must stand alone to vanquish the inheritor,*
*Water must soothe the savage beast, and*
*The wind must bow before the tree."*

Gregor blinked and sank onto the log Aimery had given up. "Conall was the one who refused the Druid way."

"I knew you would figure it out. What else can you decipher?" Aimery asked his gaze expectant.

"Obviously, Glenna is the fire and Conall the inheritor. Fiona is the water that must soothe the savage beast, and Moira the wind that must bow before the tree."

"Ah, but who is the savage beast and the tree?"

Gregor raised his eyes to Aimery. "You know don't you?"

Aimery laughed. "Maybe."

"Things would be much easier if you would just tell people."

"What would be the fun in that? You need to learn to make decisions on your own. We Fae usually just stand by and watch."

"In other words, you are telling me that Fiona and Moira will find their mates just as Glenna did."

"I knew you could use your mind when you wanted to," Aimery said with a laugh as he crossed his arms over his chest.

"If one of them makes a mistake or a wrong decision, the prophecy won't go on as planned."

Aimery thought a moment. "It might. It might not."

Gregor rose to his feet. "I have had enough of this cryptic talk. You are far worse than the Druids."

Aimery just smiled as he watched Gregor walk away. Aye, Fiona would certainly soothe the savage beast within Gregor.

\* \* \*

Gregor found Fiona beside the river. Her long dark hair swirled in the breeze as she gazed at the water, the stars twinkling overhead. It wasn't until he got closer that he saw the huge water funnel that rose above the river.

He watched as it rose higher and higher. It moved from one bank of the river to the other, the water swirling fiercely. The funnel then split in two, then split again as they danced across the water. The funnels slowed to a calmer level, and varied in size now. The feats spellbound him, and he found he wanted a closer look.

He had nearly reached Fiona when she said, "Come sit."

Words eluded him as he sank to the ground beside her. All but one funnel disappeared, and then, to his amazement, water shot from the middle of the funnel to land some ten paces away in the river.

But before he could ask how she had done it, another shot of water exploded from the river exactly where the first had disappeared. The water continued to hop along the river.

Fiona giggled beside him, and he couldn't stop the grin that pulled at his lips. He wanted to see her face, but he couldn't take his eyes from the river and her many tricks.

The water hopped toward him as the funnel slowly disappeared into the river. He opened his mouth to ask her why she stopped when he was hit in the face with water. He wiped his face while Fiona clutched her sides as the laughter doubled her over.

Gregor found himself chuckling along with her.

"You never saw it coming," she said in between the laughter.

"I'm glad to see you are in a better mood."

She sat up and wiped at her eyes. "Thanks to you."

He was glad to see a smile back on her face. "What to talk about Moira?"

The smile diminished until it was barely visible. "Nay. I would rather not hear her name again."

"She didn't abandon you. She wanted you safe while she returned to the castle for Glenna," he tried to reason with her.

"She left me. She didn't come back. She never contacted me all these years. That is abandonment, no matter how you look at it."

He sighed and gazed at the water. "You haven't heard her side of the story. You don't know what happened in the castle after she left you."

"She has had ample time to explain it to me."

He couldn't fault her thinking there. "'Tis hard being the eldest child. You feel responsible for things and when they don't turn out like you want, or expect, you are left with the guilt."

"What are you guilty of?" she asked.

"All Moira wanted was for you and Glenna was to be happy. That happiness has finally come for Glenna, and very good people raised you. Moira never had to worry about you, and she wanted you to continue on with that happiness."

"Answer me, Gregor," she demanded. "What do you feel guilty over? Why were those men trying to kill you?"

*Because I did the unthinkable.*

She turned fully toward him. "Were you exiled from your clan?"

"Aye," he finally answered.

"I recognized the plaid those men wore as MacLachlan. Will you tell me why you were driven from your clan?"

He shot to his feet. "I have told you more than anyone else since that day. I think that is enough."

"It helps if you talk about it."

"You might want to take your own advice," he said.

He had to get far away from her. He had almost told her everything. It had felt right to tell her, to share the heartache he had carried since that awful day.

But he couldn't bear to see the look on her face when he found out just what sort of man he was. That would hurt far worse than any torture.

* * *

Fiona watched Gregor walk away. Maybe he was right. Maybe she should take her own advice. It had felt good to confide her fear to Gregor. Since she no longer had the desire to rip heads off at the mere mention of Moira's name, she deemed it safe enough to venture back to their camp. Maybe Aimery would still be there. To her surprise, he sat on the fallen tree whistling as he whittled on a small piece of wood.

She stopped in front of him. "Why have you come?"

"I told you. I wanted to check on you," he answered without looking up.

"If the Fae are as powerful as the stories I have been told, then you would have known that without seeing for yourself."

A smile broke across his face. "'Tis true. I wanted to meet you before you reached the Druid's Glen."

Satisfied with his answer, she sat beside him. "The entire time I was raised with Helen and Cormag they taught me the Druid ways and how to control my power. I know all about my parents, the prophecy, MacNeil, and the Druids. But I know nothing of my sisters."

Aimery stopped whittling. "And that scares you."

She raised her eyes to Gregor who had remained silent. "Aye," she admitted. "I am terrified."

## 8

"Are you sure this will work? Gregor has no idea we are even here," MacNeil said as he and his men rode closer to the MacLachlan lands. The Shadow hadn't disclosed anything to him, and frankly he was tired of it.

"Of course, it will work," The Shadow said. "I have already told you that. You needn't worry how he will know, but rest assured he will."

"I'm going to need more than that."

In a blink, there was a blade pressed to his throat. "That's all you are going to get," The Shadow whispered.

MacNeil jerked his head away from the dagger. "I'm not so sure your plan will work. After all, your many attempts on Glenna's life failed miserably."

The Shadow cackled into the night air. "Ah, MacNeil. Always the same argument. You do worry overmuch."

MacNeil wasn't so sure. Oh, he didn't mind the killing. In fact, he enjoyed it. But he didn't have time to pillage and kill leisurely. He had a prophecy to contend with and time was running out.

If The Shadow's plan did indeed work as he intended, then Fiona would be dead in a day. Only if Gregor knew his clan would be under attack though.

And he seriously doubted that was the case.

* * *

*Blood. There was blood everywhere. Covering everything. And the screams surrounded her, as if they were trying to tell her something, begging her to listen.*

*Fiona desperately tried to see more, to see what was causing the bloodshed. The pain of the people infused her until she could barely breathe. She pushed away from them to find an older man lying on the castle steps while MacNeil stood over him laughing. It seemed vitally important that she recognize the man.*

*She concentrated all her energy to find something about the man, and then...*

"Fiona!"

She jerked open her eyes to find Gregor kneeling above her, his hands on her shoulders, his brow furrowed and his lips pinched together.

"You were having another nightmare."

It wasn't a question. She nodded and tried to turn over, but he wouldn't let her. "Tell me of it."

"There was so much blood." She ran her hand across her brow to wipe the sweat away. "I can still hear the screams."

"Anything else?"

She raised her gaze to his. "I saw MacNeil. He stood over a man on the steps of a castle that he had killed.

For some reason, I think I'm supposed to know this man."

He ran a hand down his face. "I couldn't wake you. You wouldn't open your eyes."

"I'm sorry." She sat up. "Everything is fine now."

"Nay, Fiona. It isn't." He got to his feet and began to pace. "By the saints, why couldn't Aimery still be here?"

"Aimery couldn't help me and you know it. He would say something cryptic and leave it to me to decipher."

Gregor stopped pacing and turned to face her. "Just wake up the next time."

He had been worried about her, she realized. She got to her feet and went to him. Now would be another good time to begin her seduction. His back was to her as he looked into the woods. She wanted to touch him, to feel his strength beneath her fingers.

After a deep breath, she bit her lips to plump them and ran her finger down his back. He jumped at the contact. She didn't try to hide her satisfied smile as she came to stand in front of him.

"You are worried about me. That's very sweet," she said and looked up at him through her lashes.

"Of course I'm worried. 'Tis my duty to bring you unharmed and safe to the Druid's Glen."

She gave him a dazzling smile, all the while laughing inside at how he shied away from her touch. "I am unharmed and I know you will keep me safe."

"You are my responsibility." He caught her hand as she tried to touch his face. "I haven't figured out why your feelings toward me have changed so suddenly, but I will."

"There's nothing to worry about. I changed my mind."

Gregor wasn't buying it for a moment. She was up to something. She practically purred when she talked to him, and he didn't think he could stand to have her soft hands on him again.

She drove him to distraction with the simplest smile and her touch was excruciating to bear because he couldn't have her.

"Where a woman is concerned there's everything to worry about," he said. "There are still a few hours before dawn. Get some rest."

He held his breath until she walked away. For a moment he thought she might try to press and work her wiles on him. After all, he was only a man. Alone with a beautiful woman that had intrigued him from the first moment his eyes had found her.

But she wasn't for him. He was a monster, a murderer. She deserved better than the likes of him.

Once she was wrapped in her plaid and asleep, Gregor let his guard down. Being on his family's land had made him restless. He longed to see his mother, to have her warm smile directed at him and her hands soothe away his worries.

The sun streaked over the horizon when Gregor heard a deep sigh behind him. Fiona. He watched her sleep the rest of the night until her face was etched in his memory. He had torn himself away from her long enough to make a trek to the stream to freshen up.

A brief glance showed Fiona stretching sensually as she

woke from her slumber. No other nightmares had plagued her, thank the saints.

"Good morn," she said and sat up.

He nodded because words refused to leave his throat. She looked adorable with her hair coming out of her braid as the sun shed its light on her.

She stood and walked toward him. "I'm going down to the stream to freshen up. Want to join me?"

Gregor fisted his hands to keep from reaching out to her. She had no idea how her invitation stirred him. If she did, she wouldn't be tempting him. He began to pick up their few possessions when he heard the splash in the water. It didn't take much for him to picture her naked body gliding through the water.

After a vicious shake of his head to clear the image, he called to Morgane.

By the time he readied both horses, Fiona had returned. She braided her hair as she came to stand beside him.

"I feel much better," she said. "Isn't it amazing how a bath can refresh a person?"

He shrugged.

Her laughter filled the morning air. "My silent guardian. Tell me, do you sleep at all?"

"Not much." He wondered what had made him admit that to her, but when it came to Fiona he was thoroughly perplexed. He fitted his hands around her small waist and began to help her mount.

"I know some herbs that could aid your sleep."

"I don't need anything."

Her hands cupped his face. "There are deep shadows under your eyes."

He was about to answer her when the smile slipped from her face to be replaced by a frown as if she was in deep thought.

"So much pain," she whispered. "Your eyes are so sad. I wonder why I have never noticed that before now."

He hastily sat her on the mare and mounted Morgane. "We have wasted enough time this morn," he said before nudging the mare into a trot.

With his concentration on scouting for enemies and making sure Fiona kept up, he didn't have time to think of where they were and just how close he was to his home.

It wasn't until he stopped for the midday meal that he allowed himself a deep breath. So far, they hadn't encountered any more MacLachlan men.

"You have ridden like a man possessed."

He helped Fiona dismount and quickly moved away from her. "I don't have all the time in the world to get you to your destination."

"It isn't that. 'Tis your family, isn't it?"

He ignored her and set about looking for some food. "Maybe an oatcake would stop your constant questions."

"Why don't we visit your family? I'm sure they would be delighted to see their son, regardless of what you did."

What little patience he had evaporated with her last comment. He whirled around toward her as years of rage worked their way to the surface. "You know nothing. Nothing, Fiona. Do you know what it means to be banished from your clan?"

"It means you are never to return."

"Exactly," he bellowed. "If I return I shall be killed."

She took the oatcake from his hand and sat wordlessly on the grassy mountainside. He regretted losing his temper, but at least it had silenced her. Morgane nudged him with her nose and he patted her neck to assure her he was all right.

While he nibbled on his tasteless oatcake he looked out over the Highlands. He never tired of seeing the rugged beauty of his land. The clouds filled the sky, refusing to allow even a brief ray of sun through them, but even so the land was breathtaking.

Fiona forgot to eat as she watched Gregor look over the land. He belonged here in the wild. Free from anything or anyone. He was a Highlander. Her breath lodged in her throat when he tilted his head back and closed his eyes as a breeze swept the hair from his face. Golden locks floated in the wind while his face relaxed and took on almost a boyish charm.

She had pushed him too far. She knew that now, but she had wanted to help. Her oatcake forgotten, she stood and walked to stand beside him. His breathing stopped for just a moment, and she was afraid she had intruded. However, once her eyes had found the scene before her, there was no way she was going to leave any time soon.

"With each sway of the wind, the grass changes from green to gold to red, and even purple."

"Magnificent, isn't it?"

The love in his voice would be clear to even a deaf person. "Oh, aye. 'Tis glorious."

"I used to come here often as a child."

She couldn't believe he had told her something of his life. She waited, hoping he would say more.

"You should see it in the winter when the snow is newly fallen. I could never decide when I liked it most."

She looked at him then. His black eyes were still trained on the land around them, but they weren't as sad as before. This land, his family's land, healed him at much as it troubled him. If only she knew what he kept buried inside himself, she might be able to help.

When she raised her gaze, his eyes were on her. He stared at her for the longest time, as if he wanted to remember every inch of her face. She looked her fill as well. His wide, full mouth beckoned her, promising delights she could only dreamed about. She had heard the women in her clan talk, but listening to them and carrying through with something she really didn't know anything about was completely different.

Her body wanted Gregor. And as long as she kept her heart out of it she would be safe. There was nothing wrong with taking some pleasure where she found it, and he most assuredly promised that pleasure.

Before her courage left her, she reached down, grasped his hand and brought it to her face. When his warm, calloused fingers touched her cheek, she closed her eyes and rubbed her face against his palm.

She took a step closer to him and placed her hands on his chest. The leather beneath her palms was soft, cool to the touch. Just the opposite of what he would feel. Her face was raised toward him and his hand lightly caressed her cheek. He lowered his head as his hand moved to the back of her neck.

It was about to happen. She would finally receive her first kiss.

## 9

Gregor jerked back an instant before his lips touched hers. "Nay."

Fiona laughed, but he knew it was forced. "Am I so repulsive? The men in my clan claim otherwise."

"You know you aren't homely," he said and walked to the horses.

"Gregor—"

"Enough of the tricks." He swiveled toward her to give her a piece of his mind when he found her standing with her hands on her hips and a brow arched. "What?"

"You might want to see this."

He strode to her side and saw men riding hard toward them. There was no mistaking the MacLachlan plaid. "Damn. We need to ride."

When he turned around she was already mounted. "What's taking you so long?" she asked.

He bit his tongue and leapt atop Morgane. "Ride, Fiona," he shouted.

"I thought Aimery said we wouldn't be bothered again," she shouted over her shoulder.

"These are different men. They must have been on patrol and spotted us."

"I thought the MacLachlan's were friendly."

He caught up with her and shrugged. "I would rather not find out. I want to be off MacLachlan land by nightfall."

* * *

Beathan MacLachlan comforted his grieving wife. "Are you sure it was him?" he asked his soldiers.

"Aye, laird. I would know Gregor anywhere."

"He returned, Beathan," Margaret cried. "Our only child had returned to us. Now he's gone again."

"He was with a woman, laird. They ran as soon as they spotted us," the soldier explained. "They were too far ahead for us to catch them in the hills."

"No one knows the mountains like Gregor," Beathan said. He waved away the soldiers and concentrated on his wife. "I will find him, Margaret. I promise."

He slumped into his chair before the hearth as his wife went to their chamber. If only he could undo time. He would change the past and the harsh things he had said, and done, to Gregor.

That day, so long ago, he had lost both his children. One to death and one to banishment. It had taken years for Margaret to forgive him. When word had reached them that day that Gregor was on MacLachlan land he had immediately sent soldiers to bring him home.

Only things hadn't turned out as he had hoped. His only wish was to tell Gregor he was sorry for not standing beside him, for not believing him, and to ask his forgiveness.

"Gregor, my son, please come home."

The door to the castle flew open. Beathan stood and reached for his sword as two men walked in. "Who are you?" he demanded.

"The ones who will urge Gregor to return home."

A cold chill encased Fiona. She tried to keep it from Gregor, because she knew he would think she was becoming ill from being in the rain, but he saw it anyway.

"We need to find shelter," he hollered above the roar of the rain.

She nodded, but feared even a fire wouldn't warm the chill that encased her soul. Something terrible had happened, but she didn't know what.

They continued through the downpour that had suddenly come upon them. She kept her head down while Gregor looked among the mountainside for a cave. They come across several that had either been occupied by some animal or too small.

A shrill whistle brought her head up. He pointed to his left, and she could just make out the entrance to the cave. By this time, she was willing to share the cave with an animal. The plaid she had wrapped around her was soaked through, and now so were her clothes.

She waited outside the cave entrance as Gregor looked

around. He was back in no time leading her horse into the cave. She slid off her mare and began to unsaddle the horse while he took care of Morgane. After the horses had been seen to, he tossed her another plaid.

She caught it before it hit the ground and gave him a bright smile. "It seems like you are always trying to get me out of my clothes."

He didn't comment, but she had seen the slight lift of his lips before he had turned around. While he scrounged for dry wood she hurriedly undressed and wrapped the dry plaid around her.

Try as she might, she couldn't push the fear aside that something dreadful had happened. Or was about to happen. If only she could figure out what it was. Fat lot of good her Druid powers did when she couldn't fully use them. She needed a bowl of water so she could look into it. It didn't always work, but right now she needed to try.

The problem was she didn't want Gregor to know what was on her mind. She needed to figure this out on her own, of that she was certain. She needed a little time alone, and she knew of only one way to achieve that. With the plaid wrapped around her and one arm outside of it, she made her way to Gregor.

His leather garments clung to him like a second skin as he moved. It had been her intention to get close to him again, but once she reached him, her only thought was to feel his lips on hers.

No more trickery or wiles. She truly wanted to know his kiss, the feel of his firm lips moving over her mouth and skin. Her body heated just thinking about him. She knew she would have to guard her heart well, for if it was true and all Druids had the ability to find their true mate, then she would have no control over her heart.

Unless she made sure their union was only physical and not emotional.

"Fiona?"

His voice, rich and firm, made her stomach flip flop. Unsure now of whether she wanted time alone or to try and kiss Gregor, she raised her gaze to him. There must have been something in her eyes she hadn't been able to hide because he cursed and spun on his heel as he stalked to the horses.

With a deep sigh, she turned and rummaged through her bag. She found the bowl she and Helen had painted black and poured water in it. After she arranged herself comfortably before the fire and with her back to Gregor, she gazed deep within the bowl.

In the next heartbeat the scenes of her nightmares played out before her, but only in brief glimpses. Her frustration mounted until she was barely able to control it. Then she saw MacNeil and her heart plummeted to her feet.

"Nay," she whispered.

Somehow, someway, MacNeil was responsible for the coldness that had encased her soul for the last few hours. But what could he have done? She knew instinctively that her sisters were unharmed, but that didn't help in finding out who MacNeil had harmed—or intended to harm.

A horse nicker broke her concentration. She sat the bowl down and wondered what she should do next. A look over her shoulder found Gregor staring out into the rain.

The desolation surrounding him saddened her. Before

she knew it, she was on her feet and walking toward him. He turned toward her, his black eyes filled with grief and...resignation.

Whatever he had done must have been awful for it to fill his life and have him banished. His hurt brought out the compassionate side of her, and she thought if she could take away some of his sorrow it would relieve her pain as well.

He didn't push her hand away as she brought it up to his face. The feel of his unshaven face beneath her hands was a sensation she never realized she would like so much. The whiskers prickled her palm, but the warmth of his skin in contrast was heady.

She ran her hand down his cheek to his strong jaw, all the while studying his mouth. He hadn't moved, but she could tell her touch affected him by the slight stiffening of his body.

With more boldness than she had ever revealed to herself or anyone, she leaned toward him, wanting, needing his kiss. His scent of leather, horse and sandalwood filled her senses. She sighed and slightly parted her mouth as her body came in contact with his.

He was all man. More man than she had ever encountered. He stirred her body to life, made her think of being with him as only a man and a woman could.

She was a breath away from having his lips meet her when he jerked back. Could she have been wrong about him? Maybe he wasn't her mate, because her mate would never turn away from her. Twice.

Gregor tried to ignore the hurt that flashed in Fiona's green eyes, but he couldn't. His body screamed for him to taste her, to finally know if she held the nectar of the gods in her mouth. Before he allowed himself to change his mind, he brought his hands to her face and crushed his mouth to hers.

And then he tasted rapture.

Her mouth opened eagerly for his, and the softness of her lips only spurred his desire to new heights. And all with a simple kiss.

When her arms came around him, he couldn't hold back the groan that escaped him at the contact of her supple body against his chest. He plundered her mouth as though this was his only chance to taste such bliss. Her willing acceptance of his rough, demanding kiss only made him want more of her as their tongues dueled.

His breath lodged in his chest as her fingers entwined with his hair and gently scraped the back of his neck, sending chills down his body. She was going to be the death of him. He couldn't get enough of her, and when he began thinking of lowering her to the ground to take her, he knew he had reached the stopping point.

He tried to gently pull away from her, but she refused to let go and pressed her lips to his. When her tongue swept inside his mouth he nearly gave in.

Nearly.

He jerked out of her arms. Her chest rose and fell rapidly and her lips were swollen from his kisses. It didn't help that her eyes were glazed with desire, and his body demanded release.

For him to stay this close to her would be his downfall. He had to get away from her. He turned and strode out of the cave into the rain. He let the rain wash over him as he leaned against the side of the mountain, trying to regain his senses that had went spiraling out of control at her first touch.

Damn, he was a fool to have allowed himself to taste her. He had known from the look of longing in her eyes that he needed to get away. He just hadn't gone far enough.

Now with her taste still on his tongue all he could think of was her. Why had she come to him? He closed his eyes as the rain ran down his face and onto his already wet clothes. There was no denying she had touched a part of him that he thought long buried.

That part of him had died with his sister. He had shown himself, and his clan, just what a monster he was with Anne's death. 'Twas why he had tried to refuse this mission Moira had sent him on.

He had no right bringing Fiona to the Druid's Glen, and he certainly had no right taking such liberties with one the Fae had blessed. Yet, there was no rejecting the fact that it had felt right kissing Fiona. His world hadn't been so hopeless and barren. It had almost seemed like there had been a ray of hope, but that had quickly fled once they parted.

It must be the Druid in her that allowed him to feel such things. It wasn't real, and he needed to remind himself of that.

* * *

Aimery clutched his chest as the coldness swept over him. He gazed unseeing down at the many books that littered the desk. Something evil had happened, and he could almost guarantee it was the Evil One.

He leaned his head back and concentrated. It was easy to find MacNeil. The man stank of treachery and murder. But what startled Aimery was where MacNeil was.

"MacLachlan."

There was a space beside MacNeil that Aimery knew belonged to the Evil One. Once again, the Evil One used Fae magic. Whatever time Aimery thought he had grew slim. MacNeil had arrived at MacLachlan's much sooner than anticipated, but Aimery wasn't worried about Gregor's clan. MacNeil and the Evil One wouldn't do anything until Gregor arrived.

That gave Aimery the little time he needed to continue perusing the books. Somewhere in these massive tomes had to be something about mortals or Druids using Faerie magic.

## 10

F iona stared, dazed, after Gregor. Her heart still beat wildly, and her body yearned for more of him, but she was happy. She had finally gotten her kiss and it was everything she had hoped and dreamed it would be.

She touched her lips and sighed. If only he hadn't run from her. There was no running now though. She would snare him, because after that kiss there was no use refusing that he was her mate.

With a smile on her face that she hadn't worn in months, she curled up beside the fire and tried to sleep. But sleep eluded her.

She wanted to make sure Gregor returned and didn't leave her alone. She couldn't bear for that to happen. Besides, she was the one who would leave him.

Just as she was about to start worrying, he walked into the cave. He stopped and turned toward her, and she hastily shut her eyes except for a slit so she could see him. For the longest time, he watched her before he turned his back and began to undress.

The leather was stuck to his skin from the rain. He pulled off his vest, and the expanse of golden skin that narrowed to a trim waist caused her mouth to water. Muscles rippled in his neck and shoulder blades as he moved, and it was then she noticed it. The scar ran from the bottom of his right shoulder blade, in a curve, toward his spine.

It was an old scar by the looks of it. She forgot about the scar when he slipped off his boots and began to pull down his trews. Her breath lodged in her chest at what she saw.

Just as she was about to get her first glimpse of him naked, he stopped and spun around toward her. It was all she could do to keep her breathing even and continue to pretend she slept. To her overwhelming disappointment, Gregor decided against shedding his pants and laid down by the fire. It was going to be a very long night.

She slept fitfully. Every time she woke she found Gregor awake. She knew she would never survive another hard ride without some rest and forced herself to drift off to sleep.

It seemed only an instant before the dream woke her. She opened her eyes to find Gregor across the fire staring at her.

"Another one?" he asked.

She nodded and sat up. Dawn had yet to arrive, but from the gray sky it wasn't far off. There was no use trying to find sleep again.

"And I suppose you still won't tell me about it?"

How could she tell him she had seen MacNeil murder a man, but she had no idea who this man was? It sounded strange to her ears.

"I might be able to help," he offered while stirring the fire with a stick.

She thought about his comment as she began to dress. Then she had a thought. "I will tell you if you tell me why you were banished."

"Nay."

His reply was immediate. There had been no thinking about her proposition. "Are you afraid I will think differently of you?"

"I don't think, Fiona. I know. Why do you think my clan banished me?" He rose to his feet, his anger palpable.

Her dreams weighed heavily on her, and for the first time in her life, she wanted to share them. He was about to walk out of the cave when she said, "I saw MacNeil again. He's the central part of the dreams."

That stopped Gregor in his tracks. "And," he prompted when he turned toward her. "What is he doing?"

"Killing a man. A laird of a clan by the looks of it." She raised her eyes to find one side of his mouth lifted in a half smile.

"You trust me enough to tell me?"

That brought a smile to her face. She walked to stand beside him at the entrance to the cave. With the previous day's rain finished, the new day dawned splendidly.

The sky was a dusky pink as the sun began its ascent. It cast the mountains around them into shadow, making them look like hulking black monsters.

"I know you couldn't possibly understand why I have no wish to see Moira again but that is part of the reason I don't trust people," she said.

He stood beside her, hands locked behind his back. "Aye. I think I do understand. I don't trust people either."

"What a pair we make," she said and smiled at him. Memories of the night before and their kiss ascended on her.

He stepped back. "We, ah, need to get moving."

She didn't argue as she began to pack. It wouldn't take long to wear down this wall he built around himself. The hardest battle had been fought the night before.

He wanted her. There was no doubt about that after that hungry kiss they had shared. Getting him to admit it would be another thing, but she didn't need for him to admit it. She just needed him to want her so badly that he forgot about his sorrow.

* * *

Aimery chuckled while he reclined in a chair with one of the many books in his lap. Fiona and Gregor were quite a match if he did say so himself. She was coming into her own power nicely and would soon wear Gregor down. No man could stand against something as beautiful as Fiona and not fall.

The smile Aimery wore vanished quickly as Fiona's soul deep fear penetrated him. There was only one person who could cause that kind of fear.

"MacNeil."

Aimery delved deep into Fiona's mind and saw her nightmares. He sighed. He couldn't interfere in this. MacNeil wanted Fiona and Gregor, and he was supposed to sit by and watch. There was no way he would allow that.

So far, Fiona and Gregor had figured things out, and as long as they stayed away from MacNeil he would keep the Fae out of it.

But that didn't mean he couldn't ready his army. MacNeil and the Evil One were using Fae magic. Definitely an advantage over Fiona and Gregor. Just because the army was there didn't mean they would interfere.

At least, that's what he would tell the king and queen if they discovered his plan.

\* \* \*

The sun shone bright and clear the next day as Fiona and Gregor continued their trek to the Druid's Glen. She was exhausted, but refused to allow him to see it. She didn't know how he could manage to continue after a night of little sleep, again, and she had a sneaking suspicion that he spent most of his nights like that.

Few words had been spoken since the morning had dawned, and that was fine with her. She didn't know what to say to him and, apparently, he had nothing to say to her. They had eaten the noon meal while riding, and her backside was sore and in need of a hot bath.

Gregor was different now that they were off MacLachlan land. He was more relaxed, if you could call a man as wild and untamed and powerful as he relaxed.

"We will stop early tonight," he said as they crested a hill.

Fiona was too tired to speak, but when she caught sight of the loch below, she did manage a small smile. She would get her bath after all. It wouldn't be hot, but a bath was a bath. She didn't lag behind after that and urged Gregor on. When he declared a spot for their camp, she eagerly slid off her mare and began to unsaddle her.

After she found a clean gown, she headed to the loch. But Gregor's voice stopped her.

"Where are you going?"

"To take a bath."

"Let me have a look around first. Rest here until I return," he said as he picked up his bow and arrows.

She wanted to throttle him, but he did have a point. She leaned against a boulder to await his return.

\* \* \*

Gregor scouted the area, and when he was certain they weren't being followed, he made his way back to Fiona. To his surprise, she was fast asleep. He didn't want to wake her. He had known she hadn't slept the previous night. She hadn't fooled him, he thought with a smile, although she had tried to act as perky as usual.

Morgane nickered to him and he went to care for the horses. When he was finished, he found Fiona still asleep, so he made his way to the loch. A bath sounded good, and it would be an ideal time to test himself.

After he shed his clothes, he walked into the cool loch until the water reached his knees. As the water swirled around his legs, the memories rushed to invade him. He pushed them aside and took another step until the water reached his thighs.

He tried to manage his rapid breathing to calm himself,

but there was no controlling the erratic beating of his heart. With his fists clenched, he waded until the water reached his waist.

Even with the cool water, sweat beaded his forehead. The cries of his sister rung loudly in his ears as he desperately tried to push the memories into the hole where his heart used to be.

It was too much. He would never swim again and he needed to realize that. He moved into shallower water and sat so he could begin to wash. Just as he was about to finish he saw the water ripple around him.

* * *

Fiona stretched the cramp out of her neck as she stood. She couldn't tell how long she had slept, but by the looks of their camp Gregor had already returned.

*Now where could he be...?*

Her body needed the bath, so she made her way to the dark waters. It was there she found him. He sat in the shallow water and looked out over the terrain. He looked so lonely sitting there that she wanted to go to him.

She licked her lips at seeing his skin glistening with water. Her hands fisted when she thought of how he would feel as her hands glided over his damp skin.

It would be the perfect opportunity to get his attention.

* * *

The sound of a giggle reached Gregor as he turned his head. All he spotted was feet as Fiona dove into the water.

His eyes found his clothes and gauged the distance between him and the shore. He tried to calculate if he could reach them and the rocks before Fiona broke the surface when she did just that.

"Why didn't you wake me?" she asked. Her expression was that of an innocent, but her eyes were anything but.

He knew she wanted him, but there was no way he would give in. He wouldn't have that on his soul as well. She would be brought to the Druid's Glen an innocent. He refused to think what Moira and Frang would do to him if he sullied Fiona with his dirty soul.

"What's the matter?" she asked as she swam closer to him. "Has your voice disappeared?"

"Nay," he answered. "I saw you needed the rest."

She smiled and winked, and he knew he was about to get her all-out assault. He needed to get out of the water. Fast. Before his legendary control snapped.

"That was very thoughtful of you."

*Here it comes. Prepare yourself.*

With her arms stretched out in front of her she glided toward him. "Why don't you come into deeper water? 'Tis nice out here."

*No way on God's green Earth.* "I'm sure 'tis."

"Surely you aren't afraid of me?"

He shook his head, still trying to figure out a way to get to shore quickly. To his utter amazement, she took hold of his hand. He had been so intent of finding a way out of the loch that he hadn't realized she had come up beside him.

On their own accord, his eyes traveled to the water to see if she was as bare as he, but all he found was the delectable swell of her breasts visible through the dark water. It would be so easy to give in and have her. He wanted her and she wanted him. Why should he allow something as insignificant as her innocence stop him? It certainly wasn't stopping her.

He squeezed his eyes closed and silently cursed. He was the monster his father had called him. He should have more strength than be thinking of giving in to base wants and needs. He never had a problem getting a woman into his bed.

It would just take vast amounts of control to keep Fiona off him until he delivered her to Moira and the Druid's, then he could find a nice, willing wench to warm his bed for the next month.

"Gregor?"

Her voice, smooth as silk and slightly husky, surrounded him. He opened his eyes to find her very close.

*Control. Vast amounts of control.*

## 11

S he pulled on his hand. "Let's relax in the water while we can. A little swim won't hurt anything."

"Nay." Gregor yelled louder than he intended but it had gotten her attention.

She dropped his hand and shrugged. Her hand snaked out and grabbed the chain of his medallion. "What's this?"

"A medallion that was given to me by my father."

"'Tis beautiful."

"Thank you," he said and turned away. "I should head back to camp."

"Please stay and talk to me."

He didn't have any choice in the matter if he didn't want to leave before her. He resigned himself to the fact that he would be in the water for some time. Yet, he could make the most of it, he thought with an inward smile as she turned.

Water ran in droplets down her back. Skin the color of cream glistened in the afternoon sun, and he would bet his best dagger she tasted of cream as well. Her hair had come loose of its braid to float seductively in the water. He almost reached out to touch a dark strand, but stopped himself in time.

She swam deep into the loch and, although he called out to her, she kept swimming. His fear threatened to rise up and choke him as he struggled to rein in his emotions.

"Fiona!"

Finally she turned and smiled at him. "What's wrong?"

"Come back."

"Have I frightened you?"

He didn't answer her, but waited until she was closer to him. "Don't go out that far."

"I'm a great swimmer, Gregor. You have nothing to worry fear. Not to mention I have power over water," she said. Then stopped and stared at him. "You were worried about me. Why?"

"Just don't do it. Please," he ground out.

She looked at him for several heartbeats. "All right."

Then, to his shock, she began to bath. "What are you doing?"

Her laughter filled the air. "What does it look like?" She continued to lather her slender arms, and just when he thought she would stand up, she turned her back on him.

"Tell me what you did before the Druids sent you for me."

He didn't want to tell her but knew she would keep on him until he told her. "You really don't want to know."

"Why?" she asked over her shoulder. "Will it change my perception of you?"

"Aye."

"Why don't you let me decide that?"

He sighed. She was like a swarm of gnats that would keep after you no matter how much you tried to avoid them. "I'm a mercenary."

Silence. He had hoped she wouldn't change her opinion of him, but maybe it was better that she did. Then the seduction she had in mind would cease.

"I hope you fight for good causes."

He sat in stunned silence for a moment as her words registered. If discovering he was a mercenary hadn't done it, his next statement would. "War is never a good cause, and 'tis the money I'm interested it."

She stopped her bathing and looked at him over her shoulder.

"I bet that has changed your opinion of me," he said sardonically.

She shook her head. "I wouldn't have thought that of you. You don't seem the type."

"'Tis amazing how the past will shape one's life."

"Because of your banishment, you mean."

He turned his head away from her. He couldn't meet her eyes. When she said it, it made his choice seem so unpractical and stupid.

"Why, then, did you take this task?"

What to tell her? Dare he tell her the truth? That he wanted to prove to himself? That it wasn't about the coin, but more about doing something that was right?

"Because Moira asked me," he said. It was partially the truth anyway.

"How did you come to meet her?"

She had asked nonchalantly, but he knew how much that had cost her. For a moment, he watched as she continued to wash. "I was on the wrong side of a war. Glenna and Conall helped me see that."

"So, you helped them."

"Aye."

She rinsed herself and turned towards him. "In other words, MacNeil hired you."

His heart constricted at her words. They were spoken softly, but with sorrow. "Aye."

"Why?"

"Because he was willing to pay. That's my way of life. I'm not going to sprinkle it with goodness because there isn't any. I never wanted to know why someone fought a war. I went to the person who paid the most. I'm good at what I do and men will pay handsomely to have me in their armies."

"But you are good or you wouldn't have helped my sister and Conall. Regardless of what you think of yourself, 'tis the truth."

Her words stunned him. How could she think that of him? She barely knew him. He was so lost in thought over her statement that he didn't realize she was out of the water until she called his name.

"Enjoy the sunset."

He turned back around and looked above the mountains to the sky. The sun had sunk behind the massive mountains and had turned the sky a vibrant gold and purple. The clouds that dotted the sky were turned a darker shade of purple while the loch reflected the gold sky.

It was a sunset seen once in a lifetime and one that should be enjoyed with someone.

Too bad he was alone. As usual.

\* \* \*

Fiona watched the sunset from their camp. Gregor's words had disturbed her, there was no doubt, but she also knew that he was a good man that had been knocked off the right course. A good woman could set him on that course.

*But it isn't me.*

He would return soon. She decided on her course of action while swimming and there was no turning back now. She would have him. Tonight.

And she had just the thing that would make him fall to his knees. Or at least she hoped he would.

\* \* \*

Gregor walked into the camp without looking at Fiona. He wanted to give her a fire but without the shelter of a cave he didn't know if they could chance it. The fact that MacNeil hadn't followed them worried him. They were on the shortest route to MacInnes land, so in truth, MacNeil should be trailing them.

Where the hell was he anyway? He happened to spot a place in the mountainside where they could build a small fire and still be hidden.

"I'm going to find some food," he said and grabbed his bow and arrow.

"I will get the fire started." He heard her reply as he walked away.

His father had taught him well. He tracked the rabbits and caught three of them. By the time he returned to the camp he was starving and looking forward to the meal.

"I caught three hares," he said as he walked into the camp and stopped dead in his tracks.

Fiona stood by a boulder, her leg placed on it while she bent over and fiddled with her shoe. A large amount of leg was visible to his gaze, and he hungrily ate up the sight of her.

"Oh, good," she all but purred.

Gregor jerked his gaze away from her and set about cleaning the rabbits. All the while she hummed and carried on a one sided conversation that he refused to be a part of.

He set the rabbits above the fire to cook and dusted off his hands, his mouth watering at the thought of their meal. He straightened and turned to find Fiona in front of him.

"You are an expert hunter, aren't you?" she asked and ran her finger down his arm.

His muscles twitched of their own accord and chills rose on his skin at her touch. Damn, but she was hard to resist. "I get the meal on the table."

She bit her lip and looked at him through her lashes. "So humble."

"I, ah, I need to scout around the camp again." He had to get away from her. All his blood had pooled to his manhood at her nearness. He never lost control like this and it was a bit embarrassing.

"I will be waiting." She gave him a wink and sat beside the fire.

Without looking back, he nearly ran from the camp. He waited until he knew the rabbits would be cooked before he returned to the camp.

She didn't speak to him as she began to eat, and Gregor never realized how alluring a woman eating could be. He didn't taste his food as he watched her lick away the juices from the meat, her pink tongue peeking out to tempt him.

Her lips wrapped around a piece of meat and all he could think about was her mouth on his rod. Sweat covered his body as he tried to focus on eating instead of Fiona's mouth, but it was impossible. When he could stand it no more, he rose to bury the bones.

*Just go back to camp and lie down. Don't talk to her, don't look at her. Just close your eyes and sleep.*

And that was his intention until he walked into camp and found her standing beside the fire with a plaid wrapped around her. He was about to ask her if she was ill when she let the blanket fall to her feet.

Gregor felt as though someone punched him in the gut. Fiona stood before him in all her naked glory. She was magnificent, and his eyes took in everything from her long legs, full hips, slim waist, and breasts that would certainly fill his hands.

Those hands itched to touch her, to see if she was real or a vision his mind had created to taunt him. The bow and arrows dropped out of his hands, and his sword soon followed. His feet began to walk toward her and his eyes found her face.

Her dark locks hung loose and full around her shoulders and down her back to graze her waist. As he closed the distance between them he saw the dark tint of her nipples. They hardened beneath his gaze, and he knew there was no turning back now.

## 12

Fiona held her breath and waited for Gregor to stalk away, but as he came toward her she began to breathe again. His gaze raked her body, and the smile that pulled one corner of his lips caused her body to jump in anticipation.

He continued until he stood before her. Then, he fell to his knees and wrapped his arms around her waist. She enfolded him in her arms and briefly closed her eyes as she savored the moment.

She knelt down with him and saw the desire in his black eyes. Triumph flared in her. He hadn't shunned her and she was in control. It would stay that way, too.

"Do you know what you are doing?" he asked as he ran a hand through her hair.

"Aye. Don't question this. Just accept it and let yourself feel."

He leaned forward and nibbled on her mouth while his hands brought her against him. She began to remove his vest. Her hands pushed it over his broad, muscular shoulders then ran down his back as she learned the feel of him.

His hands roamed all over her while his mouth drove her to ecstasy with his kisses. She leaned her head back when his mouth moved over her jaw to her neck.

"Hmmm. You do taste of cream."

She smiled at his words. "Do I? Is that what a woman is supposed to taste like?"

He raised his head and pushed her back until she was lying on the ground. "Only you," he said as he loomed above her.

"You still have your trews on."

He laughed and the sound warmed her heart. "So I do, but I can remedy that."

She leaned up on one elbow as he disrobed and tossed his medallion in the pile. His body didn't disappoint. His legs were just as muscular as the rest of his body, but it was the man part of him that drew her attention.

He stood straight and tall and beckoned her. She had never seen a man naked before, but she knew no man would compare to Gregor. He didn't give her long to look as his body covered hers.

"I wasn't done looking," she said.

"What's looking when you can touch?"

She raised her eyebrows at his bold invitation, but rolled him onto his side just the same. Her hands roamed over his defined chest and abdomen as his chest hair crinkled beneath her fingers.

When her hand dipped below his waist to his bulging thigh he didn't hinder her. Her hand stopped shy of touching his cock. She could feel the heat of his member, and it intrigued her even more.

She bit her lip and reached out to touch him. It was silken in texture, and it leapt at her touch. He sucked in a breath and groaned as she ran her hand over him and his sacs.

"By the saints," he moaned. "I never knew your touch could do this to me."

"And what do I do?" She needed to know how she affected him.

His eyes burned as they gazed at her. "You set me afire. 'Tis everything I can do not to take you right now."

"Then take me," she offered as a thrill shot through her at his words.

He growled and pulled her on top of him. "You shouldn't have said that," he said before his mouth crushed hers.

Even though he threatened to take her right then, he didn't. His hands were gentle, insistent as they skimmed over her body, learning her curves and giving her untold amounts of pleasure.

When his hands found her breasts and squeezed, she burned for more, and he gave it to her when his lips moved to her nipples. She cried out from the pleasure and raked her hands across his back.

He suckled until she thought she would die of the pleasure. A moan escaped when his hands skimmed down her skin until they reached the juncture of her legs. Her breath caught in her throat as she looked at him, only to find his gaze on her. She raised a hand and ran a finger over his eyebrow.

"Don't stop now," she said.

His small smile sent a buzz of excitement through her. That thrill heated when his finger grazed the most sensitive part of her. Her hips jerked toward his hand, silently begging for more of his touch.

He didn't disappoint her. His finger slipped inside her as his thumb began to circle around a part of her she didn't know could feel such intense enjoyment. Before she knew it, she felt herself building toward something.

Then, Gregor's hand left her. She reached out for him only to feel him lie on top of her.

"You are killing me with each moan that leaves those delightful lips," he whispered before his mouth claimed hers in a kiss.

His tongue slid into her mouth and around hers while his hips rocked against hers. She wrapped her arms around his neck at the same time he began to suck on her tongue. The bliss left her dazed and wanting, needing more. She couldn't get enough of him.

The more he touched and kissed her the more she wanted of him. Her heart told her to stop him before 'twas too late, but her body refused to listen. It was past the point of caring for anything other than the feelings that coursed through her.

She didn't question him when he rolled her onto her stomach and began placing kisses along her back and neck. He raised her up on her knees and pulled her back against his chest as his hands cupped her breasts.

Her body concentrated on his hands so she didn't feel his knee part her legs until his arousal grazed her throbbing center. His lips kissed her ear while one hand pulled her hips hard against him.

"This is your last chance to change your mind," he whispered. "Tell me to stop."

She took his hand and placed it in the juncture of her thighs. "I don't want you to."

He groaned and slid a finger inside of her as his other hand pinched her nipples. Her body was in a fever pitch of delight and she didn't think it could get any better than this.

"So hot and wet," Gregor said in between the kisses he placed on her neck.

Her breathing was shallow and heavy as the feeling built inside of her. His hands grasped her hips and she couldn't hold herself upright. She feel forward onto her hands and heard him growl behind her.

Gregor thought he would explode. She was everything he had hoped for and more. He had told her if she wanted him to stop he would walk away. He didn't know how he'd do it, but he would have if that was what she wanted. To his great relief she had wanted him to stay.

Now she waited for him. She wouldn't know what was to come next, but her body did. He guided the tip of his member against her. Her moan and the push of her hips against him nearly had him spilling his seed.

He slid more of himself into her until he reached her maidenhead. This was the part he hated, the reason why he shied away from innocents.

"Fiona," he began, but she stopped him.

"I know what's to come. Please, don't make me wait. I need you."

Her words brought out the beast in him. He took hold of her hips to keep her still and thrust into her and past her maidenhead.

A small gasp escaped her at his intrusion. He wanted to give her body time to adjust to him, but her hips began to move against him. He was powerless to do anything other than move to her rhythm.

He closed his eyes as he thrust harder and harder into her. He was so close to the edge he didn't think he could wait for her, but he refused to allow himself the pleasure without taking her with him.

He leaned over her and found her pleasure nub. She began to moan as his fingers circled around her nub. Before he knew it she was clenching around him. He let himself go then and plunged deep within her.

And for the first time in his life his body perceived something more than just physical release.

His response to Fiona left him with an emotion his heart hadn't experienced in years. Warmth. With his emotions in a whirlwind he couldn't utter a word. Thankfully, she didn't require any. She turned over and brought him down beside her.

He pulled her close against him and thought about what he had just experienced.

"It was just like I imagined it would be," she mumbled against his shoulder.

Gregor blinked up at the stars overhead and wondered if she realized this changed things between them.

## 13

Gregor's eyes jerked open at the scream. It took him a moment to realize it came from beside him. He rolled over and looked down to see Fiona in the grips of another nightmare as tears rolled down her face. Fear unfurled its talons in his belly as he came up on his knees over her.

"Fiona," he said and gently shook her.

"Nay," she cried out and pushed his hands away.

"Fiona, wake up."

She didn't respond to him so he sat her up and pulled her into his lap. Her tears wet his chest as he rocked.

"Please, wake up," he whispered and wiped her tears away. As he ran his hands over her eyes she opened them. "Fiona?"

"I want them to stop," she said and buried her head in his shoulder.

He wrapped his arms around her and held on tight. If it was in his power he would take those dreams unto himself, but he didn't have any power.

"Same dream?" he asked.

She nodded her head. "I saw more this time."

"How much more?"

She raised her face to his. "I saw MacNeil plunge his sword into that man on the castle steps. MacNeil laughed while he did, and it was as if he was looking at someone or something, but I couldn't see who."

"Is that all you saw?" If he were able to help her piece these dreams together then maybe, they would stop.

"The man on the steps was trying to show me something."

"You never saw it?"

She climbed off his lap and stood. "Nay. It seems important, though."

He rose to stand beside her. "Fiona—"

"I know what you would say," she interrupted him, "but I've no wish to discuss what happened last night."

"But it changes everything."

She whirled around to face him. "It changes nothing. Absolutely nothing."

Gregor couldn't believe the coldness that came from her beautiful green eyes. No emotion lay there and it scared him. She had been nothing but emotional since their first meeting. Could the dreams be doing this to her?

He didn't stop her as she turned toward the small fire that had gone out. The first rays of sunlight peaked over the mountains, and it was then he realized he had slept most of the night.

* * *

Fiona would just ignore him. At least that's what she told herself she would do, but Gregor was hard to ignore. Every time she looked at him, she could feel his hard body beneath her hands and see his black eyes glaze over with desire.

He hadn't brought up their night of passion since that morning, and she was quite happy with that. Though she wanted to let her mind linger on the amazing pleasure Gregor had given her, she couldn't. Not with the dreams harassing her. She didn't see the passing landscape as she focused her mind on her dreams.

This recent one had been the worst so far. If only she had seen what the man had been trying to show her. She wanted to talk to Aimery, but she didn't know how to call a Faerie to her, and it was unlikely that Gregor did either.

She would just have to endure the dreams until she reached the Druid's Glen, then maybe there she could determine what the dreams were trying to show her.

"Do you plan to ignore me all day?"

Gregor's voice intruded on her thoughts. She raised her eyes to find him twisted in the saddle as he watched at her. "I'm not ignoring you."

"I have asked you twice if you needed to rest."

She bit her lip as he pulled up on the reins. She didn't wish to hurt Gregor, but there was just so much going on right now. "I was thinking."

"About the dreams?" he asked. His eyes softened.

She nodded and pulled her mare to a halt when she reached him. The kindness in his eyes unsettled her. He wasn't supposed to act like this. He was supposed to go about his business as if nothing ever happened.

Why was he being so kind? It didn't help that she yearned to pull his head down for a kiss, or feel his strong arms enfold her against him. He was offering to be her strength, but she couldn't allow that.

Her eyes blurred with unshed tears at her dilemma, but she saw his hand reach for her face. She jerked away from him and wanted to cry out when she saw the shock that briefly flared in his eyes.

Once again, his eyes went back to the way they were the first time she saw him. Dead. No emotion resided in him now, and she was the cause of it.

She wanted to call him back and explain, but she knew it wouldn't do any good. The damage was done. For the rest of the day, he didn't spare her a glance as he rode hard and fast across the countryside. She wanted him to ignore her, and she was certainly getting her wish.

* * *

Aimery ran a hand down his face. Things weren't turning out as they should, and all because of Fiona and her fear of being left alone.

"What is it?" asked a female voice.

He opened his eyes to see Moira standing beside him. Before he could answer, Glenna strode up.

"Aimery?" Glenna asked. "Is something amiss? Fiona isn't hurt, is she?"

He shook his head and raised a hand when he saw more questions coming. "Fiona and Gregor are just fine. For the moment."

"Is there anything we can do to keep them safe?" Moira asked.

"They must do this on their own," he explained. "The evil that is out there is gaining strength."

Glenna began to pace. "I cannot stand this. Why can't you help?"

"For the same reason I didn't help you and Conall." He stood and put his hands on Glenna's shoulders to halt her. "You and Conall needed to work things out on your own or you wouldn't be here now."

"But if Fiona is in danger?"

He sighed. "The three of you will continue to be in danger until the time of the prophecy. There's nothing I can do about that, but that is why we gave you your powers."

"You might not be able to help Fiona, but why can't we?" Moira asked.

"There are many things that haunt her, Moira," Aimery said. "She and Gregor have a long journey to make, but if they make it here then things will turn out all right."

"What do you mean *if* they make it here?" Glenna asked. "If something happens to Fiona then the prophecy won't come to pass."

Aimery smiled. "They'll make it here. This I promise you. I won't let MacNeil or the Evil One harm either her or Gregor."

"Gregor is her mate, isn't he?" Moira asked.

Aimery nodded. "Now let us turn our thoughts to the battle that will take place with MacNeil once Fiona reaches us. We have much to prepare for. Where has Frang hid himself?"

Fiona wanted to wrap her hands around Gregor's throat and squeeze. Hard. The beast hadn't even stopped for a rest that afternoon, and she was so exhausted she could barely stand.

Storm clouds had gathered all day and they fit her mood perfectly. They had just discovered a cave when thunder rumbled loudly in the distance. She took care of her mare, and dug out some oatcakes in her bag to munch on.

She wasn't about to ask Gregor for food. He didn't acknowledge she was even with him as he started a fire then went to his horse.

It had been a draining day emotionally and physically, and all she wanted to do was sleep. After she stuffed the last of the oatcake in her mouth she laid on her side using her arm as a pillow. She tried to stay awake to see what Gregor was about, but her eyes grew too heavy.

* * *

Gregor took the saddle off Morgane and turned to find Fiona asleep. It was just as well. He found it increasingly hard to keep his hands and eyes off her. She drove him crazy, but she had wormed her way inside of him and touched places that hadn't been touched since Anne's death.

A glance from the cave showed the gathering storm. If he was lucky, he could find a small hare or two before the rain came. After he retrieved his bow and arrows, he took one more look at Fiona. He hated to wake her just to let her know he was gone hunting.

He walked from the cave and never saw Morgane follow.

* * *

*Alone. She was alone again, and it terrified Fiona. What had she done to Moira to make her abandon her?*

*Once again, Moira promised to return, and like before, Fiona stood anxiously, awaiting her sister's return. Yet, Moira never came back.*

*Fiona raced to the castle, determined to find Moira herself. She wandered the castle alone, calling out to anyone who might hear her. But no matter how loud she called or how far she followed her, Moira never appeared.*

*She was alone.*

*Then she spotted Moira's blonde head running up the stairs toward their parent's chamber. Fiona ran as fast as her five-year-old legs could go. She reached her parent's chamber to find the door open.*

*The fear dissipated as she walked toward the door. Until she looked into the empty chamber. No one was there. They had all abandoned her.*

*Moira's laughter echoed around the now empty castle.*

Fiona woke with a start. It had been years since that dream had visited her. She wiped the sweat from her brow and wondered why that dream had plagued her once again. Could it be because she was about to come face-to-face with Moira after all these years?

The need to feel Gregor's arms surround her had her

searching the cave. He was nowhere to be found. She pushed aside her panic when she realized he must be hunting for food.

She laughed at herself and walked to the entrance of the cave. The rain had finally come. She couldn't tell how long she had slept because the storm clouds made it difficult to judge the time of day.

Her mare nickered at her. Fiona turned and spotted the mare standing about ten feet from her. She walked to the horse and patted her neck.

"I'm sorry I don't pay you as much attention as Gregor does his mare, but I do have reasons," she told the beast.

The horse nudged her with its nose. Fiona smiled and petted the animal again. It wasn't until then that she noticed Morgane was gone.

Gregor had left her.

Terror wrapped its steely shackles around her. Once again, she had been abandoned, just as she always feared. It was no wonder she kept everyone and everything at arm's length.

Without thought, she plunged into the drenching rain and ran in search of Gregor. She refused to be left again. If anyone were to leave, it would be her.

\* \* \*

Gregor cursed. Between the blinding rain and Morgane following him, it hadn't been a successful hunt. Thankfully, he had discovered Morgane behind him before he had ventured too far from the cave. After he tied her to a tree, the sky had opened up and let the rain out.

He was about to return to the cave when he spotted the boar. It was only a few feet from him, and he blamed the rain for him not hearing the animal.

He would be lucky if he made it out of here alive now. After a hasty look around, he spotted a low hanging branch. If he timed it just right, he could make into the tree before the boar charged him. If the branch held him, that is.

A look back at the animal proved his worst fear. The boar had spotted him and was about to charge. He didn't have time to wonder if the branch would hold him. He jumped and grabbed hold of the branch as the boar let out a high pitched squeal. He barely got his feet up by the time the boar reached him.

Once he was safely in the tree, he laughed down at the boar. That was until he spotted something running toward him.

"It cannot be," he mumbled.

But it was. Fiona ran through the rain, and she was headed straight toward the boar.

## 14

G regor cursed again, this time much louder.

*What in the name of the saints is she doing out here?*

He would make sure to ask her that after he saved her from the boar. Too bad he didn't have a spear.

It wasn't until the boar turned toward Fiona that he realized just how close to the edge of the mountain she was. If the boar charged her, they would both go over the side.

He had to get her attention. He called out to her, but she couldn't hear him over the roar of the rain. A look down confirmed that the boar had seen her and was now hunting her.

Gregor threw a leg over the branch and jumped to the ground. If he was lucky enough, he might be able to get close enough to catch Fiona's attention. But there were a lot of 'ifs' involved.

As he ran toward her, he notched his bow with an arrow and prayed his aim was true. Just as pulled his bow back to fire he heard Fiona scream as the boar ran in front of her.

"Stay still," he whispered as he set the boar in his sights.

He released the arrow as the boar squealed his attack. Gregor breathed a sigh of relief as the animal fell to its side. He raced toward Fiona and the boar, but when he reached the spot where Fiona had stood, she was gone.

The rain slacked off enough that he spotted her running away from him. Without another look at the boar he raced after her. He deserved an explanation and by God she was going to give it to him.

He was surprised at the speed in which she ran. His anger at her near death spurred him faster.

"Fiona," he called, but she continued as if she hadn't heard him.

Twice more he shouted at her, but her pace was unrelenting. With his longer legs, it didn't take him long to catch up with her. He wrapped his arms around her and turned so he would take the brunt of the fall as he brought her to the ground.

To his utter amazement, she began to scream and hit him. He grabbed her arms and wrestled her until she was on her back, and he straddled her. Still she screamed and tried to kick him.

"Enough," he roared. "Have you gone daft?"

"You won't leave me," she ground out between clenched teeth.

"Leave you?" Then he realized what she thought. With Morgane gone, she assumed he had left her.

He let go of her wrists and rolled off her. Even though she continued to pound her fists against his chest, he pulled her into his arms. He knew how fear could overrule good judgment, and her panic proved how her fear ruled her life.

"I didn't leave you, Fiona. I would never leave you." And to his astonishment, he realized that last part was true.

After her anger was spent and she lay limp in his arms, he got to his feet and carried her to the cave. The rain was now a light mist, but all he could think about was getting her out of her wet clothes. If she let him.

Once they were inside the cave, he set her down beside the fire and smoothed back her hair that was plastered to the side of her face.

She raised her green eyes to him, and he could still see the fear in them. "I didn't leave you," he repeated. "I went hunting and Morgane followed me."

"I was sure you had...left me," she said between her teeth chattering.

"You are going to become ill yet."

Before he could move his hands to begin undressing her, she cupped his cheek and pulled his head down to her lips. His body reacted instantly to her sweet touch. He wanted her more now than he had the first time and he feared that would always be the case.

She nipped his lips, and then ran her tongue along them. Her hands entwined in his wet hair and lightly scratched his scalp. Chills ran down his body at her touch.

He pulled off her gown that had molded itself against her skin. After she was devoid of clothes, her hands began to untie his trews, and he couldn't get out of his clothes fast enough.

They fell together to the ground, their lips and hands frantic to taste and touch. Her hand glided between their bodies and found his hard, aching member. With a touch that seemed to know his every want, her hand brought him to such a pitch he almost gave in and spent himself right there.

But he wanted more for Fiona.

While her hand worked its magic, he moved between her legs and found her moist and ready. He slid a finger in her and rejoiced when he heard her sharp intake of breath.

"I need you now," she panted.

Gregor wasn't about to deny her, not when he needed her just as badly. He rose above her and positioned his cock where the tip rested against her woman's lips. Pure heaven awaited him, but he wondered if he deserved another taste.

Fiona waited for Gregor to fill her, but he continued to stare at her. She couldn't wait for him any longer. She brought her legs up and wrapped them around his waist. With a smile, she pushed with her legs the same time she raised her hips.

He slid into her hot, hard. It was everything she remembered from the previous night and more. He drove her body wild with wanting and gave her a need she didn't think would ever be quenched.

She was surprised when he buried his head in her neck and let out a low groan. She clenched around him, and he hissed as he rose up on his elbows. The passion that flared in his eyes sent a thrill through her stomach. She never imagined anyone could want her as he did.

Her mind lost track of everything except for her body and what Gregor was doing to it when he began to thrust hard and fast. A yearning so intense she thought she would burst from it curled through her.

Sweat glistened from his body. She plunged her hands into his long hair as his mouth touched her. The kiss mimicked their lovemaking, and she was panting by the time he raised his head.

His touch was unlike any pleasure she had known or would likely ever know again. He was her mate no matter how she tried to deny it. But she would leave him. She had no other choice.

She put such depressing thoughts aside as the tension built within her. She was so close to the exquisite bliss that he brought her. Then, before she knew it, her world tilted and her body spasmed around him. She closed her eyes and let the feeling envelope her as Gregor thrust fully into her, touching her womb.

His head fell back and he roared his climax. She clasped him to her when he collapsed on top of her. They lay together in the aftermath of their lovemaking. She had never known such peace and didn't want it broken by words.

When he rose, she made sure he thought she slept. It must have worked for he rolled over and pulled her into his arms just like the night before. Her last thought as sleep took her was that this could never happen again. Her heart was becoming too attached already.

\* \* \*

The morning sky burst with shades of pink and purple. A glorious morning after such a storm, but Gregor knew that was the temperamental climate in the Highlands and he wouldn't have it any other way.

He didn't try to talk of the lovemaking he and Fiona shared again. He knew better. What worried him was Fiona's fear. It probably exceeded his and, with their meeting with Moira soon, his concern doubled. Moira was the root of Fiona's fear, which could be making her have those nightmares.

His brow furrowed as he thought of how peacefully he had slept. With Fiona in his arms, he had no trouble finding sleep, but he hadn't known if she had another nightmare. She must not have for she looked in fine spirits this morning as she sent him a smile before she walked to her mare.

He walked to her to help her mount. He would take any reason to touch her now, and by the knowing smile on her face, she realized that as well. After he mounted Morgane, he looked at Fiona once more. Her dark locks were hanging free and wild this morning and he liked it. His body surged to life at the mere sight of her, but he tamped down his desire and clicked Morgane into a trot.

The morning sped by as they made good time through the mountains. When they came to the waterfall, he halted and dismounted.

""Tis beautiful," he heard Fiona say.

"Aye, 'tis. I have always favored this spot. 'Tis very peaceful."

"Are we stopping?"

He looked up at her as the sun glistened off her hair. Ah, she was a beauty. "I wanted to fill our water skins. If you need to rest we can."

"I'm fine. I say let us keep going if we can."

He nodded and bent to fill his skin when her words stopped him.

"Which path are we taking?"

He turned to where she gazed. There were two paths, one for each side of the waterfall. After the day he had been banished from his clan, he had never taken the one on the right again.

"The left," he said and leaned over the water.

Fiona gasped, and he jerked his head toward her.

* * *

Fiona stared in disbelief at Gregor as his medallion slipped from inside his leather vest. It had taken her a moment but she remembered where she had seen it before.

"The man in my dreams. He was wearing one just like that." She raised her eyes to Gregor and found his brow furrowed. How had she not remembered that after seeing Gregor's medallion when they swam?

"When did you see this?"

"Last night."

"You didn't say anything," he accused as he straightened.

"The dream only showed me the man and him pulling a medallion from inside his shirt."

She bit her lip, afraid to say the next words. "Gregor, 'tis your clan that MacNeil is after. That is why he isn't following us."

"He doesn't know who my clan used to be."

"Apparently he does. And he is going to kill the laird."

He stared hard at her for the longest time, as if warring with himself. "'Tis just dreams you are having. They don't mean anything."

"I have always had prophetic dreams. There may yet be time to help your clan if we turn around."

She watched in amazement as Gregor mounted Morgane and took the path to the left of the waterfall. "I don't have a clan," he said. "'Tis best you remember that in the future."

"I cannot believe you are going to let MacNeil slaughter your clan and do nothing about it." When he continued to ride, she jerked her mare around. "I can't, and won't, stand by when I know I can help them."

"They banished me," he roared. "They'll kill me on sight."

She raised her eyes until she found him on a hill above her. "Don't worry about them, Gregor. Think of your father and mother. Don't they deserve your aid?"

He didn't say anything, just pulled Morgane around. She waited for a moment, but he didn't return. How could she have been so wrong about him? She had thought him a good man, but she must have been wrong.

A noise behind her made her turn around and descending the path was Gregor. He rode to her and stopped.

"I promised Moira and Glenna that I would return you to the Druid's Glen posthaste."

"And so you shall. After a minor detour."

"I don't think you realize what is at stake. MacNeil *wants* me to bring you to the MacLachlan's. He means to kill you."

"He can try," she said and kicked her mare, but he grabbed the reins.

"I cannot return."

"Not even to save your family?"

"They don't want a murderer returning to the clan, regardless of his reasoning."

Her stomach fell to her feet with a thud. A murderer? Gregor? Surely, they were wrong.

"Who do they claim you murdered?"

"My sister."

## 15

F iona could only stare at him. She opened her mouth but realized she didn't know what to say to him.

His laugh surprised her. "Even you don't know what to say to that."

"I don't believe you did it," she stated.

"Are you sure?" He stared hard at her. "Nay, I don't think you are. We head to the Druid's Glen," he said and turned his horse toward the waterfall and the path to the left.

She had to think fast, to stop him. Everything in her told her they needed to go to the MacLachlan's. Now.

"Would your sister have wanted you to turn your back on your family?"

He pulled up on the reins and sat. She waited for him to say something, do something, but the moments ticked by without any movement or sound from him.

Then, he slowly turned Morgane around and looked at her. "Know this. If we go to the MacLachlan's, you could die."

"I won't die. Remember, I'm a Druid with powers. I can take care of myself."

He nodded and rode past her and turned onto the path on the right side of the waterfall. Elation filled her at her victory, small though it was. If they hurried they might reach the MacLachlan's before MacNeil.

* * *

The Shadow laughed with glee and rubbed his hands together. His plan had worked, just as he had said it would.

"What are you so happy 'bout?" MacNeil snarled as he sat beside him.

The Shadow looked at the MacNeil soldiers that milled around them in the hall. Laird MacLachlan had welcomed them, though all knew he hadn't wanted to. They had taken MacLachlan's hospitality, and would continue until Gregor arrived.

"I'm ready for a woman to warm my bed," MacNeil grumbled.

"We won't be here much longer."

"Why?" MacNeil asked and leaned close. "What do you know?"

"My plan worked. Gregor and Fiona are headed this way as we speak."

MacNeil's mouth dropped open as he stared dumbfounded at him. "How do you know this?"

"Because I do. Don't question me," he ordered. "Get your soldiers ready for battle. When Gregor crests the hill, I want him to see his clan being wiped out."

"And Fiona?"

"I'll take care of her," The Shadow promised.

\* \* \*

Gregor knew he was headed to his own death. Whether by his clan or MacNeil, he would die. There was no getting around that. He could have continued riding toward the Druid's Glen if Fiona hadn't mentioned Anne.

Fiona had been right. Anne wouldn't have let him turn away from his clan. His own death didn't matter. What mattered was keeping Fiona safe and bringing her to the Druid's.

If only he knew how to call Aimery, but the Faerie probably wouldn't help him anyway. He glanced over his shoulder at Fiona. She was holding up well under the hard ride. They had stopped briefly, but she hadn't uttered a word to him.

It had been a relief because he couldn't stop thinking about his parents and seeing them again after so many years.

"How long has it been since you have seen your clan?"

Her question made him sigh. He had been afraid she would start digging around for answers. "Too long."

"How old was Anne when she... when she—"

"Was murdered by me?" he finished for her. "Nearly ten summers."

"And you?" she asked quietly as she came up alongside him.

"Old enough to know what I should have been doing." Her unwavering stare made him realize she would keep on until she got her answer. "I was ten and six."

"So young."

"Not really. I had tremendous responsibility for my age."

"How long until we again reach MacLachlan land?"

"Two days. A day and a half if we ride hard."

"Then let us ride hard," she said and kicked her mare into a run.

She continued to surprise him. He never knew what she would say or do next, but she kept things interesting. She also almost made him believe that she found him innocent. Almost.

They didn't speak the rest of the day. Even when they stopped for the night, she immediately laid down and slept. Gregor didn't venture far from the camp as he hunted for food.

He didn't want a repeat of the previous night. Her fear had been palpable. He hadn't been that scared since Anne's death.

After he cleaned and cooked the quail, he woke Fiona. "You are going to need your strength," he said and handed her a piece of the meat.

She nodded and took the offered food. He ate slowly and watched her. If the situation weren't so drastic he would find the fact she ate with her eyes closed rather amusing. She had no more finished her meal before she was once again asleep.

He covered her with her plaid and sat to watch her for the night. His eyes couldn't get enough of this mysterious woman who had managed to worm her way into his soul.

\* \* \*

"Something's wrong," Moira said. She looked to Frang and Glenna as they sat in the Druid's Glen. "I feel it. Fiona and Gregor are headed toward danger."

Glenna sighed dejectedly. "MacNeil."

"Aye, 'tis MacNeil," Aimery said as he walked into the stone circle.

"Where are they?" Moira asked. "I cannot simply stand here knowing she's in danger."

Frang put a hand on her shoulder. "Gregor will keep her safe."

She looked toward Aimery. "Isn't there anything you can do?"

"The Fae aren't allowed to meddle in the affairs of humans."

"'Tis a lie," Glenna said. "The Fae meddled when we were given our powers."

"Maybe so," Aimery said and turned away. He took two steps then vanished.

Moira wanted to scream. This couldn't be happening. Not when they were so close to fulfilling the prophecy. Dartayous came into her line of vision and a thought took root. She took a step toward him when Glenna walked in front of her.

"I know what you are planning and I won't let you do it without me."

Moira looked down at her petite sister. Glenna may be small, but her power was great, as MacNeil had already found out. "Then come."

Dartayous stood in his warrior's stance with feet apart and hands hanging loose at his sides so he could grab any of his numerous weapons at any moment.

"I wish to talk to you," she told him. His blue eyes watched her keenly before he gave her a slight nod. He held out his arm for her and Glenna to walk first.

Once they were out of the stone circle and in the surrounding forest, Moira stopped. "I have need of a favor."

His dark brow shot up at her words. "You would ask a favor of me?"

"I have no choice," she ground out, hating to think that he might refuse her. She took a deep breath and began again. "Fiona is in danger and I cannot allow anything to happen to her."

"In other words," Dartayous said. "You want to go after her, and you need me to aid you."

"Aye," Glenna said and stepped forward. "You know how important the prophecy is, Dartayous. Won't you help us?"

"I would, but I don't think your husband would approve."

"Conall need never know."

"Really?" said a deep voice from behind them.

Moira and Glenna whirled around to find Conall standing with his arms crossed over his chest. "And just what would you have told me, lady wife?"

Moira's eyes jerked to Glenna who visibly swallowed. Glenna smiled at her husband and said, "I don't know what I would have told you and it doesn't matter now. Will you come with us?"

"You aren't going anywhere," Conall stated. "Aimery and Frang said for both you and Moira to stay here. It wouldn't do to have the three most powerful Druid's scattered across Scotland when the time of the prophecy is here."

"We would be back before then," Moira said.

Dartayous walked until he stood beside Conall. "You don't know that, Moira, and we cannot chance it. I will only take you somewhere if Frang or Aimery orders me to."

"And if I try to leave by myself?"

"Then I will stop you," he said flatly.

Anger welled up inside her. Only Dartayous could bring such emotion in her. Only Dartayous could make her hate so strongly. "'Tis no wonder I cannot stand to be around you," she said and walked off.

Glenna watched her sister leave, then turned to Dartayous. "Don't listen to her. She is angry and doesn't know what she saying."

"Moira doesn't get angry," he said.

"She is angry. She wants Fiona safe, and she is willing to do whatever it takes to make sure she is."

"Which is why I was put as her guard. I will do whatever it takes to keep her here," he said before he too walked away.

Glenna turned to Conall. "Why does Moira hate him so?"

"Only time will tell that. Come. I've something I wish to discuss with you."

"Really? What is it?"

"I need to talk about something in our chamber," he said with a wicked gleam in his eyes.

She laughed and wrapped her arm around him. "Does it perchance have something to do with our bed?"

"Aye. How did you know?"

"I'm not a Druid for nothing."

"Well, it does come in handy," he said and picked her up in his arms as he walked toward the castle.

Fiona opened her eyes to find Gregor staring at her. "Did you sit there staring at me all night?"

He gave her a heart–stopping smile. "Maybe."

She yawned and stretched. After she rose to her feet she saw the sky turning pink, signaling the rising of the sun. "Give me a few moments and I will be ready to leave."

After relieving herself, she splashed some water from her water skin onto her face. She hurriedly raked her fingers through her tangled hair and braided it.

When she returned to their camp, Gregor had already saddled both horses.

"Ready?" he asked as he helped her on her mare.

"Aye."

"Then let's ride," he said and swung up on Morgane.

She watched the ease in which Gregor weaved them through the rocks on the mountains. It on the tip of her tongue to ask when was the last time he had ridden this way, but she knew he wouldn't answer her.

Although he hadn't spoken of his banishment again, she still couldn't belief he had killed his sister. She wanted to know the story, to know what happened, but any fool could see his mouth was shut tight on that subject. She couldn't blame him. She still didn't like to talk about Moira, and what plagued him was much worse than a sister that abandoned her.

He rode well in front of her, and the path was too narrow for them to ride side-by-side, which allowed her mind to wander over everything that had happened since she had left her home.

The one thing she knew was that Gregor was a good man. Even if he did kill his sister, he had changed. He came close to being the only person she truly trusted and that bothered her to no end.

Her heart was something she had to keep shut away so she wouldn't get hurt again. But Gregor's misery pulled at her heartstrings. The one thing she could do was keep him away from her. Their lovemaking had been incredible but something she would do everything in her power not to allow it to happen again.

With him being her mate she chanced everything being this near to him.

If she didn't watch it, her heart would choose without her knowledge, and all would be lost. She would be abandoned once again.

*Never.*

Once they reached the Druid's Glen she would make sure never to see him again. It was her only option.

"Fiona," Gregor called over his shoulder as he came to a stop.

She rode up alongside him where the path widened a little. One look at his face and she knew she wasn't going to like what he had to say.

"I have to leave."

## 16

"What?"

Gregor knew by Fiona's wide eyes that she hadn't expected his words. "I cannot risk endangering your life."

"'Tis your job to bring me to the Druids."

"Aye. Alive. You will be safer if you stay here."

"Nay," she stated and kicked her mare into a walk.

He sighed and looked up at the sky. How did he get stuck with the most stubborn woman in all of Scotland? He trotted Morgane ahead of Fiona and stopped sideways in her path. There was very little room for her to go around him.

"Listen to me," he said in his most stern voice. "I will return for you."

"I'm not going to take that chance. You need me."

He winced when he heard the desperation in her voice. There was no denying the fear in her, and he was an ass for putting her through this but it was for her own good.

"MacNeil wants you. I cannot allow him to get his hands on you," he argued.

She crossed her arms over her chest and raised her chin. "Have you forgotten I have powers?"

"Nay, I haven't, but that is beside the point."

"'Tis exactly the point. I can help you," she said her eyes full of unease.

He sighed and rubbed the back of his neck, but the ache continued. With a vicious jerk of his head sideways he popped his neck and repeated it on the other side.

"This is war, Fiona. MacNeil will have innocent people mixed with his soldiers so you won't use your powers. He's not a stupid man."

She had nothing more to say, and the desolation in her gaze burned him. He helped her down and into a cave he knew was hidden behind one of the boulders.

After he killed a hare and started a fire, he stood and looked at her. She hadn't said another word to him. He hated her silence.

*Never thought I would think that.*

He wanted her to yell at him or argue, not to act as if he didn't exist.

"I will be back as soon as I can," he said.

Still, she refused to look at him. He sighed and moved to the entrance of the cave. "Stay here, Fiona. If in three days I haven't returned, head toward the waterfall and take the path to the left. You will find your way to the Druids."

He waited for her to say something. When she didn't, he walked out of the cave. There was an odd ache in his chest that he refused to acknowledge, and like every other emotion he had, he shoved it down in the darkness where his heart used to reside.

* * *

Fiona was glad Gregor hadn't seen the tears that fell down her face. She couldn't believe he had left her, regardless of the fact he said he was coming back. Only a foolish woman would sit and wait for him.

She was about to leave the cave when she realized she was scared to go on without him. This is what she had been afraid of. She didn't wish to need or want him. The tears coursed faster down her face.

It became too much to think about and she layed down. It was only midday, but she soon found herself lulled to sleep by her tears.

The dream began almost immediately. She watched Gregor fight the MacNeil soldiers as he stood on the steps of the castle beside his father. Then a man wearing a cloak stepped behind Gregor and thrust a long dagger into his back. She screamed and sat up. Despite what Gregor said, she had to follow him. She couldn't allow her dream to come true. Gregor wouldn't die, not if she could help it.

After hurriedly dousing the fire and saddling her mare, she mounted and took off after Gregor. Only a few hours had elapsed so she just might reach him in time.

She didn't want to think about becoming lost since she hadn't asked him how to reach his clan, but she hoped the path she saw him take would lead her to it. She refused to think about what would happen if she didn't find her way.

The sun had begun its descent and still no trace of

Gregor or his clan. Dread began to fill her. She was lost. She would never reach Gregor now.

She continued to follow the path, praying with each bend of the road that she would find Gregor or his clan. As she rounded one bend, she pulled her mare to a halt as she found her way blocked. Two men stood in the path, blocking her way.

Fear began to rise up in her until she noticed their glittering blue eyes. They were Fae. Relief engulfed her as she realized they could help her.

"Do you know the way to the MacLachlan's?" she asked.

Aimery abruptly stepped from behind the men. "Hello, Fiona."

She sighed and gave him a small smile. "Aimery. I'm so glad you are here. I need to know the way to the MacLachlan clan."

"Do you know what will happen if you go?" His somber voice gave her a moment's hesitation.

"Do you know what will happen if I don't?" she asked.

"Aye. I do."

His response wasn't what she expected. "Then you know I must go."

"Then you care for Gregor?"

"He saved my life. I'm returning the favor," she answered, hoping it was enough.

Aimery smiled and shook his head. "You cannot lie to me. I see into your soul. It would make your life easier if you would stop lying to yourself."

She had had enough. There wasn't time for a lecture. "Will you point the way or not?"

"You have come too far. Turn back and take the left fork you passed," he said as he turned his back on her.

She looked over her shoulder at the path, and when she turned back around, the three Fae were gone. "That figures," she mumbled and turned her mare about.

If she didn't become lost again and rode fast she might make it to the MacLachlan's before dawn.

She leaned down across her mare's neck and whispered in her ear, "If by some chance you know the way to Gregor, please take me. I haven't much time."

The mare snorted and nodded its great head up and down. Fiona sat up and patted the mare's neck. "Let's go, then," she said and clicked the horse into a gallop.

Fiona didn't know how long she rode or if she was lost. The stars twinkled above her and as long as the clouds didn't cover the moon it lighted her way. She knew her horse was tired and she began to worry again.

Surely she should have reached the MacLachlan's by now. She tamped down her fear and continued riding. It wasn't until she crested a hill that she spotted the castle below her. She couldn't tell much about it but was more concerned about whose castle this was.

She dismounted and walked her mare off the crest of the hill. It wouldn't do for her to be spotted. Once she tied the mare to a tree branch, she crept closer to the castle. She was within three feet of one of the soldiers, but she couldn't make out his plaid. Her luck held out though when another soldier walked out holding a torch. From the meager light the torch shed she spotted his kilt.

It wasn't a MacLachlan.

* * *

Gregor yearned to stretch his cramping muscles. He had been in the same position since early evening. Once he reached the castle he had scouted the area and its occupants. MacNeil and another man were inside the castle, but Gregor didn't see any soldiers.

Where were they?

From the brief view, he knew his father didn't like MacNeil and the other man there, but hadn't kicked them out. This was unlike his father.

He had also been startled to see white hair covering his father's head instead of his usual dark brown. Lines creased his face and his eyes were sunken. Gregor was shaken by that glimpse of his father, and he wondered how his mother was.

He would deal with that later, though. Right now, he needed to hide until MacNeil's soldiers showed up. While he kept to the shadows, Gregor made his way toward the side of the castle. The wood was still piled the same, and if he were lucky, his old hiding place would still be there. It took some doing, but he managed to move some of the wood and fold himself into the hole.

He not only had a perfect view of the front of the castle, but he could also see the gatehouse entrance. If MacNeil or his soldiers tried anything, he would know about it.

That had been about ten hours ago. His belly rumbled with hunger and his legs cramped painfully from being bent against his chest. He dug out another piece of bread he had stolen from the kitchen and began to eat. It would be a long time until dawn when he assumed MacNeil's troops would arrive.

He'd finished the bread when he heard shouts outside the castle gate. One of his father's men opened it and two of MacNeil's men rode inside. Gregor bit the inside of his mouth at the stupidity of the soldier at the gatehouse. The MacLachlan's didn't think MacNeil posed a threat because he had only two men with him, but they didn't know MacNeil as he did.

*  *  *

It was a MacNeil. Fiona stood frozen as the two soldiers laughed and joked about how easy it was to gain access into the MacLachlan castle. She sucked in a breath as one of the soldiers leaned against the castle wall, just inches from her. If she weren't careful, her planning would be for naught.

Slowly, she backed away from the soldiers until she could make her way to her mare. Thankfully the mare was still there. Fiona didn't know when MacNeil planned his attack, but she would be waiting.

She untied her horse and slapped it on the rump. It wouldn't do for them to see her mare in the morning. After the mare had run off, Fiona crawled in between the two trees where a bush grew. The bush offered her protection as well as a view of the castle.

Now, all she had to do was wait.

## 17

MacNeil took a large swig of his ale as he surveyed MacLachlan's hall. The laird was making it plain he wanted him to leave but he hadn't come out and said it. Yet.

His eyes traveled to his companion. He sat alone in front of the hearth, his dark cloak pulled around him. The Shadow. MacNeil snorted and drank more ale.

MacNeil's fingers itched for a battle. If he had his way he would have attacked these weak, pathetic excuses of Highlanders yesterday, but The Shadow had stopped him. And for what? For Gregor?

He didn't give a horse's arse whether Gregor saw his clan's destruction or not. Gregor had his coming very soon, MacNeil thought with an inward smirk.

"Does the ale please you, Laird MacNeil?"

MacNeil turned his head to find MacLachlan's wife, Margaret, standing beside him. "It would suit me better with a woman."

She straightened her spin as the fake smile left her face.

"If one of the women want you, then take them, but you won't force one."

"You should know better than to talk to a man that way," he bellowed and slammed his goblet down on the table.

"I think you should go to your chamber and sleep off the ale," MacLachlan said as he came to your feet. "I won't allow you to talk to my wife in such a way."

MacNeil laughed and was about to lunge over the table after the old laird when a hand clamped down on his shoulder. He didn't need to look to know it was The Shadow.

"I think the laird is correct, MacNeil. Your chamber is calling for you," The Shadow said and pushed him toward the stairs.

MacNeil started up the steps and was thinking about which woman he wanted in his bed when The Shadow's voice reached him once more.

"Remember what Lady MacLachlan said. No forcing the women."

Rage surged within him at the audacity of the man. MacNeil stopped and debated on whether to take The Shadow's head or not. After all, he was just a man, and men could be killed.

But before he got up the courage to turn around, the hairs on the back of his neck stood on end, and he had the unmistakable feeling that The Shadow knew what he had been thinking. He continued up the stairs to his chamber and forgot about killing or women.

The Shadow waited until MacNeil was out of sight

before he turned back to Margaret and Beathan. "Please forgive him. He doesn't hold his ale well."

Margaret smiled and bowed as she left the hall. Beathan began to pace. "For several days you have stayed here as my guests, and I have waited patiently for you to tell me what brought the two of you here." Beathan stopped and turned toward him. "I think 'tis time you told me."

The Shadow smiled. "You will discover all tomorrow morning, laird. I give you my word."

"I hope so, because if you don't, my men will escort you off my land."

He allowed the old laird his threat. After all, tomorrow he would be dead, so what did it hurt? He bowed and left the hall, intending to make sure MacNeil stayed in his chamber for the night. It would be just like MacNeil to do something rash and stupid and get them 'escorted' tonight.

To his relief, MacNeil was sprawled across his bed, asleep. But just to be sure, he put a spell on the door so no one could get inside the chamber and MacNeil couldn't leave.

At least until morning when he would unleash MacNeil and his soldiers.

* * *

Aimery motioned to his army of soldiers to fan out around the surrounding hills overlooking MacLachlan castle. They would stay hidden and watch as long as Fiona wasn't in danger, but the moment MacNeil or the Evil One got their hands on her, he would send his army down to destroy them.

He just hoped it didn't come to that. Fiona knew how to use her powers, and all he could expect was for her to use them to save Gregor.

A brisk wind blew off the nearby loch and pulled strands of hair into his face. He took out a small strip of leather and pulled his hair back at the base of his neck and tied it off. He wanted an unobstructed view of the battle.

Aimery's gaze found the horizon. The black sky was giving way to gray. The time drew near.

* * *

Fiona sighed and tried to rub the soreness from her neck. Before she knew what she was doing she tried to pop her neck. Just as she was about to stop, she heard a loud pop and the pain lessened.

"No wonder he cracks his neck all the time," she said as she turned her head one way then the other.

Pink and purple graced the sky as the sun began its climb. Apprehension filled her body. The battle would be today, but where were MacNeil's soldiers? Her question was answered a moment later when the ground shook from hundreds of horses that came barreling toward the castle. She glanced toward the castle, and instead of finding MacLachlan soldiers at the gate, she found the two MacNeil men.

Something had already happened inside. She couldn't decide whether to stay where she was, or attempt to get inside the castle. And where was Gregor?

Her terror grew until she shook with it. She had never

been in this situation before. What if she did something wrong?

*You already did. Gregor told you to stay in the cave for a reason.*

She ignored her conscious and looked over her shoulder where she expected MacNeil's army to ride. She didn't have long to wait as line after line of soldiers rode toward the MacLachlan castle.

"I need to get inside," she whispered to herself.

\* \* \*

Gregor fingered the dagger in his boot. 'Twas a clear shot to the MacNeil soldier by the gatehouse, but it was too soon to alert anyone to his presence. He needed to bide his time and take out as many as possible at once.

His ears picked up a voice he thought to never hear again. "Mother," he murmured as he tried to turn his head so he could see her. Unfortunately, she was in the kitchen. She must have been by the window in order for him to hear her. There was no mistaking the trepidation in her voice as she talked to a servant about the day's meals.

He closed his eyes against the stab of longing that pierced his chest. Everyone loved his gentle mother, and the fact that she feared something told him things were going awry inside.

Every bone in his body urged him to seek his mother out, but he couldn't. If he did, it would destroy every plan of attack he had. Even with the prospect of never seeing her, he stayed rooted to his spot. His parent's and his clan's safety was his ultimate goal.

They need never know he was there.

* * *

MacNeil chuckled and rubbed his hands together as he stood atop the tower. His army had arrived. All that was left was giving them the signal to invade the castle. A sound reached him, and he turned and found MacLachlan. He almost smiled at spotting the two large soldiers that flanked the old laird.

"You don't seem too happy this morn."

MacLachlan narrowed his eyes and crossed his arms over his chest. "I told your friend last night that if I wasn't told this morn what it was you were doing here, I would ask you to leave."

"Before we broke our fast?"

"If need be. I have been a patient man, but not any longer. I don't take kindly to having my family or clan threatened in any way," he stated.

MacNeil breathed in the Highland air. "You will find out soon. Tell me, when was the last time you spoke to your son?"

MacLachlan visibly blanched. "What has that to do with anything?"

"Quite a lot, actually," The Shadow said as he walked out onto the tower.

MacLachlan's soldiers took a step closer to their laird. He dropped his arms and said, "My son...is...dead."

"Strange since he worked for me as a mercenary for a while," MacNeil told Beathen and rejoiced when the old man's brow furrowed. "'Tis odd what banishment from one's clan can do to a man."

"What do you want?" MacLachlan demanded.

MacNeil stepped in front of the laird until he was almost nose-to-nose with him. "We are getting to that. I think you needs follow us."

To his surprise, MacLachlan and his two men followed willingly as he led them out of the castle to the bailey. Once there, he turned to look at MacLachlan. "You think you have taken precautions to protect your clan, to keep them safe from rogues and villains?"

"Aye," he answered. "Of course."

MacNeil laughed. "You failed," he said and pointed out to the gates.

MacLachlan and his soldiers gasped at the sight of the MacNeil men racing toward them.

"You want to know what we want?" MacNeil asked him. "We want Gregor."

MacLachlan turned angry brown eyes toward him. "He's not here."

"He'll be here," The Shadow said. "I can already feel him."

\* \* \*

Gregor's heart raced uncontrollably. His father stood with MacNeil and a man wearing a black cloak. Whatever they were telling his father had upset him for he was visibly shaken.

But when they pointed to the gates, Gregor knew they were showing his father something. He didn't have long to wonder what that something was as he felt the ground tremble.

*Horses. Lots of them.*

Gregor's blood pumped so loudly through his veins that he could hear it. It was almost time. He would finally have his chance at MacNeil.

The sound of a scream startled him. He lifted himself on his elbows and tried to see what was going on. It wasn't until he saw his father running toward the castle that he knew it was his mother.

"Nay," he yelled, but no one heard him.

The entire MacLachlan clan screamed as they tried to run from the oncoming soldiers. The sounds of children crying and soldiers yelling almost drowned out the sound of the horses.

In moments, MacNeil's soldiers thundered through the gatehouse. MacLachlan soldiers were well trained, but they didn't stand a chance against MacNeil's numbers.

Gregor had seen enough. He was about to pull the string he had tied to the wood and have it crash down on MacNeil soldiers, but then the unthinkable happened.

MacNeil and the cloaked man brought his parents to stand in front of the woodpile. There was no way for him to get out now and not harm his parents. He clenched his teeth together as he watched men he had grown up with get cut down in front of his eyes while his mother sobbed.

But it was his father that worried him the most. His father had always been a man that others wouldn't dare to cross and now he looked like he was about to collapse at any moment. As if all of this was just too much for him.

When MacNeil placed the tip of his sword against his

mother's throat, Gregor thought he would die. He bit down on the inside of his mouth until he tasted blood to keep from shouting.

It wouldn't do his parents any good if he were discovered now.

But it was MacNeil's next words that sent his blood cold. "Tell me where Gregor is, MacLachlan, or I will slit her throat."

\* \* \*

Fiona ducked her head as MacNeil's soldiers thundered past her and raced through the gates. Even above the sound of the horses she could hear the people screaming and crying.

"'Tis a slaughter," she said out loud as tears gathered in her eyes.

She hadn't been able to save her clan, but she could help save Gregor's. After the last of the soldiers had passed, she crawled out from the bush and raced toward the castle. No one paid her any heed as the battle raged around her.

It was easy enough to get through the gatehouse, but once she entered the bailey, she didn't know where to go. Chaos reigned as men fought and women and children tried to hide. Blood spilled needlessly unto the earth all around her. Her heart silently cried out for Gregor's people, but she pushed aside her heartache and scanned the bailey. MacNeil was easy to spot, but what bothered her was the other man who stood next to him.

"The Evil One," she murmured.

The two men stood with their backs to her while

MacNeil held his sword against a woman's throat. When she saw the man's face she knew 'twas Gregor's parents that MacNeil held. But where was Gregor?

She expected to see him fighting, but he was nowhere to be seen. Had she misjudged him? Had he ran instead of coming to help his clan?

## 18

"He isn't coming. You were wrong."

The Shadow took a deep breath and clenched his fist instead of hitting MacNeil. The man whined about everything. Didn't he realize that Gregor was already here? "He's here. I can smell him."

"What?" MacNeil asked and looked around. "Then where is he? I have a blade to his mother's throat."

"He's waiting."

"You are wrong," MacLachlan stated. "Gregor knows that to return would mean death."

"What?" Margaret asked. "Gregor is here?"

"Hush, woman," MacLachlan told his wife.

The Shadow chuckled. "Aye, my lady, your son is here. We called him here."

"Why?" MacLachlan asked. "What does Gregor have to do with this?"

"Everything," MacNeil hissed. "Not only did he betray me but he sided with the Druids."

Margaret shook her head. "There are no more Druids in Scotland."

The Shadow moved closer to her. She was still a pretty woman despite the many summers she had seen. Her blonde hair was streaked with white, and her eyes were a dull gray, but he would bet they had once been blue.

"There have always been Druids in Scotland. There will always be Druids in Scotland," he said. He turned to MacNeil. "'Tis time."

The Shadow heard MacNeil laugh as he motioned to his soldiers to grab MacLachlan and Margaret. There had been enough talking. He knew one way that would get Gregor out of wherever he hid.

Once they reached the castle steps, he stopped and looked around the bailey. "We need to hurry, MacNeil."

"Nay," MacNeil shouted as he dragged MacLachlan up the steps. "I have kept my tongue while we sat here. I want to savor this."

He turned his eyes to MacNeil. "We aren't alone."

MacNeil blanched and looked around the bailey. "I don't see anyone."

"And you won't either. They don't want to be seen."

"Where are you going?"

The Shadow turned and looked back at MacNeil. "Have your fun, but forget about Fiona. I will meet you at our scheduled spot."

* * *

Gregor strained to hear the words exchanged between MacNeil and the stranger. Although he knew they were looking for him, waiting for him to make a move, he waited and listened.

His mother was held by two of MacNeil's soldiers, and his father now had MacNeil's blade against his throat. Gregor looked around the bailey and saw the MacLachlan clan had put up a good fight.

There were plenty of MacNeil soldiers lying dead alongside MacLachlan men. He wished he had Conall with him. Then he could free his parents while Conall aided the MacLachlan men that still fought.

His attention was jerked back to MacNeil when he heard his mother scream.

* * *

Fiona slid between two cottages as she spotted a small group of men fighting the MacNeil soldiers who needed help. She took a step toward them and spotted a rain bucket. A quick glance around found her many more.

She took a deep breath and put all her hurt and anger into using her powers. To her relief, she heard a whoosh as the water leapt from the buckets and surged straight into the air. With one wave of her hand she called the water to her. It pooled in front of her, chest high. By this time, she had gained the soldiers' attention, as well as most of the MacLachlan's that were nearby.

When one soldier decided to pay her no heed and continue fighting, she jerked her hand toward the soldier. A stream of water shot out and wrapped around the soldiers right arm like an iron manacle. Before any of them could blink, she had the MacNeil soldiers bound.

"Get you and your families to safety," she told the MacLachlan men.

She turned and found one solider screaming for help. She didn't know how much water was left and didn't want to try and fight until she did know. With a simple thought, she had a stream of water locked around all of the soldiers' mouths and heads.

"That ought to quiet you until I deem otherwise," she told them as she began to walk away.

She turned back and looked at them. It wouldn't do for others to notice them yet. She waved her hand to the left and the six soldiers were lifted and moved to the back of a cottage.

Fiona blew out a breath. That had gone well, she thought. Until she heard a woman scream. She turned and saw Gregor's parents on the castle steps.

"Nay," she said and raced toward them.

* * *

It was time.

Gregor waited until the MacNeil soldier fighting one of his clan moved back against the wood, then he pulled the string. Wood rolled down and crushed the MacNeil soldier. Gregor sprang from his hiding place.

He ignored the blinding pain in his legs as they cramped from not moving for so long. His mother's scream echoed in his head as he raced toward the castle.

His father picked up the sword MacNeil had thrown to the steps. No sooner had his father grasped the sword than MacNeil attacked. His father fought valiantly, but he was older than MacNeil and didn't move as fast as he used to.

MacNeil's sword sliced his father's right arm and the sword clattered loudly on the steps.

"Nay," Gregor yelled as MacNeil raised his sword.

His father turned and looked at him. Gregor watched in a daze as MacNeil plunged his sword into his father's stomach. Even as his father crumpled to the steps he kept his gaze on Gregor.

His feet wouldn't move fast enough as he watched his father's blood spill onto the castle steps. This wasn't how his father was supposed to die. He had almost reached the steps when something hit him in the back. He fell to the ground and quickly rolled to his feet to see a man waiting to fight him.

He didn't have time for this, he thought angrily as he drew his sword. After he stretched his arms, he walked toward the soldier. If he wanted a fight, then he would most certainly get a fight.

Gregor raised his sword and blocked a downward slice before he pivoted and dropped to his knees. He rolled forward and leapt to his feet in time to parry a thrust into his midsection. The soldier was off balance and fell to the ground. Gregor jumped to avoid being sliced across his shins. The soldier gained his feet and charged.

Gregor spun and swung his sword toward the soldier. The soldier gasped and clutched his chest as blood oozed between his fingers. He didn't wait around for the soldier to die, but ran toward the castle.

He stopped dead in his tracks at the sight before him. "It cannot be."

"Ah, but it is," MacNeil sneered. "Isn't it amazing what lands in your lap when you want it badly enough?"

Gregor raised his eyes to Fiona and asked, "Why?"

"Because I knew I could help," she answered confidently.

"And all you got was caught," MacNeil cackled.

Fiona couldn't look Gregor in the eye once she saw his disapproval. It wasn't like she had planned to get caught, but when she had seen his father fight MacNeil, she knew what would happen.

She had rushed toward Gregor's father, hoping to save him, when MacNeil had grabbed her. He had kept a dagger against her throat so she wouldn't cry out to Gregor while he fought.

The bailey grew quiet as more of the MacLachlan clan escaped the soldiers. It made her feel better knowing that MacNeil had not slaughtered these people as he would have liked.

"What are you laughing at?" MacNeil screeched in her ear.

Her eyes found Gregor. She longed to ease his furrowed brow, but there wasn't time for words. She had to act quickly, or all might be lost.

MacNeil jabbed the dagger against her throat, drawing a bead of blood. "Answer me," he said between clenched teeth.

She ignored the prick of pain. "I'm laughing because you cannot win."

"Oh, I will win," MacNeil said. "I have you and there is nothing you or your sisters can do about. The prophecy will never come to pass."

"Don't ever say 'never.' It will come back to haunt you," she warned him as her eyes darted to Gregor's mother and the two soldiers holding her.

While MacNeil snorted in her ear, she used her magic to draw the water from a nearby barrel. She split the water into two streams and formed them like a spear as they hurdled toward the soldiers.

Each water spear hit them in the chest. They collapsed dead at Lady MacLachlan's feet. Her elation was short lived as MacNeil bellowed his fury and slashed the dagger across her arm.

A burning sting blinded her as she watched the blood flow from her arm. Dimly, as if through a long tunnel, she heard someone roar and she thought it might have been Gregor.

Before she could find him, MacNeil placed a rag over her eyes. "Can't use your powers if you cannot see, can you? You wouldn't want to hurt innocent people," he said with a laugh.

Fiona wanted to cry. She had ruined her chance at freeing them all. But she would make sure that MacNeil didn't hurt her.

"I know what you are thinking," he whispered in her ear as he led her down the castle steps.

"I doubt that."

No sooner had the words left her lips than she heard the unmistakable sound of sword fighting. *Gregor.* A finger ran down her cheek and she jerked away, knowing it was MacNeil.

"I know you will do everything possible to stay alive, but I have something that will change your mind."

*Don't ask.* "And what could that possibly be?"

"Gregor and his parents. If you don't want them to die with you, you will die without a fight."

This couldn't be happening. Why had Gregor allowed himself to be caught again? But she knew. He had sworn to Moira and the Druids that he would keep her safe.

\* \* \*

Gregor wanted to slap the smirk from MacNeil's face. The evil bastard had known he wouldn't allow Fiona to be taken and not follow, which is why he had allowed the soldier to win and take his sword. What he hadn't counted on was MacNeil bringing his mother and wounded father along.

He refused to look at his parents. He didn't want to see the condemnation he knew would be in their eyes. Once again, he had murdered. Indirectly, but he had done it just the same.

And for just a while, Fiona had made him believe he was a good man. What a fool he was. People like him couldn't change. Once a bad apple, always a bad apple.

Never before had he wanted to kill someone as much as he wanted to end MacNeil. When he had seen the blood running down Fiona's arm, all coherent thought had fled, save one—kill MacNeil.

But MacNeil had used his anger against him. Every soldier knew that you couldn't let your emotions rule you, and he had made that exact mistake. Now, he was paying for it. Not only would he watch Fiona die, but he would also have to explain to her sisters and the Druids why he had failed.

If he made it out alive.

And he didn't want to think about his parents. So far, they hadn't said anything to him, and he hoped it stayed that way. He looked up from his musing to find MacNeil had led them to the water. It wasn't long before they stood on the shores of the great loch.

MacNeil took a deep breath and said, "I think 'tis ironic that Fiona will die by the very thing she controls."

Gregor's mind raced at MacNeil's words. Surely he wasn't going to do what Gregor thought he was going to do. MacNeil soldiers, all of whom had their swords and crossbows pointed toward Gregor, surrounded him. He was powerless to do anything but watch.

Then his mother's voice reached his ears. "Oh, Beathan. They are going to drown her."

Gregor's stomach plummeted to his feet as he stared at his most feared enemy—water.

## 19

N*ay.*
Gregor refused to believe his mother's words. Surely MacNeil wouldn't dare. He took a step toward Fiona but felt a prick of a sword tip against his chest.

"Where do you think you are going?" MacNeil asked. "Could it be that you don't like the thought of Fiona drowning in the same waters where you killed your sister."

"You bastard," Gregor growled. "How the hell did you discover that?"

"It was easy, really. You would be amazed at how men will talk once their far into their cups."

This isn't how Gregor wanted Fiona to learn about what he had done, but it was too late now. MacNeil wanted her to know the details and there was nothing Gregor could do to stop him.

"Tell me," MacNeil continued as he circled Fiona. "Did Anne struggle much?"

"Hold strong, Gregor," his father said behind him.

MacNeil threw back his head and laughed. "You

banished him and refused to admit you had a son, and now you want to give him advice?"

"Leave them out of this," Gregor said. "They did what they thought they had to do."

"Aye," MacNeil agreed. "I would have done the same thing to a son that murdered my daughter. What I want to know is *why*, Gregor? She was younger than you and not a threat."

Gregor bit his tongue to keep his face from showing any emotion. He would be damned before he let MacNeil know how this affected him.

MacNeil tapped the flat side of the dagger against his palm. "Younger and a lass, so not a threat to you at all. Unless she saw you begin to be what you truly are. Tell me, Gregor, did you kill someone and she saw you?"

Gregor closed his eyes when he heard his mother gasp. He jerked his gaze to MacNeil. "By the saints, you will pay for your lies."

MacNeil laughed again. "Oh, so maybe it was just neglect that killed Anne. You should be proud of your son, my lady," he said and turned toward Gregor's mother. "His kills are legendary in the Highlands. Many lairds have paid highly for his services. I'm sure he will tell you all about them if you ask."

Gregor was fast losing the last thread of his control. He didn't know how much more of this he could take. He thought he had buried all this so deep it would never touch him again. He should have known better.

"Well, I think 'tis time," MacNeil said and took off Fiona's blindfold.

Gregor wouldn't look at her. He didn't think he could

stand to see the hatred in her eyes. It was the very reason he had refused to tell her anything about Anne and her death.

"Remember what I told you," he heard MacNeil tell Fiona before he led her to a boat and put her inside.

Gregor's heart began to pound. It had been the same boat Anne had used the day of her death. Anne's face surfaced in his memories. She grinned impishly up at him with her bright blue eyes and blonde hair as he set her in the small boat.

She had adored him and followed him everywhere. And he had killed her. What kind of brother did that make him?

"Tell me, Gregor," MacNeil said as he came to stand beside him. "How does it feel to know that you chose the wrong side this time? You shouldn't have betrayed me."

"I did the right thing. You are a fool if you think you can kill Fiona."

"I used to think of you as my best man. The one I could count on to do the dirty jobs and do them right. How could I have been so wrong about you?"

Gregor shrugged. "What you don't understand is that you are dealing with something you cannot win over. Your companion isn't here to aid you. Ever wonder why he ran off?"

His mind raced to think of some way to save Fiona, but as her boat rowed farther and farther away from him, his options became few.

MacNeil came to stand in front of him and pressed his finger into Gregor's chest. "Your words don't frighten me. Fiona will die, and the prophecy will fade into nothing."

"What's to stop Fiona from saving herself?"

"The thought of you and your parents dying."

Gregor had thought MacNeil might use something like that, but he had wanted to make sure. He turned and looked at his parents. His mother had torn part of her gown to put over his father's wound to stop the flow of blood. It had helped, but unless they got him some attention soon, he would die.

His father's eyes met his, and Gregor knew his father would do whatever it took to help. His mother smiled at him through her tears, and it gave him the courage he needed to face what was ahead.

MacNeil sneered at him when he turned back around. "How does it feel, Gregor, to see your parents after all these years and knowing that you will be responsible for their deaths as well?"

Gregor stayed silent and kept his eyes on Fiona.

"I have had enough of these games," MacNeil growled and whirled around to face the loch. "Now," he yelled to the soldier rowing Fiona's boat.

The soldier stopped, stood up and pushed Fiona over the side of the boat. Gregor reacted instantly. He elbowed the soldier on his right in the side and took the sword. With the sword in his right hand, he reached down with his left and retrieved the dirk in his boot.

The four soldiers came at him at once. He kicked one on the knee and heard the bone pop as the soldier crumpled to the ground, screaming. To Gregor's surprise, one of the soldiers ended the life of the wounded man.

Gregor lunged at one and sent him off balance. While another man attacked him, Gregor kicked the fallen soldier in the face. He threw his dirk at another and saw him fall to the ground before he turned back to the last one.

"You are no match for me," he told the soldier. "Save yourself and get out of here."

The soldier's eyes flickered to MacNeil. "Nay," he bellowed and raised his sword.

Gregor lunged and twisted. He felt his sword sink into the soldier's midsection. His gaze turned to his parents, and he was astounded to find that they'd killed their two guards, although his father didn't look well.

He took a step toward them, but his father stopped him. "Save the lass. We can talk when you return."

Gregor turned to the loch. There was no sign of Fiona. The boat that had taken her had almost made it back to shore, and more of MacNeil's soldiers were riding toward them. He couldn't take them all.

He stepped into the loch, his only thought Fiona. The water had just reached his thighs when he heard the horses splash into the loch.

* * *

Fiona surged to the surface. She stood atop the water as if it were dry land and surveyed the carnage around her. MacNeil had gone back on his promise. She should have known he would, but she had held out a shred of hope.

It didn't take long for her to find MacNeil. He rode away from the loch and his men. Apparently he thought she was dead.

She needed to find Gregor. When she spotted him fighting against ten mounted soldiers, her anger snapped.

She rose up a giant wall of water and launched it at MacNeil's soldiers. Just before the water swallowed them, she threw Gregor out of harm's way.

Once she saw the soldiers were deep within the cold loch, she calmed the water. Gregor leaned up on his elbow and shook his head. His eyes found her, and he slowly gained his feet. She quickly walked to shore and went to his parents.

"Lass, how in the world did you just walk on water?" Gregor's father asked her.

"I will be more than happy to tell you, my laird, but only once you are healed."

He coughed and blood ran from the corner of his mouth. "My name is Beathan, and there will be no healing for me. Gregor?"

Fiona moved so Gregor could be next to his father. She helped Gregor's mother try and staunch the flow of blood from her husband's wound.

"Aye," Gregor said.

"There's so much that needs to be said." Beathan stopped as another fit of coughing came. "Many times, I sent men to bring you home."

"Why?" Gregor asked.

"Because you shouldn't have been banished. We should have stood beside you."

"But I did kill her."

"It was an accident, son."

Fiona's heart ached for Gregor, and when Beathan called him son, she had a hard time holding back her tears.

"You are home now," his mother said. "That's all that matters."

"I only came to stop MacNeil. I didn't do that," Gregor said and tried to rise to his feet, but Beathan's hand stopped him.

"I lost two children that day, and have regretted it ever since you walked out of those gates. I want to die knowing you will come back and take your place as laird of this clan."

Gregor blinked. Had he heard his father right? He looked up at his mother and saw the bright smile through her tears. "What about the rest of the clan?"

"I overturned the banishment a week after you left. My men have been looking for you ever since."

Gregor couldn't believe his ears. All this time, he could have been with his family, and instead he had missed so many years. And he was about to lose his father.

"Will you come back?" his father asked.

Gregor raised his eyes to Fiona. She gave him a small nod, and he knew what he had to do. "There's one thing I have to finish, then I will return."

"Then go and finish your mission."

Gregor found his eyes misting with tears. He hurriedly blinked them away. "I will be back." He looked at his mother. "I swear, I will."

"You better," she warned before she threw her arms around him. "Now go," she said. "The clan is coming. They will take your father to the castle."

Gregor looked toward the castle and saw the MacLachlan people walking toward them. He stood and held out his hand to Fiona.

"Just a moment," she said and ran to get some of water out of the loch. She returned and knelt beside his father and held her hand over his wound. Slowly she poured the water over the wound and whispered some words.

She stood and turned to Gregor. "I've done all I can. If they tend to him quick, he will live."

He nodded his thanks. She smiled and began to walk away. He turned to his father and knelt down. "Stay alive, Father," he said.

His father held out his arm and they clasped forearms. "Go," he urged.

Gregor whistled and Morgane and Fiona's mare trotted toward them. It was time to get Fiona to the Druid's Glen.

\* \* \*

Aimery watched as Gregor and Fiona rode from the MacLachlan lands. They had managed to stay alive. He knew it would take more than MacNeil's clumsy planning to do them harm.

There had been a few times he had nearly signaled his army to move in, but the MacLachlan clan had surprised him with their courage and tenacity.

And they had survived a MacNeil raid.

If only all humans were more like the MacLachlan's instead of MacNeil.

He motioned to two of his men to follow Gregor and Fiona. Two more trailed MacNeil, but if his suspicions were accurate, MacNeil and his men would once again disappear.

"Care to explain yourself?"

Aimery turned to his queen. "Your majesty," he said and bowed. "What would you like for me to explain?"

"Oh, stop," Rufina said and flung her long, golden hair over her shoulder. "You know very well of what I speak. Now, answer me."

Aimery straightened and looked his beautiful queen in the eye. "I brought the army here just in case. MacNeil's companion is using Fae magic."

Her smooth brow furrowed. "That isn't possible. All of the Fae are accounted for, and we all know that humans cannot harness our power."

Aimery waited for her to continue. He knew better than to interrupt her thinking. While she thought, he ran his eyes over her. All Fae looked similar in height and weight. Females were slim and narrow of hip, while males were also slim but with well–defined muscles. All Fae had some form of blonde hair and the intense, unnatural blue eyes that made it easy to spot them.

His queen turned her attention back to him. "I must talk to the king. Be prepared, Aimery. You will be called to court shortly."

"You know something about MacNeil's companion, then?"

"Maybe," she said and vanished.

He sighed. If he knew his king and queen, he would be called to their side very soon. But before then, he needed to return to the Druid's Glen.

With a raise of his hand, his soldiers returned to their posts throughout Scotland.

## 20

"You fool." The Shadow took hold of a nearby limb that was lying on the forest floor and broke it in two. It was either that or break MacNeil's neck.

MacNeil shrugged and continued eating the quail. "Fiona is dead. The prophecy is over."

"She's not dead, you imbecile."

"Of course she is. I saw her fall into the loch and not come up," MacNeil said as food came out of his mouth.

The Shadow reined in his fury with great effort. "The Fae blessed all three of those girls with powers. What do you think hers is?"

"I don't know," MacNeil said with a shrug as he continued eating. Then he looked up. "Wait. 'Tis water."

"Aye, it is. So, do you think water could kill her?"

MacNeil stopped chewing and raised his eyes. "I didn't think about that."

"Exactly. You don't ever think. 'Tis no wonder Glenna was able to escape you. I also have to wonder why everyone is so terrified of you."

"I'm not known as the Butcher for nothing," MacNeil said and surged to his feet. "And I'm not an idiot. It takes a genius to take over these clans like I have."

"You destroy, MacNeil. That doesn't take a genius. That just takes enough coin to pay men to follow you," he said and walked away before he killed MacNeil himself.

He seethed and desperately needed an outlet. If only the Fae had stayed away, then he could have killed Fiona, but he couldn't take the chance of the Fae catching him. It was his plan to catch them.

One in particular, actually, he thought with a grin.

* * *

Fiona waited for Gregor to say something, but she guessed she might well be waiting for the stars to fall from the sky. Even now, as they readied their camp for the night, he wouldn't look at her.

There was so much she wanted to tell him but didn't know if he would welcome anything. Regardless, she couldn't stand the silence anymore.

"Gregor, I—"

"I'm going to hunt for some food," he said and walked away.

*Well, that went well.*

She sighed and settled comfortably against the rough boulder. It was going to be a very long night at this rate. Surely, there was some way to get him to at least listen to her.

It bothered her that Gregor hadn't even been worried that she had been hurt. Of course, with her powers, the water had healed it and washed away all trace of blood. Her flesh was still pink where the dagger had sliced open her arm.

If she healed it correctly, there would barely be any visible scar. She quickly changed gowns since her sleeve had also been cut. Before she slipped on the other gown, she ripped a piece off the bottom of the torn one and wrapped it around her healing wound.

By the time Gregor returned with a grouse that he set to cleaning, she knew he had withdrawn from her. She rose to her feet and walked toward him. When she stood behind him and he still didn't acknowledge her, she placed a hand on his shoulder.

He immediately tensed and stilled. Her heart tore in two for the guilt and shame she knew he carried. It didn't matter how hard she tried, she couldn't push aside the need she had to help him.

"I'm sorry I didn't stay in the cave," she said, not knowing where else to begin.

He nodded and went back to his cleaning.

"I thought I could help."

"You almost got killed."

Finally, she thought. "But I didn't. I knew MacNeil wouldn't be able to kill me."

"You knew no such thing," Gregor bellowed and threw down his dirk as he stood. "Do you have any idea how frightened I was?"

His words hit her like a month old loaf of bread. "Why? Because you had failed Moira?"

"Because I was afraid I had failed *you*," he finally said.

She took a step toward him only to find him backing

away from her. It took a great amount of effort but she didn't let him see how his actions hurt her.

"At least you are no longer banished from your clan."

He turned his back to her. "You don't know anything, Fiona."

"Your parents want you to return. They have been looking for you for years. There isn't much to understand."

His back stayed rigid at her words, but she wasn't done with him yet. She walked around until she faced him. "You are to be laird of the MacLachlan's."

"Nay. I will return like I promised but only to make sure my father is all right."

"I don't understand you. You have everything you ever wanted. Why are you turning your back on them now?"

"It isn't for you to understand," he said and walked away.

Fiona stared at the half–cleaned grouse. She needed to do something to burn off her anger, and the grouse was as good as anything right now. Besides, she needed to eat.

It wasn't until the grouse had finished cooking that she looked up and found Gregor striding toward her. He didn't even look at her as he helped himself to the grouse.

*Wonderful. How am I going to break through his walls now? And why do I even want to? I'm supposed to leave him, remember?*

She remembered all right, but it didn't stop her heart from wanting to mend his. They ate in silence. She didn't bother to tell him goodnight when she laid down. If he wanted to be left alone, then she would leave him alone.

All the way to the Druid's Glen if need be. She just hoped they reached it in a couple of days. It was on the tip of her tongue to ask him how far they had to go, but quickly changed her mind.

She didn't need a Highland winter to feel the chill that came from the man across the fire.

* * *

Gregor yearned to know if Fiona's wound was healing. He had forgotten about it until they had made camp and he had spotted the torn, bloodied sleeve.

When he had returned from hunting she had changed and didn't complain about any pain.

After he saw her begin to heal his father, he could only guess that she had healing abilities close to Moira's.

With everything that had happened, he couldn't sleep and instead watched Fiona. Her elegant beauty hurt his eyes to gaze upon her. She knew almost everything now, and he didn't understand why she still wished to speak to him.

It could be because she pitied him.

*I want no one's pity. Not even the woman that can move the heart in my chest.*

* * *

Aimery walked into his king and queen's court not seeing the other Fae that lined the walls in hopes of gaining an audience with the rulers. He had expected his summons, and hadn't been surprised when he was ordered to appear immediately. After walking the long length of the throne room, he kneeled in front of them and put his right fist over his heart.

"Rise, Aimery," the king said.

Aimery stood and noted that both the king and queen were distressed. "Is everything all right?"

"I'm glad you came directly," Theron said and looked to his queen.

Rufina stood, her long silver gown hugging her body. "Come, Aimery. We must talk in private."

He waited for the king to follow his queen before he trailed after them. They brought him into the room behind their thrones. He had been in this room many times.

It wasn't as opulent as the throne room. There weren't gold chairs for the rulers to sit on, or any of the numerous other luxurious items that lined the palace. Instead, there was a rather plain table and six chairs. The walls weren't painted with murals of Fae history, but instead were painted a soft blue to relax the occupants. It was a room where the rulers could be themselves and share a private word with someone.

Once in the room, both rulers let their full emotions show. Aimery was staggered to see the haggard expression on his king's face.

"What has happened?" he asked as he looked from one to the other.

The queen's hand shook as she raised a goblet to her lips. "Something I had forgotten."

"As did everyone, I presume," the king stated and slumped into a chair.

Aimery continued to stand as he waited, his nerves strung as tightly as they could be. He wanted to yell at them, but knew dire consequences would occur for such a rash action. Instead, he casually clasped his hands behind his back and waited.

His queen didn't keep him waiting long. She pushed her long blonde hair off her shoulder and sat beside her husband. "It was something you told me that made me stop and think of . . . an incident, ages ago. So long ago, in fact, that we all assumed he was dead."

"Does this have something to do with someone using Faerie magic?" Aimery asked.

"You know as well as I only the Fae can use our magic," the king said and ran a hand down his face.

Aimery couldn't believe his ears. "So this rouge Druid is one of us?"

"My brother, in fact."

"Tell him the story," Rufina said softly and drank from her goblet.

Theron nodded and motioned for Aimery to sit beside him. "It is a story that should never have been forgotten, and one that might cost us everything."

Aimery held still as his king battled with himself and the queen paced the small room.

"My brother always wanted power," the king started suddenly as he shook off his white cloak and stood. "He was actually in line to be king since he was older than I."

Silence filled the room. Aimery leaned forward. "What happened?"

"My father was told of the prophecy."

"How does that involve your brother?"

The queen came to stand beside her king. "The entire prophecy has been forgotten. It took some doing, but we managed to find the original document that it was written on."

Aimery's lungs felt as though a dragon's claw squeezed them. "What is the prophecy?"

The king raised his blue eyes to Aimery and said:

> *"In a time of conquering*
> *There will be three*
> *Who will end the MacNeil line.*
> *Three born of the*
> *Imbolc, Beltaine and Lughnasad Feasts*
> *Who will destroy all*
> *Samhain, the Feast of the Dead.*
> *One who refuses the Druid way*
> *Inherits the winter and in doing*
> *So marks the beginning of the end.*
> *For the worthy to prevail, the fire*
> *Must stand alone to vanquish the inheritor,*
> *Water must soothe the savage beast, and*
> *The wind must bow before the tree.*
> *But if the tyrant lives again*
> *The secret magic of the Fae*
> *Will be unlocked for all to witness*
> *For the tyrant to inherit the kingdom*
> *He must take the place of the noble one*
> *When the Three unite powers; In doing so,*
> *The tyrant will rule for eternity."*

Aimery sat in silence as the impact of the prophecy settled around him. "Who is the tyrant and the noble one?"

"For the longest time, no one knew. My father refused

to believe that any of the Fae would be involved in the world of man, but the prophecy was very clear on that."

The queen put her hand on the king's shoulder and said, "It wasn't until the old king was murdered that it became clear who the tyrant was."

"Your brother," Aimery said.

The king nodded. "None of us could believe it. We all knew he wanted to rule the Fae, but to also rule the world of man. Although we once lived with the humans, it didn't last long."

"Your brother was condemned because he murdered the old king," Aimery said as he recalled his teachings of youth.

"Yes, he was imprisoned."

"Where? Couldn't you bring him back?"

Theron laughed bitterly. "He was thrown into the darkness where none would follow him."

Aimery sucked in a breath. The darkness was a place that the Fae shied away from. It was oblivion. Once you went in, you never came out.

"We watched him enter the darkness," the queen said and shuddered. "That part of the prophecy was soon forgotten since the tyrant was no longer here to carry through."

"If this Evil One is your brother, how did he get out?"

The king sighed. "I don't know. He had millions of years to figure out a way though."

"Do we know who the noble one is?"

His king and queen shook their heads. He had his work cut out for him. "I must get back to the Druids. This addition to the prophecy will aid them."

"No," his sovereigns yelled.

"Ironically, you aren't allowed to tell them," his queen said. "In truth, we allowed ourselves to share more with them than we should have."

"We want to keep their world as it is. The Fae do not belong with them," the king added.

Aimery stood and began to pace as his mind raced. "How, then, did MacNeil get involved in this?"

"My brother needs a sacrifice. Someone so evil that it would take the combined powers of the three Druids to destroy him."

"What am I to do?"

"Keep a vigilant watch," his queen said. "Let us know if anything changes. Fae have already gone missing."

By the third evening of Gregor's silence, Fiona was about to scream. But in truth, it was for the best. With every minute of his silence, it made leaving him that much easier. Apparently, he didn't want to have anything to do with her, but she wasn't about to allow him to leave first.

Nay. She would do the leave–taking just as she always planned. Nothing could deter her from her course now. She didn't wish to think of the future since she didn't have a clan to return to. Even the thought of staying with the Druids didn't appeal to her because of Moira. Maybe she would stay and visit with Glenna for a while. Then...she would see what happened.

The thought of looking into her own future had crossed her mind, but she didn't want to know. She learned long ago that sometimes 'tis better not to know what's going to happen. This was one of those instances.

She glanced up from the fire to find Gregor walking away. Again. Every night since they had left the MacLachlan's he had disappeared. She didn't know where he went or why. She knew he wouldn't leave her alone. He made an oath and he would carry through with it, of that she was sure.

She watched until the darkness claimed him. Something told her they would arrive at the Druid's Glen soon, very soon. Tomorrow perhaps. Then what? Then she would concentrate on the prophecy. Everything else would be forgotten.

\* \* \*

Gregor leaned against a tree and watched Fiona. He had been surprised, but relieved, at her silence these past two days. He hadn't known what to say to her. He was afraid if he looked into her eyes he'd see her hatred of him for killing his sister.

He knew she wanted to know the story, but he would die before he told her. It was one thing she didn't need to know, no matter how hard she pried.

Tomorrow they would arrive at Conall's castle and the Druid's Glen. He wondered how Fiona would react when she came face-to-face with Moira. It didn't take a Druid to know that Fiona wouldn't ask him to stay by her side while there. She was a strong woman who didn't need anyone.

Too bad he needed her so desperately it hurt.

He ran a hand down his face. Life always dealt out the

unexpected, especially to him. He thought of his father and the words they exchanged, but no amount of words could undo Anne's death.

There was no way he could be laird of any clan after what he had done. They had been right to banish him.

"Are you always going to think that way?"

Gregor whirled around to find Aimery leaning a shoulder against the tree. "What?"

"Are you always going to think you deserved to be banished?"

"Probably."

"Only a fool would do that."

"Then I suppose I'm a fool," Gregor said and went back to leaning against the tree.

Aimery came to stand beside him. "Aren't you even going to ask why I'm here?"

"You are here to torment me."

He laughed. "Nay. I came to tell you what a great battle you put on at the MacLachlan's."

Gregor shrugged and kept his eyes on Fiona. "What do you think will happen once you reach the Druids tomorrow?"

"I think she will get to know her sisters and forget about me," Gregor said.

"What are you going to do?"

"I haven't thought about it."

"You will be double a fool if you let her go," Aimery warned.

"'Tis no affair of yours."

"Really? I beg to differ, Highlander."

Gregor faced the Fae and ground his teeth together. "I cannot let go of something I never had."

"Both of you are fools," Aimery said, disgust marring his face.

"Just keep Fiona safe. That's all I ask."

Aimery peered at him. "Is that all you want? Is there something else you want more than anything? Something you have been too afraid to even think about?"

Gregor backed away. How had Aimery found out? Even he hadn't allowed himself to think of it, even in his sleep.

"Answer me, Gregor."

He swallowed and looked at the tall Fae. Even though it was going to kill him for giving up this one and only chance, he shook his head. "I just want her kept save."

"Then, I will see to it once you bring her to the Druids," Aimery said in resignation. In a blink, Aimery was gone.

Gregor almost called him back, but decided he had made the right decision. How would he begin to tell Aimery that he knew Fiona was closing herself off to him? He would sound like a lovesick fool.

Fiona would be much better off without him. Besides, he didn't have anything to offer her, a powerful Druid. She was everything that was good and right in this world, and just because he had chosen the right side this time, didn't erase his sins.

After tomorrow, he would leave Fiona with the Druids and never look back. He had his memories. It was enough. It had to be.

\* \* \*

Fiona didn't know how long they had ridden that morning. Gregor had been in a foul mood when she had woken, and with the little sleep she had gotten, her mood matched his. She noticed they came out of the mountains and made their way over some hills. The lush green of the valley made her think of her home with the MacDougal's. She missed them terribly, but they would be avenged.

They crested one of the larger hills and she spotted a large loch. She pulled up on the reins and stopped. This was it. She had finally arrived.

She took the opportunity to look around. Off to her right was a large forest, and she knew that was where the Druid's were. Soft music filled her ears. The Druid's called to her and her soul urged her to hurry toward them.

When she opened her eyes, she found Gregor staring at her. She opened her mouth to speak, but he quickly turned around and clicked to Morgane. She watched him ride away from her, but she wasn't ready to follow him yet. This scene was her first of the Druid's Glen, and she was going to enjoy every moment of it. Just as she was about to ride after Gregor, her eyes found the gray stone of a castle.

"Glenna," she said.

*Moira.*

After all these years, she must face her elder sister. There were many things she wanted to say to Moira, given the chance, but she didn't wish to do it in front of Glenna. There would be time. She knew Moira would make that time.

Before she changed her mind, she kicked her mare into

a gallop and caught up with Gregor. But with every step her horse took, her stomach twisted into knots.

Apprehension took hold and refused to let go. She had to grasp the mare's mane to stop her hands from shaking. When they rode over a small hill and the castle came into view, she nearly lost her breakfast. In just a short while, she would have to face everything she had refused to speak about. There was no turning back now. It was a good thing she hadn't known they were so close the previous night, because she would have come up with some reason to delay their arriving.

A cry went up at one of the gatehouse towers. She was close enough now that she could see people running along the parapets. One woman in particular took her notice. Her long dark hair flowed behind her as she ran into the castle. Could that have been Glenna?

"Gregor," a shout came from the gatehouse as they neared.

He waved in response and continued riding, not giving her another glance. Despite the pain his silence caused, she knew it was for the best.

But Gregor was forgotten as she rode through the gates into the bailey. People milled around them as a tall, muscular man with long black hair strode toward them with a bright smile.

"Welcome," he said when he reached them. He turned toward Fiona and reached up to help her dismount. "You must be Fiona. I'm Conall, Glenna's husband."

Fiona leaned to the side and searched the crowd for her younger sister.

"She will be right out. She wanted to make sure she looked her best for you," Conall said.

"Oh," she said, not quite hiding her disappointment.

"But Moira is here."

And into her line of vision stepped the one person she could have lived the rest of her life without seeing again.

## 21

Fiona turned her back on Moira and tried to control her rapid breathing. She hadn't expected to encounter Moira so soon. The instinct to run had taken hold. Fiona's fingers had gathered in her skirts and slowly lifted the material so they wouldn't hamper her escape.

"Fiona?"

She raised her eyes to see a small beautiful woman standing in front of her. Dark wavy hair fell nearly to the woman's hips, and there was no mistaking those brown eyes.

Fiona blinked away her tears at the memory of her father's eyes and gave the woman a big smile. "You must be Glenna."

Before she knew it, Glenna flew into her arms and wrapped her in a tight hug. Warmth surrounded Fiona's heart and the urge to run vanished. Glenna was safe and happy. After all this time!

Glenna stepped out of her arms and wiped away her

tears. "Forgive me. I knew I would cry, but I hoped I could contain myself."

Fiona laughed with her sister as Conall walked up and wrapped an arm around Glenna. "I'm sure you and Gregor could use some rest. Come inside and we will see to your needs before the Druid's call for you."

She started to follow Glenna, but Conall's furrowed brow caught her attention. She turned and found Gregor mounting Morgane.

"Where are you going?" Conall asked him.

Gregor refused to raise his eyes as his rubbed the mare's neck. "I have things I need to see to."

Fiona stopped herself in time from crying out for him to stay. She looked down to find Glenna peering at her strangely.

"Come," Glenna said. "Let the men talk. We three sisters have much to catch up on."

But Fiona wouldn't budge. "I have no wish to speak to Moira."

There was pain in Glenna's eyes when she looked over Fiona's shoulder to where Moira stood. "But she is our sister."

"Things happened you know nothing about. I'm here for the prophecy and you. That's all." Fiona waited to feel Moira behind her or hear her voice. Instead, Glenna nodded and led the way into the castle.

Fiona sighed. She had a brief reprieve before she had to face Moira.

* * *

Gregor watched Fiona walk away without a backward glance his way. He had hoped she would at least wish him Godspeed. Maybe thank him for bringing her safely. But once again, he was the fool.

"Care to explain?" Conall asked beside him.

"Nay."

"You cannot leave yet."

Gregor looked down at the one man that had called him a friend. He owed Conall for making him see what was right and wrong, and that debt would never be repaid.

"If you need me, just say the word."

"I do need you," Conall said. "Now, get off that mare and come inside to rest."

Gregor hesitated. Something wasn't right. He had a sneaking suspicion Conall had just tricked him. "What do you need me for?"

"There's always the need for extra men for any surprise attack MacNeil might make."

"And," Gregor prompted at his friend's silence.

Conall shrugged. "I need help rebuilding the barn."

"I knew you were in too good of a mood to have someone threatening the clan," Gregor said and dismounted. "I'm a warrior, not a builder."

"'Tis all right. We will teach you," he said and clapped Gregor on the back.

*  *  *

Moira turned and made her way out of the bailey. The comfort of the forest and the stone circle would soothe the pain of Fiona's cut.

She reached the nemeton, a sacred clearing in the midst of the forest, and kneeled beside the faerie mound. Tears coursed down her face. She had longed to have her sisters together again, and hadn't given a thought that things might not be happy between them.

The last time she had seen Fiona had been the night of their parent's murder when she left Fiona to return for Glenna. Could Fiona hold some ill will toward her because she hadn't taken her back inside the castle?

Her spine tingled of a sudden. She looked over her shoulder and spotted Dartayous. Would he never leave her in peace?

"Go away," she told him.

"You are in no condition to be left alone."

"Really?" She laughed and looked up at the bright blue sky and the puffy clouds that drifted slowly by. "Are you offering me a shoulder to lean on?" she asked and looked at him.

He stiffened and narrowed his eyes before he spun around on his heel and stalked off. If there was anything she could do right, it was irritate Dartayous.

"He was right, you know."

Moira looked up to find Aimery standing beside the faerie mound. "I just want a moment by myself."

"I warned you that Fiona might be angry."

"I didn't expect her to be so angry that she would turn her back on me," Moira said and wiped away another tear that had escaped.

"Don't give up on her. She needs you more than she realizes," Aimery cautioned.

When Moira raised her eyes he was gone. She was

finally alone to shed the tears she didn't wish anyone to see. As she let loose the dam, she didn't realize she was being watched.

By the one person she didn't want to see her weakness.

Dartayous.

\* \* \*

Fiona knew Glenna wanted to ask what had happened in the bailey, but to give her credit, she hadn't spoken a word about it. In fact, Glenna had gone out of her way to talk of anything but Moira as she busied herself getting everyone a drink.

When Conall led Gregor into the hall, it didn't surprise her. Fiona had a suspicion that Conall wouldn't allow Gregor to leave so quickly.

"How was the journey?" Conall asked once they had taken a seat at the long table in the main hall.

"Fine," she and Gregor replied in unison.

She watched as Glenna and Conall exchanged a glance. "What was that for?"

"Because we can tell that something did happen," Glenna said. "But if you have no wish to explain, we understand. How would you like a nice, hot bath?"

Fiona nearly leapt out of the chair. "Aye, that would be wonderful."

"I will see to it immediately," Glenna said and walked away.

"So," Conall said as he leaned his elbows on the table. "We have been told that you already know about the prophecy and your powers."

She nodded and took a drink of the cool water Glenna had placed in front of her. Her survey of the hall left her impressed. Rich tapestries and many weapons adorned the walls. It was a hall where everyone was welcome, and one that was filled with love.

It reminded her of her foster parents. Even though she had tried to keep her distance from them, it had been impossible. There had been too much love between the two of them to be shut out. She knew that now, but it was too late.

She looked up to see Gregor, Conall, and Glenna staring at her. "What?"

"I have been calling you," Glenna said. "You seemed very far away."

"I was," Fiona answered and looked down at the table.

"Your bath is ready."

Fiona jumped at the chance to get away from Gregor. Being this close to him and knowing she would never see him again was harder than she had imagined. She smiled at Conall as she followed Glenna and sent a fleeting look toward Gregor.

He didn't even glance at her.

The rebuff stung, but it shouldn't have. They hadn't said two words to each other since they had left the MacLachlan's.

"'Tis better that he leaves now."

"Did you say something?" Glenna asked as she turned around.

Fiona shook her head. "I'm just weary from the journey."

"Then this hot bath should do you good. I'm sure everything will look different once you are rested."

The fact that Glenna had such a positive outlook on everything surprised her. From what she had learned, Glenna had been raised in the most horrible of circumstances. How could she be so happy? It couldn't be because of Conall. Could it?

Her thoughts were in turmoil as Glenna led her up the stairs and down a long hallway. The chamber was richly decorated. The bed was draped in dark blue velvet with a rather large chest at the foot of the bed. A table and two chairs faced the hearth and a tapestry showing a battle of some kind hung above it. A large wooden tub was placed at an angle beside the hearth where steam rose from the water.

Fiona loved the feel of the chamber instantly, and she couldn't wait to climb into the water. As soon as Glenna had mentioned a bath, Fiona had felt every particle of dirt on her body and clothes.

"I will have your gown washed for you," Glenna said and held out her hand.

Fiona swallowed. She had never cared to have anyone with her while she dressed or undressed. At a very early age she had seen to herself in all things. Moira's abandonment had made her dependent on one person. Herself.

She turned her back toward Glenna and hastily undressed and slid into the water. She let her gown fall at her feet and hoped she hadn't offended Glenna.

"I apologize," Glenna said. "I should have come back for the gown."

Fiona tried to tell her all was all right, but Glenna held up a hand to stop her.

"I know we don't know each other, but I want that to change. Moira and I had a rough time of it at first, but we are very close now."

Fiona began to rub her neck until she realized what she was doing and jerked her hand away.

*Saint Michael! I've already picked up Gregor's habits.*

"We are sisters and, through fate, were parted," Glenna continued, unaware of the chaos within Fiona. "Even after the prophecy, I would like us to stay close."

"I cannot make any promises," Fiona said and sank low into the water. "Especially where Moira is concerned. I came because I had to and because I needed to see with my own eyes that it was you."

Glenna smiled and wiped at her eyes. "I'm glad you are here."

"Me too," Fiona admitted. "And I can promise that we will get to know each other."

Glenna smiled brightly. "I'll leave you to your bath, then. There are some gowns in the chest for you to wear until I can get this one and your others cleaned."

Before Fiona could say another word, Glenna had departed. With a long sigh, Fiona let the hot water envelope her. Maybe it would help ease the ache in her chest as well as soothe her tired body.

* * *

Gregor clenched his hands and tried to appear as though Conall's words hadn't affected him.

"Are you even listening?" Conall asked.

"You are near to shouting. I cannot help but hear you."

"Then why aren't you saying anything?"

Gregor turned his neck until he heard it pop. "There isn't anything to say. My duty was to bring Fiona here. I have."

"But there's more to the story."

*Damn the man.*

Conall sighed loudly and leaned back in his chair. "I thought we were friends."

"We are," Gregor assured him.

"But you still don't trust me."

"That's the problem. I trusted you more than I have any man since—"

"Since?" Conall prompted.

"Since I left my clan."

Conall ran his hand down his face. "By the saints. I hope that one day you will feel like you can tell me what happened. Nothing you can say will make me think of you as anything other than a trusted friend."

*If only that were the truth.*

"What do you think of Fiona?"

Gregor wanted to roll his eyes. "You are as bad as she is with the questions. I think she's...nice."

"Did anything happen between the two of you?"

*Lots.* "We came to know one another. She's a very strong woman who can take care of herself. She doesn't need me or anyone by her side to live."

"A true Highlander's woman."

Conall's words were like salt in a wound. "Aye. She will make some man very happy."

"Why can't that man be you?"

Gregor looked into Conall's gray eyes. "If you think that, then you are a bigger fool than I thought. You know what I am. I'm not fit to be any woman's husband."

"Why don't you let Fiona decide that?" Conall asked with a satisfied look on his face.

"If you haven't noticed we haven't spoken since we arrived. To be honest, we haven't spoken in four days. Ask her what she thinks of me, and she will tell you."

"What happened to make her stop speaking?"

Gregor took a long drink of ale before he said, "She found out a wee bit of my past."

\* \* \*

"What now?" MacNeil asked as he sat atop his horse. They stood on the mountain that overlooked Conall's castle and the Druids.

"We wait. Our time is near," The Shadow said. "Stay near, but out of sight. I don't want anyone to see you."

"I can take care of anyone that stumbles upon us."

The Shadow whirled around and glared at him. "Fool. If the Druids know you are here, they will make sure they keep you until the time of the prophecy."

MacNeil couldn't hold the eye contact. He lowered his gaze. "Fine. I will make sure we aren't seen or found."

"Good. When I need you I will come for you."

MacNeil watched the man walk away. In all this time, he still hadn't seen his face. The Shadow. That's all they had ever called him, it was all he wanted to be called.

"Stupid name," he grumbled and signaled to his men to follow.

He would find them a hiding spot so that even The Shadow couldn't find them. But he knew that wasn't true. The Shadow had been able to discover things normal men couldn't.

And that's when MacNeil realized he wasn't dealing with just any man. He refused to think of it anymore, because if he did The Shadow would find out. Nay, he would keep it hidden away. Never think of it, or talk of it. Maybe then he would have an upper hand on the elusive Shadow.

His eyes followed The Shadow as he walked to the top of the hill. The Shadow raised his arms above his head and began to chant something.

MacNeil snorted. More magic. Probably concealing them so that no one would stumble upon over a hundred soldiers.

## 22

F iona ventured into the main hall after her bath. The water had done wonders to refresh her body and soul. She had dug in the trunk in her chamber and found a gown of deep red.

She had instantly fallen in love with the color, and once she had it on she doubted she would ever take it off again. It fit near to perfection with the sleeves being only a little long. Still, the scooped neck and hem was accented with a lovely cream and gold braid. All in all, it was a gown fit for royalty.

As she stood at the bottom of the stairs and stared out at the people filling the hall, she almost regretted venturing from her chamber. She was about to turn and make her way back to her chamber when she spotted Gregor.

His blonde hair was still damp from a recent washing, and his beard was gone. She was startled by his handsome, clean-shaven face. Oh, she knew he was handsome, but seeing him dressed in trews and a saffron shirt without any weapons as he sat beside Conall with a goblet in his hand stunned her.

In her mind, he was a warrior. Nothing more, nothing less. Even when she heard his father asking him to take over as laird, she never imagined him thus.

Now, before her, sat a man as he should have been. Welcomed and loved, for it was plain Conall's clan felt both for Gregor.

Her mouth fell open as a small, black-haired girl climbed into Gregor's lap. He stroked the child's hair and gave her a bright smile. The kind of smile one couldn't hold back from a child.

His reaction to the child brought tears to her eyes. She had a hard time keeping them from spilling over as the girl wrapped her arms around Gregor's neck and gave him a hug.

"That's Ailsa, Conall's daughter," Glenna said as she came to stand next to Fiona.

"She's beautiful. Even from here, I can see she has his eyes."

Glenna laughed. "That's how I discovered her."

"Discovered her?" she asked, not sure she'd heard correctly.

"Aye. She had been kept from Conall after her mother died in childbirth. Once I showed Conall, though, he's kept her by his side."

Fiona licked her lips and faced her sister. "Do you like having children?"

"Oh, aye," Glenna said as her eyes shone brightly. "And I hope one day to have one of my own."

"I'm sure you will. People as in love as you and Conall deserve much happiness."

Glenna smiled and nodded her head. "I'm glad to see you are joining us for supper. I'm also happy to see you chose that gown. I so hoped you would like it." She grabbed Fiona's hand and pulled her toward the dais.

"How could I not love it? 'Tis exquisite."

Glenna slowed her steps and leaned close to Fiona. "One day soon you are going to have to tell me what's between you and Gregor."

Fiona stiffened. "There's nothing between us. Nothing at all."

"Whatever you say," Glenna said with a shrug as they reached the dais. "But you can't lie to a Druid."

Fiona found herself seated beside Glenna and thankfully away from Gregor since he sat beside Conall. What she hadn't planned on was the arrival of Moira.

Her breath lodged in her lungs as Moira walked through the doors and toward the dais. Fiona knew no matter how hard she prayed that Moira wouldn't come to dine with them, that she would be wrong. To make matters worse, the seat next to her wasn't occupied.

"I thought it would be nice to have all of us here," Glenna said.

Fiona couldn't stand to look at Moira, so she turned her head away. Only to find Gregor's eyes on her. She knew he disapproved of what she had done in the bailey, but he didn't know what Moira had done to her. Let him disapprove. Why should she care anyway? He wasn't anything to her.

*Liar. He's your mate.*

Mate or not, she couldn't trust a man like him. He was a wanderer who didn't stay in one place too long. He even admitted that he wasn't going to be laird of the MacLachlan's. She could only assume the reason was because he didn't wish to be tied down.

Regardless of the fact he had never given her a reason, he was what he was. A warrior. The only thing they had in common was that they didn't need anyone besides themselves to survive.

When Moira took the seat beside her, every fiber in Fiona's body told her to get up and run, but she didn't wish to offend Glenna and Conall for a second time. Fiona sat rigid as a post and kept her gaze straight ahead for fear of clashing looks with Gregor once more.

"I cannot believe after all this time we are all together," Glenna said happily. "We're a family again."

If Glenna noticed that neither she nor Moira agreed with her statement, she made no mention of it.

"Tell me about your foster parents, Fiona," Glenna said. "I was so happy to learn they were good people."

"The MacDougals were excellent people and very close friends with our parents."

"Were?" Conall asked.

"No sooner had Fiona and I departed the MacDougal's than MacNeil attacked," Gregor answered for her.

"You should have told me," Glenna chastised Fiona. "I'm so sorry."

Fiona nodded and blinked rapidly at the onslaught of tears that Glenna's words brought. She turned her ear to Conall then.

"What happened?" he asked Gregor.

"They nearly reached Fiona before I did. MacNeil and his army pillaged and killed like all their other raids."

"Did Cormag or Helen survive?"

"Nay," Fiona choked out.

Gregor slid his glance to her before he turned to Conall again. "Fiona went back when she saw the smoke. We managed to enter the castle without being seen and found Cormag."

"You weren't able to save him?"

Fiona stared hard at Gregor as she waited for his response.

"Nay," Gregor finally answered. "They had tortured him to gain information about Fiona. How he managed to stay alive that long I'm not sure."

"And Helen?" Glenna asked.

Fiona had never found her foster mother but by Gregor's look and the shake of his head, she was better off not knowing what they had done to her.

"He wasn't alone," Gregor said after a moment of silence.

"The same cloaked figure that tried to kill Glenna and Ailsa?" Conall asked through clenched teeth.

"Aye."

Glenna leaned forward and eagerly asked Fiona, "Did you see him? His face? What did he look like?"

"Even at the MacLa—"

"He kept the hood up," Gregor talked over her.

Fiona narrowed her gaze at him. Why wasn't Gregor going to tell them about the attack on the MacLachlan's? Surely that would be useful information.

Unless he didn't want them to know of his clan and the banishment.

The truth hit her like a battering ram. The only reason she knew was because she had been there. She would wager her best gown that no one knew anything of Gregor's past. She still didn't know exactly what had happened to Gregor's sister and doubted she ever would.

Gregor wanted his secrets kept safe. And she would guard them as long as he stayed out of her business with Moira. He seemed to understand her silence as he gave a quick nod of his head.

When Fiona sat back, she found Glenna, Conall, and Moira staring between her and Gregor. At this rate, her and Gregor's secrets wouldn't be kept for long, she thought as she picked up her fork and bit into the roasted quail and carrots.

With such delicious food, she forgot about Moira sitting beside her until she turned to comment on the great food. The smile died on her lips when she looked into Moira's green eyes.

"Fiona," Moira began.

But she lowered her gaze before Moira could continue. How could she have forgotten who sat next to her?

"Eventually you will have to talk to me."

It was on the tip of her tongue to tell her exactly what she thought of that comment, but she kept silent. It was the only way she could deal with things, because if she began her tirade against Moira, there was no telling when it would stop.

After holding such anger inside for ten and eight years, there was too much of it to allow only a little loose.

"Please. We're sisters," Glenna beseeched as she leaned close. "I've dreamed of the moment where we would all sit together. And this isn't how I envisioned it."

Fiona had had enough. "We don't always get what we want. That's life."

"It doesn't have to be," Moira said. "I heard you might be angry with me. I'm not sure for what, but I'm willing to find out why."

Fiona felt trapped. Who would have known that coming to this place to meet up with her sisters would do this to her? She wanted to scream and cry all at once. Her emotions inside were twisted into such a knot that she was too confused to think straight.

*'Tis because of Gregor.*

"Nay," she whispered. It couldn't be because of him, it had to be because of Moira. Her gaze was drawn to him, and despite her trying not to, she looked at him. Ailsa was again in his lap. The beautiful child looked comfortable and he appeared content to have her there.

She didn't look away when Gregor's eyes found her. His gaze held her intently, as if he tried to tell her something, but she couldn't see anything other than the desire in her own body.

It became difficult to stay in her chair. Even as Glenna and Moira continued to talk, she didn't hear them. Her focus was Gregor and the memory of their lovemaking.

She swallowed as the image of his black eyes filled with desire and wanting flashed in her mind. He had given her pleasure before he had taken his own. Even the way he had touched her body had been almost reverent. His gentleness and passion brought heat to her body even now.

What was wrong with her? Never in all her years had she been so emotional. It must stop. Now.

"Excuse me," she said and rose from her chair. She couldn't leave the hall fast enough.

Gregor watched her leave and debated with himself for all of a moment before he sat Ailsa down and followed Fiona. He didn't speak as he hurried to the stairs.

Fiona's quiet attitude had bothered him since their arrival. She didn't look comfortable here and it worried him. He didn't want to be bothered by her, but he couldn't seem to help it.

She had been in his blood since that first night they joined bodies. His eyes sought her out wherever he went. If she happened to be near him, he found it impossible to do anything other than stare at her. The fact that she had ignored him only hardened his resolve to keep his distance.

He stayed because Conall asked him to and because Conall was a friend. He didn't have many friends, so ones like Conall he made sure he kept. So, instead of leaving and putting as much distance as he could between him and Fiona, he stayed. But he would make sure it wasn't for long. Just long enough to finish the barn and see Fiona settled with her sisters.

Besides, from the hints Aimery had given him, Fiona would find her mate just as Glenna had. Frankly, he didn't wish to be here for that. It was hard enough knowing he couldn't have her now, but it would be nigh impossible once she discovered her mate.

He wondered why Conall had told him where Fiona's chamber was located, but now he was glad of it. She had fled so fast he hadn't been able to find her.

Now, as he stood outside her chamber door, he had to question his sanity. She wanted no part of him, yet he was going to put himself through all kinds of hell just to make sure she was all right.

"What are you doing here?"

He turned to find Fiona next to him. "I came to check on you. You ran from the hall so quickly I knew something was wrong."

She sighed and pushed strands of hair out of her face that had come loose from the braid. "I just needed some air."

"You don't like it here?"

"I'm glad I finally got to see Glenna, but..."

"You could have gone without seeing Moira," he finished for her.

She raised her face and gave him a small, sad smile. "Aye. I cannot help it."

"I understand."

Suddenly the hallway where they stood became too crowded. He knew the instant she closed herself off to him. When her tongue darted out to lick her lips he had to stop himself from taking her in his arms and kissing her.

He tamped down his growing desire and tried to think of anything other than the feel of her soft skin beneath his hands, her soft moans as he slid into her, and her cries of pleasure as he brought her to ecstasy.

His gaze rose to her face and there was no mistaking the desire there. She might pretend she was immune to him, but she wasn't. Words weren't needed as they each took a step that put them in each other's arms. In all his years with women, never had one woman made his body tingle with just the thought of her.

Yet Fiona did just that, and it scared the hell out of him. He crushed her soft body to his and ravaged her mouth. His tongue dueled with hers, taking all of her into him as her hands clung to his neck and shoulders.

Blood pounded loudly in his ears as he pushed her against the wall and pressed his aching manhood into the juncture of her thighs.

"Gregor," she whispered in his ear.

He nearly died from the pleasure her lips gave him as they trailed from his neck to his ear where she lightly nipped the lobe.

"If we don't get inside your chamber soon, I'm going to take you right here," he told her.

She smiled brightly and reached over to unlatch the door. It was all the invitation he needed. He picked her up and carried her through the threshold, stopping only long enough to close the door with his foot.

He didn't spare the chamber a glance as he sat her on her feet. She was all he wanted right now, and he would do almost anything to have her in his arms for just one more night.

"I swore I wouldn't let this happen again," she said with a sad smile.

"I'm just too hard to resist."

She cocked her head to the side and raised a dark brow. "Maybe."

"Or maybe," he said as he brought his hand up to her face, "you know we are good together."

Her forehead furrowed deeply and she stepped away from him. "What did Conall tell you?"

"Conall told me nothing. Why do you think he would say anything about you?" he asked.

"Conall asked about us, didn't he?"

She was becoming frantic. He had to stop this nonsense and get back to where they were.

"He did, but I informed him there was nothing to tell. You have no need to worry."

"You don't understand," she cried and turned her back on him. "I should never have given in the first time."

Gregor reached out to touch her but stopped. Whatever bothered her, consumed her. She had no wish for his comfort. "You regret our lovemaking."

Her silence was all the answer he needed. He walked from the chamber before he made a bigger fool of himself. Friend or not, he couldn't stay here any longer. Tomorrow morning he would inform Conall of his decision.

\* \* \*

Fiona waited. All Gregor needed to do was touch her and she would take comfort in his strong arms. She needed him right now, needed him more desperately than she was willing to admit.

When she heard the chamber door close, she never felt more alone in her life. If not the whole of Scotland was at stake, she would never have come.

And she would never have known Gregor.

That was the crux of the matter. Gregor. She wondered if anyone had ever refused their mate and what had happened to them. She would find out tomorrow when she went to see the Druids.

Sleep would be difficult with her body on fire for Gregor, but she would manage it. She didn't have a choice. Laughter from the hall below reached her. Love and happiness filled this castle. Too bad she would never allow herself to share in any of it.

## 23

F iona breathed in the fresh morning air as she stood on the castle steps. Clouds filled the sky, threatening rain, but it was still a beautiful morning with the sun breaking through the dense clouds.

"Are you ready?"

She turned to Glenna. It was time to see the Druids. "Aye."

Her sister led them led them to a cave entrance. Upon their arrival yesterday, she hadn't had taken much of a chance to look around the bailey, but surely, she would have noticed a large cave.

Fiona stopped. The dark expanse that loomed in front of her brought back the memories of the night their parents were murdered. She hadn't liked walking down the dimly lit hall and had always talked Moira into going with her.

"I was scared of it the first time, too," Glenna said.

"I'm not scared. Just remembering."

"You were terrified, darling," Conall said to Glenna as he walked up.

Fiona turned to find Conall and Gregor beside them. Glenna had said nothing about them accompanying them.

"But it wasn't the dark," Conall continued. "Do you know what she is afraid of, Fiona?" he asked with a big smile.

Glenna playfully punched him in the stomach. "I will tell her, you oaf. You will only make it worse than it was." She turned to Fiona. "I was afraid of spiders."

"Was?" Conall chuckled. "You still are."

"I'm getting better." Glenna crossed her arms over her chest and raised her chin.

"Spiders?" Fiona finally asked.

"Aye. I hate them. All those legs." Glenna shivered and rubbed her hands on her arms.

Conall sighed loudly. "I guess that means we'll be going the long route."

"That's right," Glenna said and took Fiona's arm. "You had to bring it up, Conall."

Fiona looked over her shoulder at Conall who was smiling widely as he clapped Gregor on the back. Just what were they doing here?

"How did you sleep last eve?"

"Wonderfully," Fiona lied to Glenna. Thoughts of Gregor had kept her awake the entire night.

"Good. I was worried about you."

Fiona swallowed hard. Glenna had been worried about her? "Why?"

Glenna looked at her as if she had suddenly grown horns out of her ears. "Because you are in a place you would rather not be, because you lost your foster family, because I know there are things that are bothering you, and because you are my sister."

Fiona had never been so humbled in her life. "Even after the way I acted at supper."

"Of course," Glenna said. "Whatever is between you and Moira can be fixed."

"I don't want it to be fixed."

"Why ever not?"

"For too many years I have lived with this anger in my heart."

"Exactly. That's why you need to get it out so you can be happy."

Happy. What was that exactly? She listened as Glenna described her life as they walked through the gates. Her attention strayed from Glenna's words when she caught sight of the forest.

When Glenna steered her in that direction, Fiona almost jumped for joy. She knew who lived in that forest. The Druids.

Even though Helen had been a Druid and had taught her everything she knew, they had to keep their identity a secret. Here, at MacInnes Castle, everyone knew what she was and still accepted her.

But she knew that was only because the MacInnes clan had hidden the Druids for centuries.

The music she heard yesterday reached her once more. She stopped and listened for a moment.

"Beautiful isn't it?" Glenna asked. "It soothes me."

Fiona nodded because words had become lodged in her throat. The music did ease away her anger and balance her somewhat.

"I wanted to bring you yesterday, but I knew you needed your rest."

Fiona couldn't help but smile at Glenna's enjoyment of life. How could MacNeil have raised this small, enchanting creature that was her sister? Surely she had been lied to.

"What?" Glenna asked.

"You are so happy and full of life."

Glenna smiled and lowered her head. "And you wonder how I can be such and have been raised with MacNeil?"

Fiona waited until Glenna lifted her head. "Aye." She followed Glenna's gaze and found her staring at Conall.

"It was him. He did it. He and Moira brought me to where I am today. He never gave up on me, even when I wanted him to."

She watched as Conall looked up from his conversation with Gregor as the men slowly walked toward them. He smiled at Glenna and blew her a kiss.

Fiona turned away and looked to the forest, but still that image of Conall blowing a kiss to her sister was etched in her mind. She could have that, too. All she had to do was open her heart to Gregor. It would be so easy.

*And the pain would kill me when he left.*

"Come. I cannot wait for you to meet everyone," Glenna said and urged her toward the trees.

Fiona was glad to forget about Gregor and false dreams. She had other things to concentrate on.

As soon as they entered the forest, calmness overtook her. Magic filled the air just waiting to be released. Helen had told her of this place, but to actually experience it was amazing.

She ran after Glenna though the trees, feeling younger and more carefree than she had in years. Glenna's laughter was her guide as she wound her way through the giant trees.

Just as she caught sight of Glenna, she turned and looked over her shoulder. Gregor followed close behind her, but it was the pain she saw in his eyes that bothered her.

*I did that. I put that pain there.*

"Come. The stone circle is just up ahead," Glenna called out to her.

Fiona looked away from Gregor and stopped. Gone was the tranquility as her heart was once again filled with turmoil. She followed as Glenna and Conall ran through the trees.

Their love was so strong, so true, that nothing could break it. They were bound in this life and the next. Forever.

Then Fiona rounded a tree and came to stand beside Glenna and Conall. Before her stood the massive stone circles her foster mother had described to her.

"It looks exactly like Helen told me it would," Fiona said and reached out to touch one of the stones.

From the corner of her eye, she saw Gregor walk up to join them. Despite what she wanted to feel, she was happy that he shared this with her. After everything they had endured, it was only right that he was beside her.

Glenna sighed happily. "Let's go inside."

Fiona's gaze briefly traveled to Glenna before coming back to the stones. In that short time, a veil had been lifted and she could see inside the circle. The circle housed hundreds of Druids ranging in age from the very young to the very old.

It was pure paradise inside. While outside the circle it was overcast with the smell of rain in the air, inside the circle the sun shone bright. She stepped inside as Glenna tugged on her arm. It was then she noticed Aimery beside an old man. At least, she thought he was old because of the long white beard and hair, but as she walked closer, she saw that he wasn't as old as she thought.

His skin wasn't wrinkled and his blue eyes weren't faded. He might not look old, but his soul was.

"Welcome home, Fiona," he said was a kind smile. "We've been waiting for you."

She remembered him instantly. "Thank you, Frang."

"Ah, so you remember me?"

"What I remember is that you looked... older," Fiona answered as she tilted her head to look at the Druid High Priest.

"I've been trying to get him to tell me his age since I first came here," Glenna said.

Frang gave Glenna a small smile and turned back to Fiona, except he looked behind her instead of at her. Gregor.

"Step forward, Gregor," the high priest bid.

Fiona couldn't hide the chills that swept over her as Gregor walked past her and brushed her arm with his. When she raised her gaze it was to find Frang staring intently at her.

"You did your task well. I knew you were the right man to bring Fiona home," he said and handed Gregor a small bag.

There was no mistaking the jingling of coin. "You were paid?" she asked Gregor.

"I told you I was sent to bring you here."

"But you never said you were paid," she argued. The fact that he wouldn't look at her only made her angrier.

"It doesn't matter," Frang said and stepped toward her. He wrapped his arm around her shoulder. "Come. There are many things we need to discuss."

She allowed him to take her away. As soon as his hand had touched her, some of her anger faded. "How did you do that?"

He laughed and guided her through the many boulders inside the circle. "Nothing gets by you."

"You aren't going to tell me, are you?"

"Helen has taught you well."

She chuckled to herself and gave up. "Helen was an excellent teacher."

"She showed you how to control your powers?"

Fiona nodded. "At a very early age, in fact."

"I knew they were the right people to raise you," he said with a smile.

"Why didn't you take me in like you did Moira?"

He paused and looked at her. "Everything happens for a reason. One child brought into the circle isn't cause for gossip, but two? There was no way I could bring both of you."

"So Moira leaving me that night was for a reason?"

"She didn't leave you."

Fiona wanted to scream. "Why must everyone argue with me? I was there."

"You were meant to go with the MacDougal's, but

enough of that talk. Let us speak about something else," Frang said. "Tell me of Gregor."

"He brought me here," she said and refused to say more.

"He is your mate. You know that, yet you deny yourself and him."

Her head jerked toward him. "How do you know this?"

"You are easy to read. Your emotions are like Glenna's, they are for the world to see. If one knows how to look."

His wisdom did little to soothe her. "You don't approve of my denying him as my mate."

"You know I don't. One must never deny their mate."

"Why? Surely there have been people who did."

Frang sighed and sat on a small boulder. "Aye, there have been. I don't think you are going to like what I'm about to tell you."

She waited for him to continue. "The confusion you feel will only grow. You will never be content with anything or anyone. You will long for death and become malicious."

"I have dealt with most of that for ten and eight years. I will be fine."

He watched her carefully. "If you think so."

"Fiona," Glenna called.

"Go to your sister," he told her.

Fiona hurried to Glenna. She was afraid if she stayed she would learn more than she wanted to.

Frang watched Fiona leave. They had a tough road ahead of them. He never imagined her to be so bitter.

"Why didn't you tell her what would happen to Gregor if she doesn't acknowledge him as her mate?"

Frang didn't turn toward Aimery. He had known the Fae had been there the entire time. "It wasn't the time. She needs to find out slowly. To rush her would be a grave mistake."

"Something is happening."

His tone alarmed Frang. He turned toward the Fae. "What is it?"

"The Evil One is near, very near. And Fae have gone missing."

"What?"

"My queen has been difficult to reach. Watch yourself, Frang. I have a feeling the future is about to be changed."

## 24

Gregor stood away from Conall and Glenna. He loved being with the Druids and experiencing the magic they lived by, but he didn't feel as though he should be here.

His gaze found Fiona as she walked toward Glenna. Frang was no longer with her, and he wondered what their discussion had been about. The one person he noticed absent was Moira.

His eyes scanned the area until he caught a flash of white blonde hair before she disappeared behind one of the giant stones. Moira was giving Fiona time to get to know the Druids without her near.

He looked to Fiona and found her deep in conversation with Glenna. Fiona hadn't wanted him here today. That had been painfully obvious when he stepped into the bailey. He and Moira had something in common, and maybe he could help Moira.

If he could help reconcile Moira and Fiona before he left, then he would feel as though he accomplished something. He slipped away unnoticed and walked to where he had glimpsed Moira. Her long, white blonde hair was easy to spot through the dark foliage and boulders.

She walked away from the center of the circle. Gregor lengthened his stride until he neared her. That's when he felt the presence behind him. He pulled his sword from his scabbard at the same time as he whirled around to face his opponent.

He stopped his sword from slicing into Dartayous a hair's breadth away. Dartayous never moved. He stood as still as a statue while his bright blue eyes stared at Gregor.

"By the saints! I could have killed you," Gregor said and sheathed his sword.

"Afraid not, my friend. What is your business with Moira?"

Gregor had seen much since coming to MacInnes Castle and the Druid's Glen, but the Druid Warriors were different. Especially Dartayous. There was something about this warrior that made men like Gregor stand up and take notice.

"I want to talk with her about Fiona," Gregor finally answered.

Dartayous snorted. "Good luck. She's in a surly mood and her nails haven't been retracted since Fiona came. Watch yourself."

His warning surprised Gregor. He had known Moira to be the epitome of calm and grace. For Dartayous to suggest that Moira raised her voice was unthinkable.

To his utter amazement, Dartayous slipped away without him noticing. That bothered him immensely. He was supposed to be a great warrior who perceived things.

Was he losing his edge? Was his mind too occupied with Fiona?

Whatever it was, it had to stop. And maybe Moira could aid him. It wasn't hard to find her. She stood on the cliff where Conall and Glenna had been married, overlooking MacInnes Castle. It was a breathtaking spot.

"I come up here often," Moira said. "I love to look down at Glenna and Conall and know that they are happy and at peace." She turned and looked over her shoulder. "You are troubled."

"I have been troubled for many years. Nothing will change that," he said and walked to stand beside her. "'Tis a beautiful spot."

"Tell me of your troubles."

"Actually, I came to talk with you about Fiona." He felt rather than saw her stiffen. "She holds a lot of anger inside of her."

"That is evident to see."

Gregor was beginning to think he should have heeded Dartayous' advice. Even though Moira hadn't raised her voice, it had become decidedly icier.

"She needs some time," Gregor continued. "She lost the MacDougals and found out you had known where she was all these years. She didn't take that well at all."

"I wanted her to have a normal life. Something Glenna and I never had the chance to have."

"You should tell her that."

Moira laughed. "She won't acknowledge me. What makes you think she would listen to anything I had to say?"

"I don't know," he sighed. "I know she's giving you a difficult time, but I wanted you to understand why."

"You aren't telling me everything, are you?"

He looked into her green eyes that were so like Fiona's and wanted to tell her. But it wasn't for him to speak of. That needed to come from Fiona.

"'Tis the truth I'm not, nor should I."

"It doesn't matter," she said. "What matters is that you got her here. Safe and sound, just like I asked. I knew I had chosen the right man."

Gregor ducked his head. He liked the pleasure her words gave him. If only he was as good a man as she thought him to be, but he knew she would change her opinion of him if she knew everything.

He looked up to find her staring at him.

"You worry overmuch," she said.

"Do I?"

"I cannot read your thoughts," she assured him. "I can tell that you have old memories that you have buried deep within you."

He turned away and made sure no emotion showed on his face. "You are guessing."

"Nay. 'Tis clear to see if one knows how to look. Frang taught me that."

"I didn't come here to discuss me."

"So much pain," she said and ignored his words. "You try very hard to appear detached and unaffected and you have fooled many people."

"But not you," he bit out.

"Nor Fiona."

His breath lodged in his chest. How had she known that?

"I've seen the way Fiona watches you. She feels your

pain yet wants to keep you at arm's length. Why is that?"

"She's a Druid. I don't claim to understand you or your ways."

Moira laughed. "Good answer."

"It was a mistake coming to speak with you."

"Only if you don't heed my words," she warned.

He stopped as he began to turn away. "And what words are those?"

"Don't keep those dark memories buried. Remember that regardless of what you think of yourself, you are a good man."

He nodded and walked back toward the stone circle. He had come to speak of Fiona, but in the end, Moira had turned the conversation to what she wished to discuss. He should have known better than to try to talk to a Druid.

By the time he reached the circle, Glenna and Fiona sat with the other Druids. He briefly wondered if she had noticed his absence, but knew he was only hurting himself with those kinds of thoughts.

"Where did you venture off to?" Conall asked as he came to stand beside him.

"I went to talk to Moira to try and give her an idea of why Fiona is doing what she's doing."

"She changed the subject on you, didn't she?"

"Aye."

"Glenna does that when she doesn't wish to talk about something. Still, it was good that you tried. I didn't realize you had come to care for Fiona that much."

Gregor ground his teeth together. Damn. He'd have to watch himself. "Don't assume more than it is."

"And what is it?"

*The truth? That I cannot get her out of my mind, that I think about Fiona constantly.*

"I think 'tis much more than you are telling me, but I'm a patient man. I can wait."

"You will wait for eternity, then. There's nothing to tell." It didn't help when all Conall did was give him a knowing smile.

Gregor rubbed his neck as the tension built. He raised his eyes to find Fiona's gaze on him. She hastily looked away, but not before Conall saw it.

"I know that look."

"What look?" Gregor asked, not holding back the sigh.

"The look that says there is much more between the two of you than either is letting on."

"Let it be," Gregor said before he walked away.

Conall caught up with him as he left the stone circle. "You're leaving."

"I have to," Gregor said.

"I really could use your help. Give yourself some time here to rest. Ailsa doesn't wish you to leave yet."

Gregor knew he was staying the minute Conall had said Ailsa's name. "You just had to use Ailsa."

"I know how much you adore her. If that's the only way I can hold you here, then I will use it."

"A real friend would allow me to leave," Gregor said and turned to face him.

Conall's gray eyes twinkled. "A real friend would make you stay. A real friend would show you what you have to gain by staying. A real friend would try to give you the happiness they have."

\* \* \*

Fiona couldn't take her eyes off Gregor and Conall. From the look of resignation on Gregor's face and the elation on Conall's she had a feeling things were about to change for her.

"Well, it looks like Conall won," Glenna beamed next to her.

Fiona slid a glance at her sister. "What?"

"Conall told me last night that he had a feeling Gregor was going to leave even though Conall asked him to stay."

Fiona ignored the flash of panic that ensued upon hearing Gregor's intentions. It didn't make sense for her to feel that way since she told herself she didn't want to have anything to do with him. She was the one that was supposed to leave. Not him.

"What made Conall think Gregor meant to leave?" she finally asked.

Glenna smiled widely and shrugged. "I suppose it could be because of the way Gregor looks at you."

Fiona didn't bother to respond because Glenna would believe nothing she said.

"I cannot believe you aren't going to admit that you have seen him look at you with longing."

Fiona found herself rubbing her neck and quickly stopped, but not before Glenna's eyes followed her hand. "Gregor looks at a lot of people. I'm no different."

"I admit to not knowing Gregor that well, but I will tell you that I have never seen him act like this before."

"Like what?" Fiona couldn't help but ask.

"Like he cannot wait to leave. 'Tis as if he thinks if he stays that something will happen."

*Something has already happened.*

"After Conall and I married we could tell he really didn't want to leave. I saw him looking around the bailey at the people, especially Ailsa, and he couldn't hide his longing. I wish I knew what happened in his past."

"Nay, you don't." As soon as the words left her mouth, she regretted them. She squeezed her eyes closed. "Please, Glenna, don't ask."

She heard Glenna sigh loudly. "All right. But one day I would like to know. There is so much pain in him."

"He left the glen because he came to retrieve me," Fiona said to change the subject.

"Aye. Moira thought he would be the perfect man to send. Not many clans in the Highlands will interfere with Gregor. I suppose it has something to do with his livelihood."

"Being a mercenary," she finished for Glenna.

"He told you?"

Fiona nodded. "Not at first. Trying to get him to speak of his past is like trying to move a mountain."

"'Tis the truth." Glenna laughed and pointed to her husband. "Conall seems awfully pleased with himself."

"So he has convinced Gregor to stay?"

She must not have kept the disappointment from her voice because Glenna turned toward her with a deeply furrowed brow. "I thought you liked Gregor."

"I like him fine."

"Then why don't you want him here?"

Why indeed? Because if she saw him another day she

would give in to her desires. Because she found herself wanting to soothe the pain from him. Because of so many reasons she didn't want to name. Not to Glenna or herself.

"What happened on the journey?" Glenna asked. "Did he hurt you?"

"Never," Fiona said much too forcefully. "I just like my distance."

"From everyone."

It wasn't a question, and she knew she had hurt Glenna. The words hung between them like a stone wall.

"I won't intrude again," Glenna said before she rose and walked away.

Fiona wanted to call Glenna back but couldn't find the words. Since she had arrived she managed to hurt everyone around her. She didn't know what made her act this way, and it seemed to be getting worse by the day.

\* \* \*

*So close, yet so far away.*

The Shadow moved closer to Moira. He couldn't get too close because that Druid Warrior was near and would sniff him out. Something wasn't quite normal about that warrior.

He would have to see what he could discover to make sure Dartayous didn't get in his way. But right now, he just wanted to gaze upon Moira's beauty. He closed his eyes and imagined her lying naked upon the ground before he covered her with his body.

"Moira."

His eyes jerked open at the sound of Dartayous' voice. He was near, very near.

"I'm not ready to return," Moira said as she continued to stare out over the cliff.

"He's here."

That simple statement made her whirl around, the bottom of her gown swishing around her legs. "Who?"

"You know of who I speak."

The Shadow ducked as Moira's eyes scanned the surrounding trees and boulders. Neither of them could see him, but the warrior was able to sense him.

He wanted to scream his fury as Moira quickly walked past Dartayous. The Shadow had a mind to follow. Until he saw Dartayous draw his mighty sword.

"Not today," The Shadow whispered. "But one day soon, Moira."

## 25

Fiona walked beside a now subdued Glenna as they left the stone circle and forest. She could hear Conall whispering in Glenna's ear to make sure everything was all right. She lagged behind, not yet ready to return to the castle and to give Glenna and Conall some privacy. Only a little ways behind her, Gregor followed.

Everyone gave her a wide berth and she couldn't blame them. Her wicked tongue had managed to hurt everyone, even the stoic warrior who had brought her here and saved her life.

She wanted to run and hide, but that would be the coward's way out. And she wasn't a coward.

"I see you managed to wound Glenna."

She wasn't surprised by Gregor's statement. "Unintentionally, but nonetheless, I did."

"At least you admit it. What has come over you?"

Her eyes didn't need to see his face to know that he was annoyed. "I don't know. I told you I shouldn't have come."

"You really didn't have much of a choice."

"True."

He stopped and put out a hand to halt her. "They are your sisters. You cannot replace them. Take my word for it. Let go of the past."

"I see those words are easy for you," she said as anger welled up in her at thinking of the past. "Have you done the same?"

She quickly turned away so he couldn't see the tears in her eyes. Once again she managed to speak without thinking, and this time she had gone too far. What Gregor lived with was much worse than her own problems.

"Gregor, I'm sorry," she said and turned around. Only to find herself alone.

She deserved to be alone. She had hurt the one person who still spoke to her, and the damage she did was probably irreparable.

Returning to the castle wasn't something she could do now. Nor could she return to the Druids and chance a meeting with Moira. She looked at the trees surrounding her. This was a large forest, and she would see where it took her.

Despite her resolve not to, she couldn't help but realize that no one noticed her absence. She had hurt everyone with her cruel, hateful words. She stumbled through the forest not paying attention to where she was going or the beautiful things around her. It wasn't until she walked into a clearing that she took notice.

"A nemeton," she murmured. "A sacred clearing in the midst of a forest."

Helen had told her the nemeton was like a fortress of

nature separated from the rest of the world and sacred to the Druids.

Magic drummed around the clearing and Fiona realized why when she spotted the Faerie mound. Her heart lightened from the heavy burden she had been under as the magic seeped through her. She found herself lulled by the peace and tranquility of the nemeton.

And she was content to stay forever.

She had just begun to explore the trees and bushes surrounding the nemeton when evil sliced through her soul and coldness began to overtake her. She recoiled from the hawthorn bush she had been studying.

Her eyes scanned the trees beyond the hawthorn, but she couldn't see anything. Yet, her body sensed the evil nearby.

"Leave now."

She whirled around to find a man she had seen inside the stone circle. He wore trews like Gregor's yet they weren't quite leather nor where they a common material.

It was obvious by the many daggers and swords he wore that he was a warrior. But it was his eyes that captivated her. The intensity of his blue eyes reminded her of someone, but she could not remember who.

"Don't just stand there, woman. Get away. There is evil here."

"I know," she answered and walked toward him. Instantly, the evil dissipated until she could barely sense it. Once she got even with the warrior, she tilted her head back and looked into his face. "'Tis behind me."

"You shouldn't be alone," he said and drew his sword.

Fiona's eyes were drawn to the unusual sword. From

the tip to the hilt, the blade was smooth on one side and jagged on the other. The blade had teeth.

Her gaze then caught sight of the unusual ring on his right hand and the Celtic tattoos as well. "Can you see it?"

"I can smell him," the warrior said.

Fiona opened her mouth, but the warrior stopped her. "He is about to attack. He wants you dead. I would suggest that you run as fast as you can to the stone circle. I will hold him off."

She didn't hesitate, but lifted her skirts and ran for her life. Her ears picked up the sounds of footsteps behind her, but she refused to look back. If she did, she might trip and fall, and then where would that leave her?

"Faster," the warrior bellowed behind her. "He is after you!"

She burst through a group of trees and spotted the circle ahead of her, but just when she thought she might make it, she was jerked back. The cold seeped into her skin and around her heart. The breath left her in a whoosh. As she struggled to breathe, she waited for her death.

When she finally caught her breath, she opened her eyes to see Aimery and a score of Fae surrounding her.

Aimery held out his hand and helped her to her feet. "Are you all right?" he asked.

Warmth once again filled her. "I am now. Where is the warrior that helped me?" she asked as she searched the faces around her.

"He is following the evil that was after you."

Death had narrowly passed her over, and she would be sure to thank the warrior later. "I'm glad you were here."

"Did you see him?"

The hope she heard in Aimery's voice made it hard for her to tell him. "Nay. I sensed the evil the same time the warrior came upon me."

"That warrior's name is Dartayous," Aimery explained as he led her into the stones. "He is the best Druid Warrior there is, and 'tis his job to guard Moira."

"Guard Moira? Are you afraid she is going to run away?"

Aimery shook his head and his long blonde locks barely moved. "You, Moira, and Glenna are in constant danger until the time of the prophecy. Dartayous is able to smell the evil."

"Just as I felt it."

"Aye. The Evil One attacks when you are alone. If you stay with someone, you should be fine."

Moira walked up then, her green eyes looking Fiona over. "Are you all right?"

Fiona nodded, unsure of the concern in her sister's eyes.

"It was the Evil One," Aimery said.

"'Tis a good thing Dartayous was near," Moira stated and looked over her shoulder.

Fiona followed her gaze and spotted the Druid Warrior. The tension between the two of them was palpable, and Fiona found herself curious to know why.

She watched as Dartayous shook his head, and she turned her head in time to see Aimery sigh and briefly close his eyes.

"Maybe he should guard Fiona instead of me," she heard Moira say.

"Nay," Aimery said. "Dartayous will guard you."

Fiona watched as Moira took a step closer to the Faerie. "What have you seen?" she asked him.

Aimery looked away from Moira. "Nothing. 'Tis blocked. But my instincts tell me the Evil One is after you."

"Then why the attack on me?" Fiona asked. "If he wants Moira, why bother with me or Glenna?"

"What do you mean? You haven't seen anything?" Moira asked.

He ignored Moira and turned to Fiona. "He wants Moira."

That's when it hit Fiona. The Evil One wanted her and Glenna dead, but he *wanted* Moira. The distress that caused her didn't sit well.

"Answer me," Moira demanded of Aimery.

"I don't know why," he retorted, his voice dangerously low. "'Tis never happened before."

Fiona listened closely to the conversation, but it was the quick furrow of Dartayous' brow when Aimery said he couldn't see the future that triggered something within her.

"Who has the ability to hinder your sight?"

"Only the king and queen," Aimery said. "And they have not issued such a decree."

Fiona wasn't able to ask more questions as Aimery took her arm. "Come," he said. "I will return you to the castle."

She didn't wish to return to the castle, but she also knew there was nowhere else for her to go. Much to her disappointment he took her through the caves.

It was dark and damp, but with his fast pace she didn't have much time to look around. By the time they reached the bailey she was out of breath. She turned to Aimery only to find he was no longer with her.

She didn't think she would ever get used to the disappearing Fae. After a deep breath, she made her way to the castle. No one stopped her or questioned her. Glenna, Conall, and Gregor were nowhere to be seen either.

Her chamber was the best place for her at the moment. She quickly made her way into the castle and up the stairs. Once she was safely inside her chamber, she locked the door and sank onto the bed.

Her first day here had been a disaster and it wasn't even noon yet.

Gregor lifted the board and placed it in the spot that Conall had designated. As soon as he left Fiona, he had come straight here to begin work on the barn. He hoped the work would take his mind off her, but so far he hadn't been that lucky.

He was sure as he sweated under the sun that Fiona was with Glenna inside talking of everything but him. Even if she did manage to say anything about him it wouldn't be good. He didn't know why he continued to put himself through the torture of being near her.

Yet, he allowed Conall to talk him into staying, but only until the barn was finished.

Then he must leave for good. Nothing could make him stay, not even little Ailsa. When the noon hour came, he took a brief respite with the rest of the men and ate a quick meal before he was back lifting the wood. The exertion on his body would make for a full night's rest. He wasn't taking any more chances of restless nights with thoughts of Fiona in his arms.

He would sleep this night even if he had to drink himself into oblivion.

The next time he looked up, it was to see the sun sinking into the horizon and Glenna striding toward them. Sometime during the day, Conall had come to work beside him, but Gregor had never known.

"The barn has come far this day," Glenna said as she leaned over and placed a kiss on Conall's lips.

Conall laughed and took a long drink of water. "Aye. With Gregor working like a madman, this should be done in a couple of weeks."

"I was just working as any normal man would," Gregor said as he took the water skin.

"If you call that working," Conall said with a laugh. "I finally gave up talking to you after being ignored. You must have much on your mind, my friend."

Gregor ducked his head. He did have much on his mind, but that didn't mean he should ignore friends. The problem was he had never known Conall was even beside him. Hopefully he didn't offend too many men this day.

"Where is Fiona?" Glenna asked as she looked around.

"Fiona? She's not here," Conall said.

Dread quickly spread through Gregor. "I thought she was with you."

"The last time I saw her was when we left the circle," Glenna said.

Gregor cursed. "We had words and I left her in the forest, but I assumed she would follow you back to the castle."

"Don't panic," Conall said as he wrapped an arm around Glenna. "Let's look in the castle first before we send up an alarm."

Glenna raised fright filled eyes. "She could be with Moira."

"Doubtful," Conall said and turned her toward the castle.

Gregor hurried after them. If anything happened to Fiona, the blame would lie with him. Once again, he had let his emotions rule him. That was the reason Anne died, and he couldn't bear to think that, once again, it had claimed a life. Especially Fiona's.

Once they reached the castle, they separated and began to search. All Gregor could think about was not so long ago when they searched for Glenna only to find someone had tried to kill her.

With every corner he turned he expected to see Fiona lying lifeless in front of him. But to his relief, he didn't find her like that. Glenna's voice reached him. Fiona had been found.

"Thank you," Gregor said and raised his face to the ceiling. "Thank you."

## 26

Fiona jerked awake at the sound of something banging against her door—hard. She slowly sat up when the knock sounded.

"Fiona?"

She sighed when she heard Glenna's voice and hurried to unlatch the door.

"There you are," Glenna said and stepped into the chamber. "We have been looking for you."

Conall walked up behind Glenna and gave Fiona a smile. "You had us all worried."

"I have been in here all day," she said.

"That's why I said to look in the castle first," Conall said. He patted Glenna's arm. "I'm off for a bath."

"Aye, you stink," Glenna called after him with a smile.

Fiona couldn't help the sinking feeling in her heart to learn that they had just realized no one knew where she was. She put aside her hurt and looked at Glenna.

"I'm sorry," Glenna said.

"You're sorry? 'Tis I who should apologize," Fiona said.

"My words were overly harsh. I don't know what has gotten into me of late."

"It doesn't matter." Glenna put a bright smile on. "Now, 'tis almost supper. Will you be joining us this evening?"

Fiona couldn't believe that Glenna was giving her a second chance after the way she had treated her. "Of course," she said and was truthfully looking forward to it.

"Good. I shall see you within the hour."

Once Glenna left, Fiona sat in front of the hearth and unbraided her hair. She ran the brush through her hair and found herself thinking about Gregor. Had he helped search for her?

Probably not, she decided.

Not that it mattered. She was supposed to have forgotten all about him by now. But that was harder to do than she realized. It could have something to do with the fact that he was still here. Or, it could be something more.

Frang's words came back to her then. Could he be right or was he just trying to scare her into accepting her mate? Either way, it was working.

The thought that she might live a happy life like Glenna's was almost enough to make her give in and accept Gregor. Almost.

But the thought of him leaving was enough to keep her resolve to stay away from him firm. Regardless of how she desired him or how he made her feel when his hands and mouth were on her. She would stay away. And that meant living a lonely life.

*I will be lonely either way once he leaves me.*

But what if he didn't?

*What if he did?*

It was the same argument she had had with herself from the first moment she realized Gregor was her mate. Nothing had changed, despite her learning to trust him a wee bit. After all, he had saved her life. That did deserve a smidgen of trust. Just a smidgen, but more than she had given another person in her life other than her foster parents.

If she wasn't careful, she would hand him her heart to do with as he pleased. The fact was he was still at MacInnes Castle and would be for some time, if Conall had his way. Which meant she would have to face Gregor again, and probably tonight.

"Might as well look my best," she said as she ventured to the chest in front of the bed.

She opened the lid and found all of her gowns freshly washed and folded. At the top was the gown that had always been Cormag's favorite. Her foster father had often said the green came close to matching her eyes. She had never thought her eyes were as remotely pretty as the green of the gown. The gown was made of a green somewhere between the color of the leaves in the spring and the hue of an emerald.

Her eyes were just a plain green. Not as mystical as the gown or as lovely as an emerald, nor as beautiful to look upon as the green of the trees. Still, the gown gave her fond memories of her foster parents. She decided to wear it to honor them.

She managed to quickly bathe. Once she was dry and dressed in the gown, she sat before the small fire in the hearth and combed her hair.

Afterward, she let the fire dry her hair as she prepared herself for the evening. Moira would most likely be there as well. Regardless of her feelings, she was going to smile and make everyone believe she was happy. She wanted to put Glenna at ease, even if that meant speaking to Moira.

That thought sent a stab of anxiety through her. Gregor had been correct. She was going to have to talk to Moira whether she wanted to or not. She just hoped she kept control of her tongue and didn't lash out as she had with Glenna and Gregor.

She left her hair hanging loose around her and smoothed her gown nervously. Her plaid she left off since she didn't feel as though she belonged to a clan anymore.

Before she changed her mind, she hurried from her chamber and down the stairs. She stopped on the last step and surveyed the great hall, as was her habit. Many people were already there and seated, but there was no sign of Moira.

Fiona looked toward the dais and saw Glenna wave to her. She smiled and walked to her sister.

"You look radiant," Glenna said as she approached.

Fiona smiled and lowered her gaze to hide her embarrassment at the unexpected compliment, a compliment that brought a rush of pleasure. Maybe she did look half as good as Glenna said.

"Glenna's right," Conall said as he stood. "The green is perfect for you. You outshine everyone here. Except my wife, of course."

Fiona watched as Conall leaned down and kissed the top of Glenna's head. A stab of jealousy so sharp and true throbbed within her. It would be so easy to have what they shared. So easy...and so difficult.

She took her seat and tried not to notice that Gregor wasn't in attendance.

"He will be here," Glenna leaned over and whispered.

"Who?" she asked in an effort to appear unaffected by his absence.

Glenna laughed and patted her arm. "You cannot fool me, dear sister. 'Tis your eyes. They give you away."

Fiona turned to Glenna, prepared to tell her that there was nothing between her and Gregor, when he walked through the door. She feasted her eyes upon him, as did every other female eye in the hall, which bothered her much more than she liked.

His hair, never free of the two small braids, was pulled away from his face. He walked like a man confident in himself and his ability, and it was that that drew women to him like flies to honey.

Fiona found she couldn't look away from him, even when Glenna spoke her name. And when he smiled at a passing woman, she was astonished to feel envy at not receiving that smile herself after everything they had shared.

Her breathing quickened when she noticed his eyes roaming the hall. She hoped he would notice her, and then prayed he wouldn't all in the same breath.

Then his eyes came to rest on her.

He halted in his tracks as he simply stared. Her breath lodged painfully in her lungs as she waited for him to say something, do something. His head swiveled around at the sound of his name. Fiona looked down to hide her disappointment.

It was silly to be jealous of a child, especially one as sweet as Ailsa. Still, when she looked up and found Gregor looking at Ailsa with adoring eyes, she couldn't help the feelings within her.

She pushed aside thoughts of Gregor and turned to Glenna. The food was delicious and so was the company. She laughed at the stories Glenna and Conall told of their first meeting and made sure she paid attention, even though her mind and gaze ventured to Gregor often.

"Where did you go today?" Conall asked.

Fiona thought back to the nemeton and the icy fingers of evil that had nearly captured her. Instead of ruining the nice evening with such horrendous talk, she said, "I went for a walk."

"What happened?" Glenna asked. "Did you run across more Druids? The woods are a wonderful place to be, very beautiful, peaceful."

"Aye. Beautiful," Fiona said and swallowed past the memory of the nemeton.

Regardless of how well she thought she hid her feelings, Conall must have seen something, for he asked, "Where exactly did you venture?"

"The nemeton."

Glenna signed. "'Tis one of my favorite places. No evil would dare to approach that place."

Fiona didn't answer. She couldn't. Lying to her sister and brother-in-law wasn't something she wanted to do, but she also didn't wish to tell them the truth and worry them.

"Something happened," Conall said.

Fiona glanced at his face and saw the determined glint of his eyes. Her gaze slid to Gregor and found him avidly listening before she looked at Glenna.

As nonchalantly as she could, Fiona reached for her goblet and said, "It seems the Evil One Aimery speaks of has returned."

"What?" Glenna asked, her voice shaky and low as if it pained her to even consider Fiona's words.

Conall scooted his chair back and crossed his arms over his chest. "I think it time you tell us the entire story."

"There really isn't much to tell," Fiona said, trying to downplay it. "I went for a walk and encountered the Evil One. Dartayous arrived and escorted me back to the stone circle where Aimery walked me back to the castle."

Glenna covered her eyes with her hand. "Oh, Fiona, you should have told me sooner."

"Why?" she asked as the table was cleared. "'Tis over and done."

"I have the feeling there is much more to the story than that," Gregor spoke for the first time. "Maybe we should have Dartayous sent for."

Fiona didn't want them to do any such thing, and Gregor knew it. "Oh, for the king's sake," she said with a loud sigh. "It was not as bad as you will make it out to be, which is why I didn't wish to tell the entire story."

"Tell us," Conall demanded.

Fiona leaned back and clasped her hands in her lap. She didn't wish to think about how close she had come to death, but it seemed she had no choice.

"I was at the nemeton studying a lovely hawthorn when I felt something...cold...evil. Before I could move,

Dartayous was there calling me to him. Once I reached him, he unsheathed his sword and told me to run for the stone circle. I was nearly there when—"

She closed her eyes at the memory of the heaviness, the darkness that had enfolded her.

"When?" Gregor prompted.

Fiona locked gazes with him, needing his strength to finish. "The Evil One caught me."

She heard Glenna gasp, but refused to look away from Gregor. "The blanket of darkness and the cold surrounded me. And then, just as soon as it had hit me, it was gone. When I opened my eyes, Aimery and Fae were standing all around me. The rest you know."

"Dear God," Conall said and ran a hand down his face.

Gregor simply stared at her.

"I know now to stay near the castle and the Druids at all times," Fiona quickly said.

Glenna wasn't soothed. "But what if something had happened?"

"It didn't," Conall appeased Glenna. "Fiona is smart. She will heed things now."

The somber mood that had taken over was dispelled by the shout for music. To Fiona's delight, the bagpipes were brought out, as well as a fiddle and a lyre.

Tables and benches were moved to make room for the dancing, and soon the entire hall was filled with music and laughter. At first, Fiona sat and watched the dancers. Glenna and Conall were one of the first to begin once the music started.

Fiona's eyes found Gregor standing against the wall talking to a pretty blonde. She wasn't given long to be jealous, though. Conall pulled her from her seat and danced her around the room to a fast jig. She was breathless and laughing so hard she could barely stand, but she was having the time of her life.

And when she didn't think she could dance another step, the music ended. There was an odd light in Conall's eyes as he continued to dance her back toward her seat. Except he didn't bring her to her chair.

Instead, he swung her away from them. Fiona didn't know where she was headed until she collided with a chest of solid muscle and felt strong arms lock around her. Gregor.

She raised her head and looked into his black eyes. There was no emotion evident on his face, and her smile quickly faded. Before she could utter a word, he whirled her around so that his back was to the crowded hall while hers was against the wall. This left her hidden to everyone except him.

He reached up and touched a strand of her hair that had fallen over her shoulder. As he twirled the strand around his finger he closed his eyes and sighed.

Did he even know what his actions did to her? The hall and all the people ceased to exist in the tiny world Gregor had placed them in. When he opened his eyes and brought his hand to her face she didn't stop him. She kept her gaze on him, fascinated by the sudden show of emotion.

His thumb traced her bottom lip while in his dark depths the pain and loneliness surfaced to be seen by one person. Fiona.

"Your smile makes my heart sing," he said, the baritone of his voice low and husky. "But when I see a frown I would gladly crawl on my belly through the fires of Hell to see that smile once again grace your beautiful face."

No one had ever spoken such words to her, and they brought tears to her eyes. His words were from the heart, something he kept hidden from the world.

A tear escaped and rolled down her cheek before she could stop it, but she didn't care. She wanted him to know his words had affected her.

Gregor wanted to taste Fiona's sweet lips. All he had to do was lean down. He began to do just that when something splashed onto his hand. He blinked, unsure what it was. Then he raised his gaze to Fiona's face.

Her green eyes glistened with unshed tears. But why? Then he recalled his words, words that had only been spoken in his head, but now had somehow made their way past his lips.

He took a step back. "Leave. Leave now before I do something you will regret."

She shook her head and stayed where she was.

Didn't the wench know how close he was to losing control over himself? He wanted her like he had never wanted a woman before. She was near, yet out of his reach. He could never have her again. She had made that painfully clear.

To have her looking at him as though she wanted him to kiss her was too much. He was only a man after all. There was only so much torture he could take.

He quickly walked away from her before he threw her over his shoulder and made his way to his chamber. Just thinking about it made him sweat with a need that had become unbearable of late.

Some air would be just the thing, he decided as he made his way up to the battlements. It was then he spotted Moira hiding as she looked down from the stairs at the hall below.

* * *

Fiona licked her lips and almost called Gregor back. Maybe it was for the best that he left. Yet, she couldn't help but wonder why he had said those beautiful, wonderful words to her.

It wasn't a trick. That wasn't something Gregor would do. Those words had indeed come from his heart, and if his startled expression told her anything it was that he was surprised he had said the words.

She looked around the hall. The dancing and merriment continued. Her eyes caught the sight of Glenna and Conall as they smiled up at each other, the love shining in their eyes for all the world to see.

Fiona closed her eyes. She could still feel the strength of Gregor's arms around her, the safety his body brought her.

Maybe it was time to give in. Maybe Gregor could help dispel the melancholy that surrounded her.

* * *

Gregor stepped onto the battlements and spotted Moira. She looked up at the moon, her hands holding onto the stone as if to anchor her.

He looked around for Dartayous but didn't see him anywhere. "Am I disturbing you?'

"Not at all," she said without looking at him.

He stood beside her and looked out of the calm waters of the loch. "Why didn't you join us for the meal?"

"It had been my intention until I saw how at ease Fiona was. I didn't wish to disturb that."

He nodded. "Where is Dartayous? He is always near."

She snorted and turned to face him. "He is here. I can feel him. He just doesn't wish to be seen at the present."

"Ah," Gregor said.

"I wish she would talk to me."

Gregor saw her pain and knew she had been hiding it from everyone. They had much in common. "She will. Give her time."

"We don't have much time."

"As a Druid, you should know there is much within Fiona that is in turmoil."

She wiped at her face and he was surprised to see tears. "Moira?"

"I'm fine," she said as the tears poured down her face.

Without thinking he drew her into his arms to offer what comfort he could. "All will be well."

She looked up at him and placed her hand on her cheek. "You are a good man, Gregor."

Fiona ran up the steps, excitement coursing through her. It felt right to be giving in to her desire for Gregor. She rounded a corner to find Dartayous blocking her way.

"Don't go up there," he told her.

"'Tis only Gregor. I have a need to speak to him."

He refused to move. "Let it wait until morning."

"What is wrong with you? Most everyone here has been urging me to talk to Gregor. That is all I wish to do. Now, please move."

For a moment, she thought he might argue with her, then he slowly stepped aside. When she went to walk past him, he put a hand on her arm. "I will ask you once more. Let it wait until morning."

Why did he want her to wait? Something wasn't right. Then it dawned on her. Someone was with Gregor.

She jerked her arm out of his grasp and ran up the last remaining stairs. As she stepped out onto the battlements, she wished she had listened to Dartayous, for standing in each other's arms was none other than Gregor and Moira.

Anger and resentment pooled in her stomach. Gregor dropped his arms from around Moira as Moira stepped away from him. How dare Moira seduce Gregor! Fiona took a step toward them to tell Moira exactly what was on her mind. Then, she remembered how she had pushed Gregor away.

Mate or not, she hadn't claimed Gregor as hers, and, therefore, he was available.

Even to Moira.

Tears quickly gathered in her eyes. She turned away before they spotted them.

\* \* \*

Gregor stood dumbfounded at the sight of distress on Fiona's face. The fact she was upset at him comforting her sister didn't make sense to him. He started after her only to have Dartayous step in front of him. "Get out of my way," he told the warrior.

"You have done enough damage this night," Dartayous said as he looked from him to Moira. "Leave Fiona be."

Gregor opened his mouth to argue only to find that Dartayous was gone. He looked over the stone wall at the bailey below and saw Fiona running toward the caves. It wasn't long before Dartayous followed her.

"I'll be damned if he's going to comfort her," he mumbled and charged after them.

"Don't," Moira said as she stepped in front of him. "She won't believe you now."

Gregor clenched his hands as his eyes followed Fiona into the caves.

\* \* \*

Fiona ran into the darkness of the cave, but she welcomed the shadows. They hid her pain and tears. She walked through the darkness, unmindful of where she was going. She just wanted some time alone.

She turned a corner and found a long stretch of cave with six torches lighting the way. Her mind refused to worry about finding her way back. She would think about that when the time came. As she walked through the cave, a sudden chill overtook her.

There was no mistaking the coldness that enveloped her. The Evil One had returned. She slowed her steps and concentrated on using her ears to hear anything unnatural. Her eyes scanned the cave walls, searching for him. Then, the torches blinked out.

Not only was she on her own and didn't have a weapon, she didn't know her way around the caves. And what had Dartayous told her? Never to be alone. Yet, that's exactly what she had done.

"We meet again."

The voice as frigid as the dark of winter surrounded her. She wrapped her arms around herself for warmth.

"Did you actually think you could escape me for long? There isn't anyone here to save you now."

The voice was all around her, keeping her off balanced and confused. "I don't need to be saved."

"Really?" The voice laughed eerily.

Her instinct told her that he was near, very near. "I am a powerful Druid."

"Ah, yes. But you are lacking one thing. The water in which to use your power."

Fiona tamped down the growing dread and straightened her spine. If she were to die, she wouldn't do it cowering in front of a man who refused to show himself.

His laughter rang through the tunnel. "Cowering or not, you *will* die."

The tunnel burst with light as the torch nearest her blazed to life. Her gaze found the man. He stood, turned at an angle in front of her. The cloak still concealed his head, but she might be able to get a brief look at him. If she was lucky.

Slowly, his arm lifted to show he wielded a sword. And it was pointed at her heart. "'Tis time to die."

The scream lodged in her throat as he made his attack. She fell to her knees and rolled away from him. Her legs got tangled in her skirts and she couldn't get to her feet in time.

She struggled to free her legs so she could kick at him, but she knew she had failed when she heard his laughter. How could she die this easily? The Fae had blessed her with special powers. But how did one defeat something as evil as the thing standing above her?

"Nice try. I had really hoped you would give me more of a fight," he said and raised his sword over her heart.

## 27

Fiona's only thought as the sword plunged toward her was of Gregor. If she were to die, it would be with the memory of Gregor. She closed her eyes and recalled the feel of his lips on hers.

But there was no pain, only the sound of a roar of rage that filled that cave to a deafening pitch. The howl bounced off the stone walls until she had to cover her ears or chance going deaf.

After a moment she lifted a hand from her ear and heard only silence. She opened her eyes to find Dartayous standing over her. His sword was outstretched, preventing the Evil One from killing her.

"Don't you have anything better to do?" he hissed at Dartayous.

"I cannot stand your stench."

While they battled wits, she crawled backward until Dartayous no longer stood over her. When she hit the cave wall she climbed to her feet, never taking her eyes off the two men.

"You cannot stop me. Nothing will stop me from gaining all the power," the Evil One stated.

"There is a way to stop you."

"But you don't know what it is," he taunted.

"Maybe not, but I think I could find out."

The torches once again extinguished and the coldness began to ebb.

"Fiona?"

She stretched out her hand. "I'm here, Dartayous."

Something bumped into her hand, and she touched the fabric of his vest. Then, she knew it was Dartayous.

Before they took two steps, the torches once again lit themselves. "That's really beginning to unsettle me," she said.

She didn't know what surprised her more, his chuckle or seeing Glenna, Conall, and Gregor running toward them.

"Are you all right?" Glenna asked when she reached them.

Fiona glanced at Dartayous. "I am now."

"It seems you have been in the right place at the right time lately," Conall said.

"It seems you have been doing a lot of that lately," Gregor said as his voice dripped with sarcasm. "I thought it was your duty to guard Moira?"

"I'm a Druid Warrior. I aid any Druid that needs it."

"Fiona, what made you run in here?" Conall asked.

She didn't look at Gregor. "I encountered Moira."

"I see," Glenna said.

Fiona knew Dartayous wanted to leave. "Thank you. I'll be fine now."

"Will you truly?" Dartayous asked, his eyes boring into hers.

His blue eyes held hers for a long moment. He had seen what had happened on the battlements, but wasn't going to share it with Glenna and Conall. She nodded and watched him walk into the darkness of the cave.

Conall's brow was raised when she turned back to them. "What did he mean?"

"Nothing," she lied. "Would you be offended if I said I wanted to stay with the Druids tonight?"

Glenna stepped toward her. "Something happened. Won't you tell me?"

The kindness in her sister's brown depths nearly undid her. She swallowed and tried to smile. She failed miserably. "I just need some peace."

"You will find it within the circle." Conall's face was lined with worry, and she found herself growing to love her new brother-in-law.

Glenna nodded and stepped into Conall's arms. "Maybe 'tis best. Especially, after the attempt on your life this afternoon."

She didn't bother to tell Glenna of the recent attack. There was no need to worry her sister. There was no more talk as Fiona followed them to the stone circle through the caves. She really needed to remember this route for future use, she told herself.

When they arrived, Frang waited for her. "Dartayous has already informed me of what transpired."

She paused as she walked past Glenna. "'Tis just for a wee bit," she told her only to have Glenna's arms wrap around her.

"Stay safe, sister," Glenna whispered in her ear.

Fiona looked back to find that Gregor was no longer with them. Her heart ached terribly, but she would push it aside for now. Frang wrapped an arm around her as they entered the circle. The peace she sought eluded her still, but maybe she hadn't given it enough time.

"Do you wish to talk about anything?" Frang asked her.

She shook her head. "I just wish to be alone."

"Then, I shall make sure of it." He led her to a room hollowed out by one of the giant boulders that were everywhere.

She walked inside to find it roomier than she had imagined it would be. The welcoming glow of a fire lit the room. A bed had been carved out of the stone and many blankets were piled on it.

"I hope you find everything suitable."

She smiled at the Druid priest. "I thank you for making me welcome here, and this will do nicely."

"Before I go, I think you ought to know a little more about what will happen if you refuse your mate. You might be able to live your life with what I described, but for your mate, it will be ten times as worse. Both of you will wander each of your lives alone and bitter, never knowing what love is." He stared at her a moment. "Good night to you."

After Frang departed, she sighed and sat on the bed. Surprisingly it was comfortable, yet she couldn't think about a stone bed being comfortable after Frang's words. Now she knew she wouldn't sleep this night.

\* \* \*

Fiona came awake with a start. Her breathing was labored even to her own ears. She looked around and saw only the dying embers of the previous night's fire.

But the dream stayed with her. She sat up and wrapped her arms around her legs. There was no denying that her dream had been the future. And what a bleak future it was.

She was cruel and said harsh things to anyone who came around her. Nothing brought her pleasure. Not the sunsets, flowers, or the sound of children's laughter. She was alone. Forever.

Because she had turned away her mate.

The desolation of the dream still claimed her. She had thought the stone circle and the Druids would bring her peace, but there was no peace to be had.

*There is one way to have peace.*

It was too high of a price for her to pay, though. She climbed out of the bed and readied herself for the day. When she walked from her little chamber the sun already shone brightly.

No one bothered her, just as Frang had promised, as she walked among the Druids. Her feet took her toward the forest. Out of the corner of her eye, she spotted Dartayous.

She turned her head and gave him a smile. He nodded briefly, but she didn't dare stop. Wherever he was, Moira was close by. So far, she had been lucky in staying away from Moira and not having to talk with her.

With her mind occupied by her dream, she didn't pay attention to where she went, but she did know she was being followed. She looked over her shoulder and spotted Dartayous.

"Shouldn't you be guarding Moira?" she asked him.

"She is being kept inside the circle. You have yet to find your way."

She shrugged and looked out over the cliff. "What a beautiful spot. You can see everything."

Silence. She breathed in the clean air and tried to regain some of the calm she had possessed while at the MacDougal's.

When she opened her eyes she had regained some of the serenity. She looked down at the bailey of MacInnes Castle and wondered where her home would be. It couldn't be with Glenna as long as Gregor resided there, yet it couldn't be with the Druids because of Moira. She couldn't even stay alone because of the Evil One that roamed the hills.

She would do better at the castle. At least there she could ignore Gregor. Moira wasn't so easy to ignore. With her mind decided, she turned and began the descent to the castle only to be stopped by a voice in her head.

*"I will make your decision very easy."*

She gasped and took a step back. Instantly, Dartayous was at her side.

"What is it?" he asked, concern lacing his voice.

*"Since you won't claim your mate, I think 'tis time he died."*

"Nay," she screamed and ran toward the castle, knowing in her gut that Gregor was indeed about to die.

Dartayous stayed by her side as she ran into the bailey. She stopped and searched for Gregor, but couldn't find him.

"Who are you looking for?" Dartayous asked.

"Gregor."

"He is building the new barn."

She raced toward the back of the bailey only to find it blocked with people. There wasn't time to spare, so she took the stairs to the battlements. Her eyes searched the men until she found him on the roof. She sighed her relief to see him safe and sound.

"What happened?"

She turned to Dartayous. "Nothing." Her gaze found Gregor again.

His muscles glistened in the morning sun as he brought the hammer down to nail a board. She licked her lips when she saw the muscles in his back and shoulders flex as he lifted a large board to another man.

"Nothing," she said again as Gregor went back to hammering. She was about to turn away when a loud crash stopped her.

She screamed Gregor's name when she saw the barn begin to collapse. There wasn't time for him to jump off the top of the barn by the time the frame cracked around him. To her dismay, the frame splintered and sent Gregor plunging to the ground. She pushed past people and ran toward the barn. She needed to be with him.

With the help of Dartayous, she made it through the throng of people milling around the barn. Wounded men littered the bailey, but it was Gregor she was concerned with. And when she saw Conall lifting boards away from something, she knew it was Gregor.

Her heart beat painfully in her chest as she watched Conall and Dartayous try to reach Gregor. Tears blinded her vision as the wails of women nearly deafened her. She fell to her knees beside Gregor when Dartayous and Conall cleared the debris around him. With a shaky hand, she reached toward his chest to see if he still lived.

Conall placed a finger beneath Gregor's nose. "His breathing is shallow. We must tend to him immediately."

"We'll never get him into the castle. 'Tis too far," Dartayous said.

She lifted her gaze to Conall who stared solemnly at Gregor. "There is a cottage just past the blacksmith's," he said softly.

"We don't have time to waste," she urged.

Conall's eyes jerked to hers. "Right."

Thanks to Dartayous and Conall, they managed to carry Gregor into the empty cottage. "A widow lives here. Right now, she is in the castle helping Glenna. I will have her stay there until..."

"He will be fine," she stated while praying her words were true.

"I need to see about my other men. All you need should be inside. I will return later." With that Conall walked away.

Dartayous touched her arm. "Do you need anything?"

"A miracle," she told him.

"If you need me, just say my name. I will hear you."

"Thank you," she said and turned to enter the hut.

Once inside, she noticed Dartayous had started a fire and had begun to heat water. She couldn't stop her hands from trembling as she reached out to touch Gregor.

His face, arms, and chest were crusted in blood. With a bowl of water and a cloth she cleaned off the blood and hastily stopped any cuts that continued to bleed freely.

When she came to his face she realized one of the cuts

that ran from his right temple down to his ear would have to be stitched. As gently as she could, she washed the area and prepared a needle and thread. She prayed he stayed unconscious as she stitched him. With every prick of the needle, she expected him to jerk awake, yet amazingly, he stayed asleep.

By the time she was finished, her gown clung to her skin, and she had to wipe the sweat off her face. She had just finished removing his boots when the door to the cottage opened.

"Conall just told me," Glenna said as she hurried inside. "How is he?"

"I don't know."

"Moira really needs to be here. I don't know enough to help you." She inspected Gregor's head wound. "Good stitching."

"Thank you," Fiona said.

At this point, Fiona would have welcomed Moira with open arms if she could help Gregor.

"I don't know when Moira could get down here since she is helping the other wounded men," Glenna said as she continued to look over Gregor.

"I will see to him." Fiona turned to stroke the fire, and tried to recall every bit of wisdom Helen had imparted on her regarding healing.

"I think his ribs are broken."

Fiona swallowed. "I know. I will see to it."

Glenna touched her arm. "Let me help you while I'm here. It will take forever for you to do it by yourself."

She nodded, thankful for the extra hands and Glenna's calm demeanor. "Thank you."

They both turned back to the bed. Gregor lay motionless with only his trews and boots on.

"We really need to remove his trews."

Fiona bit her lip. She didn't mind removing them, but she didn't want Glenna to see him.

"I won't look. I swear."

She turned to her sister and smiled. "I know."

Together they managed to get his boots and trews off without moving him too much. Fiona covered him as soon as the trews began to come off and ignored Glenna's small chuckle.

While Glenna went in search of bandages for his ribs, Fiona wiped down his chest again with the heated water. He hadn't moved or made a sound and it frightened her. What if he never woke? It had happened before while she was with the MacDougal's.

"I want to get him bandaged before he wakes," Glenna said as he walked up with an armload of bandages.

Fiona looked down at Gregor's still form. "What if he doesn't?"

"Don't give up hope."

She looked at Glenna and smiled through her tears. "I have been such a fool."

"Then you can tell him when he wakes. Now, let us hurry."

While Glenna wrapped him in the bandages, Fiona rolled him from side-to-side to help her. With every moment that passed without him waking, her worry multiplied.

She was beside herself with unease by the time they were finished, but she refused to let Glenna know.

"I will have someone check on you in a bit. If you need anything let me know."

"I will," Fiona promised as her gaze was drawn to Gregor.

"Everything will be fine."

Fiona nodded and turned to her sister. "Will it? What if I told you the Evil One did this?"

Glenna's mouth dropped open. "What?"

"I heard his voice in my head telling me what he was going to do."

"Frang needs to know this."

"Aye," Fiona agreed. "But right now, I need to concentrate on Gregor."

Glenna stared at her a long moment. "All right. I will be back as soon as I can."

Fiona twisted her hands and looked down at Gregor. She didn't like being alone and not knowing what to do.

"Food," she suddenly said. "When he wakes he is going to be hungry."

She immediately set about rummaging in the tiny cottage and found the ingredients for a simple soup. Between cutting up the vegetables and checking on Gregor, the morning flew by with the speed of a falcon.

With the soup done and waiting for Gregor to wake, Fiona took her seat by the bed. She couldn't stand to sit and watch him, she needed to touch him.

She filled another bowl with warm water and pulled the blanket down to his waist. The bandages went from his waist to just under his shoulders. He would be in much pain when he woke, she thought.

After she wrung the cloth, Fiona wiped it across his

wide shoulders and down his neck. Even lying motionless, his power was evident. That power stunned her, especially because he had been so incredibly gentle with her.

She wiped his arms, careful around the cuts and scrapes he received during the fall. Too bad she didn't have anything to put on the cuts. Then her eyes fell on the bowl of water. She did have something to help him.

With her eyes tightly closed she tried to remember the words Helen had taught her and she circled her hands over the bowl. She opened her eyes to see the water swirling on its own and nearly shouted with joy that she had remembered the correct words. With a fresh cloth, she dipped it into the water and ran it over the cuts.

The water hissed as it made contact with the wounds, but before her eyes she saw them begin to heal. When that task was done, she sat back and folded her hands in her lap. There was nothing for her to do but wait. Wait and pray that he survived.

The day dragged on incredibly slow. She didn't expect to see Glenna or Conall until the next day. They had wounded of their own to tend to, but it would have been nice to have the company.

She had snacked on the bread she had found on the table and had tried the soup. It was awful. Even fouler than when she had attempted it at the MacDougal's. She had almost thrown it out, but figured she would eat it later. Besides, she didn't wish to waste anything. Maybe Glenna would bring some food from the castle for Gregor to eat when he woke.

*If he wakes.*

She pushed aside that negative thought.

*He will wake. He has to.*

When the chair became too uncomfortable to stay in a moment longer, she rose and walked the cottage. It was a nice cottage, rather small, but clean. She imagined there had been children here once, their laughter filling the house with love.

She would gladly take this tiny cottage and have someone who would forever stay with her than a castle and all the riches in Scotland. She would even give up her powers as a Druid if the doubt in her heart would go away.

But it was a dream. She was who she was. Nothing would change that.

Her walking took her to the window. As she looked out, she watched the setting sun over the loch. It was a beautiful sight, almost as glorious as the ones she and Gregor had watched together.

If only she could go back to those days when they were alone. She might do things differently, if given the chance.

"Wishful thinking. You must stop that," she told herself.

She needed to concentrate on Gregor, and then once he was well she could continue her thinking about what she should have done. Until then, it was a waste of her time. After the sun had set and the darkness began to close in, she shut the window and went to stir the soup. She wished she had her materials to make a tapestry. It would occupy her thoughts. If only for a little while.

It was sometime around midnight that something woke her. She sat up in the chair and looked around the cottage. It must have been her imagination, she decided, and turned to check on Gregor. That's when she noticed his ragged breathing.

"Nay," she cried and leaned over him. "Gregor, don't leave me. Not like this," she said as panic set in.

She wiped him down again, but nothing helped his breathing. She checked his cuts to see if any were infected, but there was nothing. Helplessness set in like an unwanted sickness. She had never dealt with anything like this before and didn't know what to do. There wasn't time to get Glenna, nor would she leave Gregor.

But she refused to sit and watch him slowly die before her eyes. There must be something she could do. Then she recalled something Helen had taught her.

"'Tis worth a try," she said.

She knelt by the bed and held her hands palm down above Gregor's chest. She breathed in deeply and began to concentrate on Gregor's breathing.

"Give him my strength," she whispered.

Her hands began to shake as the force of her powers took hold. "Give him my strength," she yelled.

Her eyes flew open as her breath left her. "Dartayous," she whispered before she fell to the floor.

## 28

D artayous jerked as if an arrow had imbedded in his chest. Fiona had called to him. "We must go," he said as he took hold of Moira's arm.

"I have work to do," she replied without looking at him.

He turned her around to face him. "Fiona needs you."

Moira searched his face before she nodded and followed him from the castle. Dartayous was to the point that he had been about to carry Moira out of the castle if she hadn't agreed.

Something dreadful must have happened to have Fiona call him. His stride was long and Moira nearly had to run to keep up with him, but his instincts told him not to tarry.

"What's happened?" Glenna asked as she and Conall caught up with them.

"'Tis Fiona."

"Where is she?" Glenna asked as she looked around.

Dartayous didn't really have time to explain, but he knew he had to. "She called to me. She's in some kind of danger."

No more words were spoken as they hurried to the cottage. He burst through the door first and found Fiona lying on the floor beside the bed.

Moira pushed past him and ran to Fiona. She touched her and sighed. "Get her on the bed," she told Dartayous.

"What happened?" Glenna asked.

Moira checked Gregor as Dartayous laid Fiona beside him. "She gave him her strength. He was dying."

"Was?" Conall asked.

"She saved him."

Conall leaned over Fiona and peered closely at her. "But will she be all right?"

"Aye. She just needs to rest," Moira answered. She held her hand over Gregor and closed her eyes. "His ribs are broken."

Dartayous watched as she ran her hands over Gregor's chest and whispered words. She had used most of her strength this day to heal the many wounded and he knew she wouldn't last much longer. He hurried to her side and caught her as she began to fall.

"I healed them, but there will still be some soreness," she told Conall and Glenna. She stood out of Dartayous' arms and walked to the other side of the bed to Fiona.

She placed her hand on Fiona's head and leaned down to whisper in her ear. Dartayous was ever amazed with Moira and her healing ability. Some might say the greatest gift the Fae had given her was the power over wind. He would say it was her healing.

He noticed the shallow parlor of her skin and knew she needed rest. Immediately. "Are you finished?"

She nodded. "They will be fine after some rest."

Glenna hugged her. "Thank you, again. You have done much for my people this day."

"We will never be able to repay you," Conall said.

"Just give me many nieces and nephews," Moira told them. "That's payment enough."

Dartayous placed his hand on Moira's back to guide her out the door. He needed to get her to the stone circle where she could recover her strength.

"I'll have Aimery send some guards," he told Conall.

"Good," Conall said. "I was just about to suggest that."

Fiona sighed and stretched her arms above her head. Her eyes slowly opened. She was rested and her back didn't ache from sitting in the chair, which was odd. It wasn't until her hand touched the blanket that she realized she was on the bed.

She slowly sat up and looked at Gregor. His breathing was normal and his cuts looked like they were almost healed. How was this possible? She wasn't fool enough to believe she had done it. Which left only one possibility. Moira.

Dartayous must have brought Moira, she deduced, and slowly inched off the bed. She hated to say it, but she owed Moira a huge debt of thanks. Once she had washed her face, she took her seat beside the bed. She found it impossible to keep her eyes open, and it wasn't long until she began to doze.

\* \* \*

"I'm tired of waiting," MacNeil said as he paced. He was the Butcher of the Highlands, yet The Shadow would have him hide in the woods like a coward. No more. The prophecy was soon to commence, and he wanted one of those wenches taken care of now. He drew his sword and walked toward his men, but he didn't get far.

"Halt, MacNeil."

He jerked at hearing that voice. For days he had waited for The Shadow to come. Now he came just when he was about to rally his men.

"I'm through with you," MacNeil told him, refusing to turn and look at him.

"I don't believe so. You need me, and you know it."

MacNeil whirled around to face him. "Do you think I haven't heard how you tried to kill Gregor? Yet you didn't succeed."

The Shadow lifted his shoulders in a shrug. "Maybe. Maybe not. I'm close. So very close. Are you willing to risk your life on a few days?"

MacNeil mulled over his words. "I give you three more days. After that, me and my army will take care of this ourselves."

\* \* \*

Fiona jerked awake just before she hit the floor. She wiped the hair out of her face and arched her back to stretch out the kinks. When she lowered her arms, she noticed Gregor's eyes were open.

"By the saints. You are awake," she said and touched his arm.

"I would have tried to catch you, but I don't think I would have made it in time." He graced her with a hesitant smile that made her heart soar.

"How can you jest when you are injured?"

"'Tis my wonderful charm."

She laughed and smoothed the hair from his forehead. "I'm just glad you are awake."

"How long since the accident?"

"A day, but it seems like an eternity."

He smiled again and covered her hand with his. "You took care of me?"

"Aye. Glenna and Conall had their hands full with the other wounded. You were brought here."

She became uncomfortable under his gaze. He tried to look inside her, and she couldn't blame him. After keeping him at a safe distance, she suddenly cared for him while he was injured. She would be wary, too.

"Hungry?" she asked. Anything to break the eye contact.

"As a matter of fact, aye."

She jumped up, glad for something to do. Until she noticed that all the bread was gone and the only thing left was the soup.

"I must go to the castle for food," she told him and headed to the door.

"Is that not soup I smell?" he asked, stopping her in her tracks.

*Saint Francis' knobby knees.*

She didn't have much of a choice now. She turned and headed to the hearth. Her gaze didn't meet his as she spooned the soup into a bowl and handed it to him.

"Is something wrong?" he asked.

She shook her head.

"Then look at me."

With a sigh she raised her gaze as he spooned the first bite into his mouth. She tried not to wince when he swallowed as she waited for him to say how awful it was. It wouldn't have hurt her feelings, because she knew she lacked cooking skills. It was just something she had never caught on to.

"'Tis good," he said and took another bite.

She blinked back the tears because she knew he lied, but the fact that he had cared enough to tell her he liked it meant so much to her. "You don't have to lie," she told him.

He laughed and sat the spoon down. "Why would you think I lied, lass?"

"Because I know how awful it is."

"I admit it isn't the best, but I have eaten worse."

She met his gaze and soon they were both laughing. How was it that he always had a way of making her feel good?

"You'll need more than that," she said still laughing. "I need to go to the castle for some real food."

"I would rather you didn't leave."

The laughter died on her lips as he once again stunned her with his words. She knew he wasn't afraid, so could it be that he wanted her company? "All right."

* * *

"Something is troubling you?" Frang asked Aimery.

"If the Evil One is attacking others beside Moira, Fiona

and Glenna, then I must report to my king and queen. Things have gone astray."

"How astray?"

"I haven't heard from the king and queen. That in itself it extremely odd."

Frang rubbed his beard. "The rogue Druid is causing more damage than you expected."

"He's more than a Druid," Aimery admitted and looked over the Druids within the circle.

"What are you saying?"

"Nothing yet. I will keep some Fae around to keep watch over the lasses. I must get to the king and queen."

"Are you sure 'tis safe?"

"The Land of the Fae is the safest place to be."

"Is it, I wonder? This rogue Druid is using Fae magic. I think I would be worried about him visiting your land."

Aimery's brow furrowed. "He wouldn't dare."

Frang tried to question Aimery more, but the Faerie quickly disappeared. Something strange was happening, and it didn't take a Druid to foretell that.

\* \* \*

Gregor couldn't take his eyes off Fiona. Her caring for him had a strange effect on him. Every time her hands touched him, his heart pounded loudly.

He had been tempted to pull her down on him, but the fact he could barely take a deep breath stopped him. Soon, though, he would give in to his desires and suffer through the pain, if he was able, to hold her in his arms.

"I need to check your stitches."

He jerked at the sound of her voice so near him, then sucked in a breath at the pain.

She reached out and touched his arm. "I'm sorry. I didn't mean to startle you."

"You didn't," he said through clenched teeth. "I will be fine."

Her raised brow said she questioned his words.

He didn't bother to say more as her soft hands gently touched the side of his face. He wasn't worried about a scar, but he was worried about how she would look at him now. Would she recoil in distaste?

"Is something wrong?" she asked.

He waited until she finished her inspection before he said, "Nay."

"The stitches should come out soon. 'Tis healing nicely."

"Thanks to you," he said and reached for her hand. "Thank you for tending to me."

She ducked her head and he could have sworn that she blushed. "It wasn't all me. Moira helped heal you with her powers."

"But it is you that is here now."

Her eyes jerked to his face. When her lips parted he stifled a groan. She had no idea the carnage she left in her wake. "May I ask you something?"

He waited, afraid of what she would ask, but knowing that he would answer it. No matter what it was. "Aye."

"Tell me what happened to your sister."

He sighed and looked away. Maybe it was time to tell her. Then she would leave and let him forget about dreams he couldn't hold onto.

"Did I tell you Anne was very beautiful?" he asked and patted the bed for Fiona to sit.

She shook her head and laced her fingers through his after she sat beside him.

"She was. Even at her young age, the lads chased after her. But she wanted no part of them." He laughed, recalling old memories. "She would ask me what I thought of some of them. If I didn't like them, she wouldn't give them a second thought."

"She adored you."

He nodded. "That day she had asked me to take her on the boat. I hadn't wanted to, but she had begged, and I could never say nay to her."

He stopped, unsure if he could continue. Then, Fiona gave him a smile.

"I put her in the boat, but then a young lass that had caught my eye walked up. Anne said she would stay in the boat while I talked with the lass for a moment. I never thought Anne would actually try and row the boat herself."

"There was nothing you could have done to stop her," Fiona said.

"I shouldn't have talked with the lass," he roared. He closed his eyes and shook his head from the pain in his ribs and his stupidity at not staying with Anne. "I looked up when I heard the lass gasp. Anne had rowed out and had lost one of the oars. She couldn't get back."

He took a deep breath and struggled to breathe as his memories crashed in on him of that day.

"She stood up and began yelling for me. I ran into the water telling her to sit down or she would overturn the boat. She couldn't hear me, and before I knew it, she was in the water."

"Didn't she know how to swim?"

"Aye. I taught her myself, so at first I wasn't worried. I knew I could get to her in time. Until she didn't surface. Then I remembered the currents that run through our loch. Many of my clansmen had died from those currents. It was why Anne wasn't allowed to venture out too far."

"What happened?" Fiona asked softly.

"I dove under the water. The current hadn't taken her far, but it had tangled her in the kelp. She couldn't get loose, and no matter how hard I tried to get her out she wouldn't come loose."

"Didn't anyone come for help?"

"The lass must have called for help, but by that time it was too late. Anne died in my arms, and I was also caught."

"Everything happens for a reason, Gregor. You must know that. 'Twas, as your father said, an accident."

He looked into her beautiful green eyes. "I killed her. Why should I be alive and not Anne?"

"First of all, you didn't kill her. You tried to save her, and nearly died yourself. Isn't that enough punishment?"

He didn't answer her. His punishment was living while Anne was in the earth. She had been so full of life and beautiful. She should have lived to get married and have children, not die in her brother's arms.

"Look at me," Fiona demanded.

He raised his eyes to her.

"I wouldn't be here without you. Glenna wouldn't be with Conall without you, and Ailsa wouldn't be here without you. Did you stop to think about any of that?"

"The pain won't ever go away. I can't let it."

"Why? Because you think you'll forget Anne if you do?"

*How had she managed to figure that out?*

She rose from the bed and put her hands on her hips. "I expected better of you. You, of all people, should know that you can mourn the loss of someone without punishing yourself for it."

He watched as she began to tap her toe in annoyance. If it wasn't such a serious situation he would be laughing.

"I don't think Anne would have wanted you to live like this. I think she would have wanted you to be happy."

"You think so?"

She looked around the room and licked her lips. "Aye."

"Do you want to make me happy?"

He knew the question startled her, and by her furrowed brow she was contemplating how to answer him. He didn't expect her to answer really, but he liked to see her squirm.

"How?"

The fact that she answered at all scared the hell out of him.

"How, Gregor?" she asked and moved closer to the bed. "What is it that could make you happy? Have you ever been happy since Anne's death?"

His throat refused to work and he tried to swallow. Fiona had sat on the bed and began running her finger down his chest. "Aye, I have been happy."

"When?"

He decided if there was a chance, even a remote one, that he could have Fiona in his life, he'd take it now. "When you are in my arms."

Her green eyes jerked to his face. She looked deep into his eyes and leaned forward. Her lips parted as her breasts pressed against his chest. It was the purest form of torture. He gripped the blanket to stop himself from grabbing a hold of her. At least, that was his intention until her lips touched his, then he forgot about everything except her.

## 29

Fiona gave up trying to resist Gregor. There was no point in it. When he said he was happy when she was in his arms it had broken a piece of her defense. Now, as she tasted his lips and had his arms around her, she had to wonder why she ever tried to avoid him. He touched her deepest places, as only a mate could.

She moaned as his hand found her breast. "You are injured."

"I'll survive. I have got to be inside you," he whispered against her neck. "I feel as though I'm dying without you."

She let him roll her over until he was on top. He gazed down at her, and she couldn't deny the feelings that showed brightly in his eyes. It would be so easy to tell him that she cared for him.

*Cared? You do a lot more than care.*

That was true, but she wasn't ready to admit how she really felt. Not even to herself.

"Do you wish to stop?" he asked.

She shook her head and wrapped her arms around his neck. "I'm through running from you."

"Damn good thing, woman, because I couldn't stand much more of it."

She laughed, but it was quickly cut off as his mouth covered hers. It was a kiss meant to claim her, to remind her that she belonged to one man. Gregor. They shoved the blanket from him and off the bed. She couldn't get enough of him. Her hands roamed over his back and shoulders as he kissed her until she was breathless.

She pulled back and placed a finger over his mouth when he started to talk. After she scooted out from beneath him, she rose from the bed and began to undress. The look on his face as she removed her gown fueled her own passion. When she stood naked in front of him, he held out his hand.

"I couldn't resist you the first time I saw you like this. I knew then I would never be able to refuse you."

His words brought a goofy smile to her lips. She was sure she was acting like a young lass with her first love, but she didn't care. Her heart felt lighter and freer than it had in months.

She gently pushed him back on the bed and climbed on top of him. "With your injuries I don't want you to overexert yourself."

"We wouldn't want that," he said as his hands cupped her breasts. "God, woman, you have no idea what you do to me."

Her heart fluttered at his words. She lowered her head and placed kisses on every one of his cuts he had received in the accident.

"I need you, Fiona," he groaned.

She understood his desire, and she was just as ready. She rose up and positioned him. Then, she slid down until all of him was inside of her. A sigh escaped her. Having him deep inside made her feel as though she was no longer alone. Almost as if she were a half of something that was finally made whole.

She began to move her hips back and forth. He groaned and grabbed her hips. Already the tension was building. His hand reached down between their bodies and began to caress her.

"Gregor," she screamed right before the world shattered around her.

She heard him grunt and clasp her hips in a tight hold and knew he had followed her. She held herself up by her arms on either side of him as her breathing went back to normal.

He reached up and parted her hair that had fallen around them like a curtain. "You were made for loving," he said before he kissed her chin. "But only by me."

* * *

He was through waiting. He, Alisdair MacNeil, wasn't a patient man. Regardless of what The Shadow said, he would move his men. His spies had seen how vulnerable Conall's castle was, and if he timed it right, he could do away with Gregor slowly and painfully.

Then, he could kill Fiona and not have to worry about the prophecy.

"Go," he ordered four of his men. They would be the

lookouts, and if they saw a chance to attack, then they would send word.

This would be over soon. It was getting too close to the time of the prophecy to leave matters into the hands of a man who didn't have a name.

If he was a man at all.

* * *

Aimery walked into the throne room to find it void of anyone. It explained why he hadn't been able to contact his king or queen, but it didn't explain where they were.

His instincts told him to run, but his oath to his king and queen halted any thoughts of fleeing. They were in danger and he would risk his new bow made of enchanted oak that the king's brother had a hand in this. They had all been fools if they thought he wouldn't venture back into the Land of the Fae.

"Fools we were, then," he mumbled and continued to search the room for any clues.

When he had been over the throne room as well as the three rooms behind it four times, he began to walk from the room, intending to check the rest of the castle, when a voice stopped him.

"I always hated the colors in here."

Slowly, Aimery turned around and faced his sovereign's throne. Standing between the two solid silver chairs was a hooded figure. "Well, that explains my king's absence."

The figure took a quick step toward Aimery. "The throne should have been mine," he roared.

"But you couldn't wait for it, so you killed your own father. Tell me, what is your real name?"

An eerie laugh filled the room. "Wouldn't you like to know? I bet my brother or his wife could tell you."

And with a wave of his hand Aimery looked up and saw two figures being lowered from the ceiling. They were tied with their hands above them.

Aimery rushed toward them but found himself being thrown backwards as he landed with a thud on the white marble. He raised his eyes to the cloaked figure.

"I would have thought you would know I wouldn't let you near them. I have been told how intelligent you are," he said to Aimery. "Obviously, I was misinformed."

Aimery got to his feet. "How long do you plan on keeping them thus?" he asked and pointed to his king and queen.

"As long as it takes to take over the world," he cackled. "Speak, Theron."

The king turned to Aimery. "Do not worry about us. You must save the others."

"I would expect such words from you."

Theron turned to the cloaked figure. "Show yourself, Lugus. Why are you hiding behind a cloak?"

Aimery watched as Lugus jerked open his arms and the cloak fell away. Dark blonde hair and the blue eyes of the Fae met his gaze.

"Satisfied?" Lugus asked his brother. He lowered them until they hung inches off the floor.

Aimery stood still as he watched Lugus walk toward his queen. When Theron tried to speak, Lugus held up a hand, taking away his king's voice. But Lugus, it seemed, had forgotten about him for the moment as he stared at the Faerie queen.

"Oh, Rufina. You were supposed to have been my bride. 'Tis a pity really, but in the end I found someone much more deserving than you to rule the world by my side."

Aimery had seen enough when Lugus touched his queen's face. He charged Lugus, but was brought up short and jerked into the air.

"You didn't think I had forgotten you, did you?" Lugus asked. "I have big plans for you." He tapped his chin as Aimery continued to hang in the air. "Now, where should I put you?"

Aimery tried to break free of his hold, but Lugus' power was too strong. With his last effort, he concentrated all his magic together and propelled it toward Lugus.

It worked to break Lugus' hold and Aimery came crashing to the floor.

"Run!" Rufina told him.

Aimery got to his feet and ran to the door. He placed his hand on the door to open it when he was jerked backward until he was held in the air in front of Lugus.

"You didn't think I would let the Noble One go free, did you?"

Aimery looked to his king and queen as the realization sank in. He was the Noble One, and without him, Lugus would take over the world.

\* \* \*

Gregor woke to the most delicious feeling in the world. Fiona was in his arms, her head on his chest, fast asleep. He was content and happy for the first time in his life.

She stirred and tilted her head back to look at him. "Did you sleep well?"

"Better than ever." Which wasn't a lie. The only times he seemed to actually sleep was when she was in his arms. "And you?"

"Wonderfully."

Her smile lit his day even though the sun had yet to rise. "How can you make a man feel invincible?"

She laughed and ran her finger across his chest. "I didn't know I had that power."

"Aye, woman, I feel as though I could slay a dragon with my bare hands just knowing that I could return to you."

She sighed and her warm breath on his skin sent chills down his body. "That would be rather difficult since there aren't dragons in Scotland."

"How can you say that? It wasn't too long ago that you didn't know that the Fae existed. Who knows what else is hidden from us."

She sat up and it was all he could do to keep his eyes on her face and not her plump, full breasts. He gave up and reached up to cup a breast. He ran his thumb across a nipple and saw it harden. He laughed when she swatted his hand away and playfully punched him on the leg.

"What's the matter?" he asked her. "You don't like my touch?"

"I like it so much that I can't think when you are touching me, and I wish to talk."

He sat up, leaned against the wall, and pulled her with him. He ignored the pain in his ribs. The last thing he wanted was for her to know he was still in pain, because she'd immediately get off the bed.

"Then talk, but make it quick. I have a need to be inside of you again," he said and ran his hand through her dark locks.

She moaned and snuggled against his chest. "Then I will be sure to make it quick."

"I hope so."

"Now, tell me about your dragons."

He shrugged. "I'm not sure why I said that. I had a dream about them last night. They were beautiful."

"What did they look like?" she asked and tilted her head to look at him.

"They were all different colors. Some were red, some black, some green, and some white. Every color you could imagine."

"Where they good?"

He ran his hand down her bare shoulder. "Some were good, some evil. Just like men."

"What happened in your dream?"

"The sky was filled with dragons while Fae, Druids, and men battled on the ground."

She rose up and touched his face. "I believe that your dream was giving you a glimpse of what was to come."

He kissed her and smiled. "It was just a dream. It meant nothing."

She lifted a dainty shoulder. "If you say so."

"Now, let's stop talking."

"What did you have in mind?" she asked, her voice lowered a pitch.

"This," he said and slid his hand down her body until he touched the juncture of her thighs. He sighed when his fingers felt her wetness.

"I want you," she said and sucked on the lobe of his ear.

"I was never one to turn a lady down." He came over her and ignored the pull in his ribs.

He wanted to love her slowly this time, and he would, despite any pain. He kissed her deeply and almost lost himself in the kiss. Before she locked her arms around him, he moved down and kissed her breasts. His mouth feasted on her ripe breasts until she pushed against him with her hips.

His mouth trailed kisses down her stomach to her thighs where he teased her with his tongue. He would get close to her womanhood, but would never touch it.

Her breathing was ragged and she held onto his arms with a death grip, moving beneath him. Until his tongue flicked across her woman's lips and she went rigid.

Fiona gloried in the pleasure Gregor gave her. She hadn't thought his mouth could make her feel any better, until he kissed her in her woman's parts.

Pleasure pure and exquisite ran through her as Gregor brought her closer and closer to her fulfillment. It hit her suddenly and he held her hips as she jerked with each spasm that jolted her.

When the climax passed, she looked up to find him leaning over her. She smiled and took hold of his cock. "Shall I return the favor?"

"Not today. Right now, I want to feel you around me."

She guided him to her and sighed as he filled her until he touched her womb. When he began to move she was surprised to find the tension building once again.

"Come with me," he urged as his pace quickened.

She gave in as the world shattered around her once more. She saw Gregor throw back his head and roar as he, too, climaxed. He fell on top of her and she wrapped her arms around him. She had been a fool to avoid him. Peace was once again in her life.

*He's your mate.*

Aye, he was her mate. She would admit that now. But only that.

It was his moan as he moved off her that got her attention. "You are in pain."

"Only a little," he said and tried to sit up. "They're just sore."

"At any rate, 'tis time to take the stitches out," she said and rose from the bed to dress.

"Now?"

"Tis as good a time as any."

She laughed when she heard his groan. "I would rather have some food."

"After I tend to you."

She got the scissors and began to remove the stitches. When the last stitch had been removed she sat back and looked at the wound. She let out a breath she hadn't known she held.

"Is it that bad?"

His question startled her. "It looks better than I thought it would. I was worried that I would mar that handsome face of yours," she teased.

"It doesn't pain you to look at me?"

His insecurity pained her. "Gregor," she said and turned his face to look at her. "You are the most handsome man I have ever seen. This scar only adds to your handsomeness, not distract from it. It shows the world what a great warrior you are."

"I don't care about what the world thinks of me, woman," he said, his black eyes showing his anxiety. "I care what you think when you look at me."

"Then you have nothing to worry about, because all I see is a man who could conquer the world."

His eyes held hers for a moment before he looked away and chuckled. "Do you always know what to say?"

"Nay," she answered and leaned over to kiss his cheek near the wound. "I say what my heart tells me." She bounded off the bed before he could grab her. "'Tis time to eat."

"Good. I'm famished," he said and rose from the bed.

"Careful," she warned when he began to pull on his trews.

"Who undressed me?"

She couldn't meet his gaze as she searched the cottage for food. "Glenna and I did."

"Glenna?" he asked, his voice holding a note of hysteria.

She couldn't hold the laugh in. "'Tis all right. I had no wish for her to see you, so I covered you with a blanket before your trews came off."

"'Tis a good thing, too. I've no wish for Conall to know his wife saw me naked. He might begin to wonder why she started lusting after me."

Her laughter filled the cottage. "Your conceit knows no bounds."

His smile brightened her day. He had smiled more in the past day than he had the entire time she had known him. She also kept a smile on her face until she realized there wasn't any food in the cottage except the soup.

She turned to the hearth and stirred the pot of soup. "All there is to eat the soup."

Strong arms came around her. "It isn't as bad as you believe."

"I've tasted it, Gregor. I know how bad it is."

"Not to me," he said and nuzzled her neck.

She looked over her shoulder at him, intending to tell him he was lying again, when a knock sounded on the door.

## 30

Fiona and Gregor turned as one to the door as it opened and in came Frang, Moira, and Dartayous. Fiona jumped out of Gregor's arms.

"I apologize for the intrusion," Frang said he walked forward and took Fiona's hands. "We came to speak with you about what happened."

"You mean Gregor's accident," she said. "You want to know what I heard."

"Heard?" Gregor asked.

"Please, sit," Fiona directed them. When Gregor continued to stare at her, she led him to the head of the table. "Sit," she said and pushed him down.

She took the seat between Gregor and Dartayous. Across from her sat Frang and Moira. "How did you find out?"

"Glenna," Moira said.

Fiona nodded. "There isn't much to tell. I went to stand on the cliff overlooking the castle when I first heard the voice in my head. I knew it was the Evil One."

"Because this wasn't the first time he had spoken to you," Dartayous stated.

"What?" Gregor asked. The anger in his voice was evident.

She put her hand on his arm to calm him. "He confronted me in the caves after I had seen you and..." She couldn't finish. It still pained her to know that he wanted Moira as well.

"I followed her," Dartayous continued. "He tried to kill her, but he was stopped."

"By you," Gregor said.

His clenched hands and angry black eyes warned Fiona that he was about to explode. "It doesn't matter."

Gregor looked down at the table. She knew they had much more to discuss once their visitors departed.

"Go on," Frang said.

Fiona licked her lips. "The voice in my head told me that he would kill Gregor. I ran down to the castle, but didn't reach him in time before the accident."

She watched as Frang rose from the table and began to pace. "Your words trouble me," he said. "There is much going on that troubles me. The fact that Aimery cannot be found is the most troubling of all."

Fiona gasped at his words. "What?"

"Aye, 'tis true."

"We aren't getting answers, but more questions," Dartayous said.

Fiona's instincts told her they hadn't seen the last of the Evil One or MacNeil. "Then what do we do next?"

"Wait," Frang said. "I want someone with you at all

times," he told her. "Gregor, you should be able to handle that task willingly. How is the healing coming?"

"Slowly, but surly," Gregor answered. "I will guard Fiona with my life."

Frang nodded. "As I knew you would. We will leave you, then. If you need anything, you know where to come."

Fiona saw them to the door then turned to Gregor. "Why are you upset because Dartayous saved me?"

He slammed his hands on the table and came to his feet. "Because it should have been me."

"You were occupied," she said as anger enveloped her. "As I recall, Moira was in your arms."

"I was comforting her."

"Why you? Why not Dartayous? After all, he is her guard," she argued.

He walked to her. "I don't know where Dartayous was. I came out on the battlements and found Moira there."

"Isn't it enough that she abandoned me? Does she have to take you, too?"

Silence reigned and she slowly raised her eyes to Gregor's. She had said too much. "I was under the impression you didn't want me," he said softly.

"I was wrong."

He pulled her into his arms. "That's all I needed to hear."

\* \* \*

The meeting with Fiona and Gregor troubled Moira. Once they returned to the stone circle, she went for a walk. She knew better than to think she was alone. If she looked behind her, she'd find Dartayous.

And it didn't bother her that Dartayous was there now that she knew the Evil One had attempted to kill Fiona. First Glenna and now Fiona. Would she be next?

"Moira?"

She turned toward the voice to see William walking toward her. Of all the days she wanted to walk alone William had found her. "Hello," she called and continued walking.

It wasn't that she didn't like William. He was very sweet, but somewhat of a pest. He plagued her steps like an unwanted gnat and was forever wishing to speak with her. She had been relieved when he had gone on a small pilgrimage to other stone circles. It was the truth that she hadn't expected him to return so soon. She hastily chastised herself for feeling that way toward another Druid.

"I want to show you something," he said.

Fiona looked at the older Druid. For some time now she had known he wanted to be more than friends, but she didn't have the heart to tell him nay. He was kind, even if he was annoying at times.

His dark blonde hair, graying at the temples just a wee bit, was left long. He was what others would call handsome, and she did find his face nice to look at. Just for a moment he seemed other than a simple Druid, but she shook away her thoughts.

"I really don't have time today," she told him.

He took her hand and pressed it to his heart. "Please."

How did one say no to that? "All right, but just for a moment."

His eyes, normally a hazel, seemed bluer today. Almost the same shade as Aimery's. How strange that was, she thought.

"Come then," William said and pulled her down a path through the forest.

Moira stated to look back to see if Dartayous followed, but knew that he did. He would always be near, at least until the prophecy was over. Then, she would lose him for good.

"'Tis just over here," William said.

She looked around. "I don't see anything."

"I know," she heard right before she lost her sight.

Dartayous knew something was wrong. Moira simply didn't vanish. That was for the Fae to do, and she most certainly wasn't a Fae.

"Where the hell is she?" he growled as he searched the forest in vain.

It wasn't until he passed the same tree three times that he knew he was going in circles. He was a child of the forest and could track anything. There was only one reason he could now fail.

"Fae magic."

Never before had he failed, and the one time that he did was the most vital. The Evil One had Moira. There was no doubt about that.

Which explained why he could no longer *feel* her.

* * *

The door opened to the cottage and admitted Conall, Gregor was glad for the company. He had become lonely after Fiona had gone to the castle for food.

"How are your men?" he asked after they clasped forearms and had taken a seat at the table.

"Doing well, thanks to Moira. Thought you could use some ale."

Gregor took the bottle and poured them each a cup. "Thank you. It was much needed."

"I hear that things between you and Fiona have gotten better. Are you willing to tell me now what is between you?"

For a moment Gregor stared at the table. "I guess there's no use hiding it. I want her. Have wanted her from the moment I saw her in the MacDougal's bailey."

"What stopped you?" Conall asked. "I have seen you around women, my friend. You don't have a problem getting any one of them into your bed."

Gregor laughed. "Fiona isn't just any woman. For the first time since—" He stopped.

Fiona was the only one who knew about Anne.

"Since?" Conall prompted.

"Since I left my clan, she's made me want things I hadn't dreamed of thinking about."

He looked up and saw Conall grin. "Ah, I know that feeling. Was the same with Glenna. And now?"

Gregor shrugged. "I'm not sure. There is so much going on at the moment we haven't really had time to talk."

"So you care for her. That's good. But, do you love her? Are you willing to fight for her?"

Gregor looked into Conall's silver eyes. "I would fight for her."

"But do you love her?"

He swallowed. Love? Is that what made his heart beat faster when Fiona was near and made him feel as though his heart was being ripped out when he thought he would never have her.

"I have never loved a woman as you speak of."

"Enough of this," Conall said and slammed his cup on the table. "You look fit enough for me. Want to get out of this cottage and use your sword again?"

Gregor looked around. He liked having Fiona wait on him and see to his needs, but he was much better. Besides, with the threats to her life he needed to use his sword again.

He rose and reached for his sword by the door. "After you," he told Conall.

\* \* \*

Fiona walked beside Glenna when the unmistakable sounds of sword fighting reached their ears. They took off at a run toward the cottage she and Gregor had been staying in.

When the cottage came into view and she spotted Gregor and Conall practicing she couldn't believe her eyes. It was too soon for Gregor to be doing this kind of exercise. She and Glenna stayed out of sight, but close enough so they could see what was going on.

"He's hurting," she said when she saw Gregor wince.

"Conall is going easy on him. This will do Gregor good."

"Not when he winces every time he lifts his arm," Fiona said. She couldn't stand to see him in pain. "And what if he opens the wound on his head? I've no desire to stitch him again."

"He's a warrior," Glenna said, but Fiona wasn't listening.

She walked in between the men and faced Gregor. "What are you doing? You aren't ready for this."

Gregor cocked his head to the side and gave her a heart-stopping grin. "It doesn't hurt."

"Really? Then why do you grimace when you raise your arm?" she asked.

He stepped toward her and leaned close. "I need this. I'm a warrior. I've sat abed much too long as it is."

She hated it when he was right. Beneath the sun and fresh air he had come alive again. Color had come into his skin and the wind blowing through his hair made him look almost good enough to eat.

With a nod, she turned to go into the cottage when his hand snaked out and caught her. She turned toward him and found a wicked gleam in his eyes.

"It touches me that you care so much," he said.

"'Tis not caring, but not wanting to mend more damage," she retorted.

"Saucy wench," he said and slapped her on the behind with the flat of his blade.

Before she could respond to him Glenna and Conall's laughter reached her. She was a bit embarrassed that they had seen the playfulness between her and Gregor, but then again she had admitted he was her mate. The fact that admission was only to herself didn't matter one whit.

"There's no need to watch them train," Glenna said. "Why don't we go for a swim?"

"Now that sounds wonderful," Fiona said. But the frown on Gregor's face stopped her. "What is it?"

"If you wish to swim, I will accompany you."

"I will be fine. Don't forget that I can control the water. I won't drown." That seemed to alleviate his fears somewhat and she hurried off before he found something else to argue about. Before she and Glenna reached the loch someone called for Glenna.

"Don't worry," Fiona told her. "I can call out to Gregor if need be."

And in truth she looked forward to a little time alone. It had been awhile since she had taken a swim. She hurried to the water and quickly shed everything but her shift.

She walked into the water and sighed as it swirled around her. Not until the water reached her neck did she stop. She ducked under to wet her hair and began to swim.

Too bad Gregor wasn't here, she thought.

Gregor couldn't concentrate. All he could think of was Fiona in the water. Regardless of what she said, he couldn't help but worry.

"What is it?" Conall asked after he narrowly sliced open Gregor's chest.

"I need to check on Fiona."

"'Tis more than that, isn't it?"

He sighed and rubbed his neck. "My sister drowned."

"That's all I need to know," Conall said. "I understand your fear. Go to Fiona, then."

Gregor knew Conall could have pulled the entire story out of him, but he hadn't. "'Tis good to have you for a friend."

Conall laughed and pushed him toward the loch. "Have fun. I will keep everyone away so you two can have some privacy."

The smile died on Gregor's face as soon as he turned away from Conall. He wouldn't be satisfied until he saw Fiona with his own eyes. He topped the hill and saw her swimming gracefully through the water.

At one time he had loved the water that much, he mused as he leaned on his sword. Since he wanted to give her some time alone before he made his presence known, he took a seat beside a boulder so he would have something to lean against and watched her.

She still wore her shift. Too bad about that, he thought. He briefly thought about joining her in the water, but knew he would embarrass himself. There would probably never come a day when he could get into water over his thighs again.

Movement in the trees behind Fiona caught his eye. He rose and tried to holler down to her when he saw a cloaked man but found himself unable to speak all of a sudden.

*Fiona!*

\* \* \*

Fiona surfaced and wiped the water from her eyes. She was thoroughly enjoying her swim and couldn't wait for Gregor to join her. She spotted him jumping up and down near the loch, but she couldn't make out what he wanted. Then, she felt the coldness of evil and knew she was about to die.

There wasn't time to tell Gregor she loved him. She opened her mouth to shout it to him when pain exploded in her head and the world went black.

## 31

"Nay," Gregor screamed as his voice suddenly returned. He ran down the hill unmindful of the rocks or the fact that he could barely breathe from the pain in his ribs.

He had to save Fiona.

While he ran, he watched her float beneath the surface. He could either follow the Evil One into the forest, or save Fiona. The Evil One would just have to wait because Fiona needed him.

His feet hit the water and he didn't stop. Not even when the fear threatened to take hold. Nothing mattered but Fiona. The panic set in as it always did when the water reached his thighs. He tried to keep going, but his feet wouldn't move.

"Not now," he cried as the terror took hold.

He pictured the kelp wrapping around Fiona as it had Anne and he snapped. He roared up at the sky and dove into the water. As soon as the water hit his face he lost control. He began to thrash around in the water trying to reach the surface. His lungs burned for breath, and he knew this time he would die.

And fail once again to save someone that he loved.

Aye, he loved her.

*Then don't give up.*

He broke through the surface of the water and took a deep breath. His ribs ached painfully, but it didn't matter. He took a deep breath and went under again. This time to save Fiona.

Her white shift caught his eye. She wasn't far from him, and he quickly reached her and brought her to the surface. As soon as his head broke the water he began to holler for Conall.

Gregor carried her to the water's edge and laid her down on the sand. He leaned over her and saw that she wasn't breathing.

"Don't do this to me, Fiona. You promised that everything would be all right."

Conall and some of his men arrived and knelt beside her. Conall put his hand on Fiona's chest and sighed. "She's gone, Gregor."

"Nay," Gregor roared. "I won't let her die. She can't die on me," he said and pushed on her chest. "Breathe. Breathe, damn you."

He continued to push on her chest, unmindful that tears coursed down his face. He had finally found someone he could love, someone that made the pain disappear, and he had lost her.

Conall reached for his hands, but Gregor shoved him away. "I can't give up," he said and laid his head on her chest. "Fiona," he said and covered her mouth with his.

"Come back to me," he whispered and blew his breath into her mouth.

He leaned up when she began to cough. Gently, he sat her up and held her while she vomited the water she had swallowed. He smiled through his tears, not caring that Conall and his men saw.

"Fiona," he said and turned her face to his.

She smiled weakly. "Hello."

He tried to get to his feet and carry her to the castle, but his ribs reminded him that he wasn't healed.

"Here," Conall said. "I will take her."

Gregor climbed to his feet, keeping his arms around his ribs, and ran after Conall and his men. When they reached the bailey, Glenna waited for them.

"I already have a chamber ready," she said.

Gregor followed them into the chamber. He still couldn't believe she was alive, and he wanted to stay by her side to make sure. He helped Glenna get Fiona out of her wet shift.

"Where is Moira?" Conall asked.

Glenna looked up from tending to Fiona. "I don't know."

"What?" Gregor asked.

"I've been calling to her," Glenna said and covered Fiona with a blanket. "Neither she nor Dartayous has come."

"Something is awry."

"Exactly," Conall said.

\* \* \*

"'Tis time," MacNeil rallied his men. "We have become fat and lazy. The men that ride with me are lean and hungry from battle. Are you those men?" he shouted.

A resounding 'aye' rent the air.

"Then we attack. Remember," he reminded them. "Gregor is mine."

"What of The Shadow?" someone hollered.

"He has abandoned us. We can do this on our own. We are warriors!"

* * *

"My laird," a man said as he came into Fiona's chamber.

Gregor looked up to find the man shifting from one foot to the other. Gregor turned to Conall and watched him walk to the man.

After some hurried words, Conall turned to him. "I hope you're healed."

"Why?" Gregor asked as he rose to his feet.

"MacNeil has returned. He wants you."

"Then let it begin."

"Wait," Glenna stopped them. "You cannot go. The Fae are missing and I don't know where Moira and Dartayous are."

"Which is exactly why we must go," Conall told her.

"It could be a trap."

Gregor leaned down and placed a kiss on Fiona's forehead. "Then might I suggest that you keep a look out of the window so you can aid us if needed?"

Glenna nodded and ran into Conall's arms. "Be careful."

"I will, though I don't think 'tis going to matter. MacNeil has come for Gregor, not me."

"You cannot kill him," she warned Gregor.

"The hell I can't," Gregor said. "He's done enough trouble."

"If you kill him, then the prophecy will never come to pass."

"You ask the impossible," he said and walked out of the chamber.

* * *

Moira tried not to panic. She knew Fae magic had been used on her, but that didn't stop the terror at not being able to see. And where was Dartayous? He was supposed to guard her. Had he been a part of this?

Surely not, she thought. That would be too great of a betrayal.

"There's really no need to be afraid."

She stopped struggling against her bonds and stilled. "Who are you?"

He laughed close to her ear. "You know me as the Druid William, also as the cloaked figure that attempted to kill Glenna and Ailsa."

A shocked breath burst from her lips, dread turning her blood cold. It couldn't be true.

"But," he continued. "You will come to know me as Fiona's killer and master of Scotland."

She listened as he moved to her other side. When he leaned down next to her, she instinctively jerked away.

"However, you will only remember me as your husband."

She bowed her head and tried to concentrate on his words, but it was nearly impossible as her stomach roiled viciously.

"Oh, aye, Moira, I've coveted you," he said, his voice near her ear. "I've longed to take you, and I've had plenty of chances."

His hot breath on her neck made her ill to her stomach. Somehow, she found her voice. "What did you do with Dartayous?"

William laughed, the sound grating and altogether evil. "You can forget him. If he isn't already dead, he soon will be. As a Druid warrior never fails, he will take his own life to make amends for his failure."

"But he didn't fail. You used magic."

His hand trailed down her jaw. "So smart. 'Tis why I want you by my side as I rule Scotland and the rest of the humans."

"Never."

"Oh, you'll change your mind. Never fear," he said and kissed her cheek.

"That will be hard to do since the prophecy will never come to pass without me and my sisters performing the ceremony."

Silence met her words. "Another Druid can take your place."

"Nay. 'Tis in the prophecy. If you had read it you would know."

A hiss and a curse reached her ears before more silence.

\* \* \*

Fiona slowly opened her eyes. "Gregor?"

"Fiona," Glenna said and leaned over her. "Thank God. I've been so worried."

"Where is Gregor?" she asked as she scanned the room and spotted Frang. "What's happened?"

Glenna and Frang exchanged a look. "A lot, actually," Frang finally answered.

Fiona could tell by their tone that whatever it was wasn't good. She sat up and grabbed her chest. It burned like fire had been poured down her throat. Then she remembered what had happened. "Is Gregor all right?"

"He's fine," Glenna said. "He saved you from drowning."

"Where is he now?"

"Fighting MacNeil."

That wasn't what she had expected to hear. "We must help them," she told Glenna.

"You are in no condition to get out of that bed," Frang advised.

"I cannot lose him," Fiona argued.

"Why?" Frang asked. "Give me one good reason to allow you to get out of that bed and leave the castle."

"I love him."

He smiled. "About time," he said. "Glenna, help your sister get dressed so that the two of you can stop Gregor from killing MacNeil."

Fiona licked her lips and wanted to laugh. She'd confessed aloud that she loved Gregor. Her heart felt as though it could fly. She was free, free from the bonds that had chained her for years.

And she must tell Gregor. She wouldn't allow that chance to pass her by once again.

\* \* \*

Gregor flexed his hand and tried to take a deep breath. It was still painful, and he ended up coughing.

"You aren't ready for this," Conall said next to him.

"It doesn't matter. The battle is ready for me."

"I have your back," Conall said as they walked out of the gates.

Gregor spotted MacNeil immediately. "Are you ready to die?"

MacNeil laughed loudly. "I came for your head, Gregor MacLachlan."

"MacLachlan," Conall said.

Gregor gnashed his teeth. "Later. I will tell you everything."

"I will hold you to it, my friend," Conall warned. "If I had known you were a MacLachlan I would have pressed you more to learn what happened."

Gregor snorted and turned to his adversary. "Enough talk, MacNeil," he shouted. "Draw your sword."

MacNeil did as requested and kicked his horse into a run. Gregor looked around and spotted the boulder next to Conall. He shoved Conall out of the way and quickly jumped on the boulder just as MacNeil reached him.

With a roar he leapt off the boulder and grabbed

MacNeil as they fell over the horse. They both landed with a thud and rolled to their feet, swords drawn.

Gregor laughed. "Your age is showing, old man. I hope there is more to this fight than that."

MacNeil stepped and sliced his sword toward Gregor's head. Gregor easily blocked it, and slashed at MacNeil's chest. MacNeil jerked back and saw the thin line of blood.

"You'll pay for that," he said and charged again.

\* \* \*

Moira heard the sounds of swords clashing the same time as William.

"I will kill him myself," William hissed.

"Who?" she asked.

He didn't answer her and she sensed that he had walked away. She tried again to loosen her bonds, but the rope was unlike any she had ever encountered.

Where was Dartayous?

Her fear for her sisters and the Druids had nearly swallowed her. She had always been strong, but she was finding it hard to stay that way when the Evil One had caught her. How could they have been so blind as to not see that it was William? It all made sense now.

William had left shortly before Glenna arrived for his pilgrimage, and he hadn't returned until just now.

"Dartayous," she whispered. "Please hear me. I need you."

*Please don't let Fiona be dead.*

\* \* \*

Gregor stepped aside and brought his sword down and around to block MacNeil. He thrust his sword, but MacNeil jumped out of the way before more blood could be drawn.

Without hesitating, Gregor raised his arm over his head and brought his sword down. MacNeil managed to block the slice that would have cut open his face. But Gregor wasn't deterred. He used the force to push MacNeil to the right. He then used his left hand to grab MacNeil's shoulder and kicked his feet out from underneath him.

Before he had a chance to plunge his sword into MacNeil, the aging laird managed to roll away and jump to his feet. Gregor grinned when he saw the anger in MacNeil's eyes, because angry men didn't think clearly.

Lugus couldn't believe his eyes. MacNeil was about to die by Gregor's hand, and that couldn't happen.

"You will pay for this, MacNeil," Lugus vowed. He could either keep Moira or save MacNeil since he couldn't move Druids like he could others.

Besides, if he was to take over Scotland, then he needed to save MacNeil.

He fisted his hands and felt the urge to kill. He had finally gotten Moira, and now he was going to release her. All because MacNeil couldn't listen to an order.

With just a thought, he released Moira.

Gregor saw MacNeil swing an underhanded slice toward his stomach and stepped inside to trap MacNeil's sword arm. Gregor then pushed MacNeil away while slicing open the top of his right shoulder.

MacNeil grabbed hold of his bleeding arm and dropped his sword. Gregor threw down his sword and circled MacNeil.

"You don't deserve a warrior's death," he said. "After the havoc you have plagued the Highland's with, you will die without your sword."

Gregor knew that was the greatest insult he could give MacNeil. A warrior wanted to die a warrior, at any costs. He got the reaction he wanted when MacNeil bellowed and swung his fist at his head.

Fiona, with Glenna by her side, watched as Gregor stepped forward and took hold of MacNeil's arm with his left hand. He then sent his elbow into MacNeil's jaw before he back fisted him.

MacNeil staggered back, but quickly attacked Gregor again. This time, he took a swing at Gregor's jaw. Gregor put up his left arm as a block, then sent his own fist into MacNeil's jaw.

Fiona was about to use her powers, but stopped when she realized Gregor didn't need her help. He had MacNeil right where he wanted him. But MacNeil's soldiers were about to interfere.

She raised her hand and a wall of water the height of a grown tree rose out of the loch. The sound reached the soldier's ears and they backed away from Gregor and MacNeil. It was what Fiona wanted, but she would keep the water wall up in case one of them tried to help MacNeil.

"Gregor cannot kill MacNeil," Glenna said.

"I don't think anyone can stop him. Even Conall is just standing behind him," Fiona pointed out.

"Frang refused to allow Conall to kill MacNeil. For whatever reason, the prophecy must come to pass. MacNeil must stay alive until then."

Fiona looked from her sister to Gregor. "I won't let him kill MacNeil," she promised. Then her gaze found Dartayous as he ran toward Gregor and Conall. "If he's there, then where is Moira?"

Glenna's brown eyes held much anxiety as she turned to her. "He would never leave Moira."

"So that leaves only one conclusion. She's gone."

"I cannot accept that," Glenna said.

* * *

Moira blinked and stared around at the trees. She hastily looked around but found no trace of William, or The Shadow, or whatever his real name was.

She didn't question her returned sight, nor did she sit and wait for him to return.

She jumped to her feet and raced toward the castle. Her feet flew even faster when she heard the sound of battle. With her stomach in her throat, she burst through the forest and spotted the fighting. Her eyes scanned the crowd to see Gregor, Conall, and Dartayous fighting. Her gaze then swung to the castle and she spotted Glenna and Fiona.

Relief filled her. Fiona wasn't dead. Tears gathered in her eyes. If it took another three lifetimes she would give Fiona the time she needed to heal.

\* \* \*

While Gregor had MacNeil, he sent another fierce back fist into his nose. Blood spurted everywhere as bone crushed beneath his fist.

MacNeil doubled over and screamed in pain. Gregor took a step toward him and slammed a fist into his shoulder before taking hold of his neck to keep him still while he jerked his knee into his face. MacNeil fell to the ground, holding his face.

Gregor's rage simmered to a barely controllable level. "'Tis time to die," he said and took hold of MacNeil's neck to break it.

In the next instant, he was flat on his back, unable to move. He opened his eyes through the force and spotted the Evil One grab MacNeil. And then, as fast as he had come, he was gone. Gregor sat up to find only Conall and his men around him as MacNeil's soldiers rode away.

Then, he spotted Dartayous. "Where is Moira?" he asked as he gained his feet.

Dartayous looked down at the ground. "I have failed. The Evil One took her. He used Fae magic to hide her from me."

"What?" Conall and Gregor asked in unison.

Frang spoke as he walked up, "You didn't fail, Dartayous. The Evil One has freed Moira. For the time being. He cannot transport a Druid because of the powers that Druids hold."

They all turned to see Moira, Glenna and Fiona running towards them. Gregor had never been happier to see Fiona. He wrapped his arms around her and swung her around.

"I thought I had lost you," he said as he sat her on her feet.

Fiona smiled through her tears. "Never. I realized when I was hit over the head that I hadn't told you something."

"It doesn't matter. You are alive. That's what I care about."

"We are mates," she said and put her finger on his lips. "I've known from almost the beginning, but I tried to deny it. No longer. I want the world to know that we are bound. From now to eternity. I love you, Gregor."

"I will love you always."

She forgot about everything and everyone as his lips claimed her in a kiss that only a mate could give. It touched her very soul and gave her the peace she'd been seeking. All was right with the world now.

The sounds of cheering broke into their world. She and Gregor broke apart and were engulfed in hugs from Conall and Glenna.

Fiona turned and spotted Moira. It was time to put the past behind her. She closed the distance between them. "I'm sorry. I should never have shut you out of my life."

Moira shrugged and smiled. "You were hurt. I understand. I should never have left you that night, nor should I have kept away all these years."

"It doesn't matter now," Fiona told her. "We are together. At last. Mother and Da would be proud," she said and pulled Glenna to her.

They wrapped their arms around each other. Three

sisters, blessed by the Fae and rulers of a prophecy, had finally been brought together.

Happiness engulfed Fiona and her gaze met Gregor's. With his love, she could do anything, and with her sisters beside her she felt complete.

"For eternity," Gregor mouthed to her.

"For eternity," she vowed.

## 32

The merrymaking continued through the night. Fiona and Gregor stayed by each other, never venturing far.

"What's next?" Conall asked them.

Gregor had confided everything to him after the battle, and it had only deepened their friendship. "I must see to my father."

"The prophecy is still a little ways off. There is time," Fiona said.

Conall nodded. "Will you take over as laird?"

"If the clan will have me."

Fiona smiled brightly. "They will have him. They need him."

The arrival of Frang dampened everyone's spirits. Fiona and the rest followed Frang into the solar. "What has happened?" she asked.

Frang sighed deeply and seemed to age before her eyes. "The Evil One is not only the rogue Druid that tried to kill

Glenna and Ailsa, but also a Fae. He was known to us as William. He has taken Aimery prisoner."

"What does that mean for the prophecy?" Gregor asked.

"It means," Frang said as he looked to Moira. "You must find the key that will allow you to enter the world of the Fae and free Aimery."

Moira's brow furrowed in confusion. "Why me?"

"Glenna and Fiona each had a journey to make to arrive here, and so must you. If William is here when the prophecy takes place, then he will assume control."

"Control of what?" Glenna asked.

"Of all of Scotland and the world. He must not succeed."

They all turned to Moira. "Then I shall depart immediately."

"With Dartayous," Frang said.

Moira and Dartayous exchanged a brief look.

Fiona ran to embrace Moira. "Be careful. If you need us..."

"I know," Moira smiled and hugged Glenna. "Get to Gregor's father. He has stayed alive in hopes of his return. Don't keep him waiting any longer."

Fiona nodded and stepped into Gregor's arms once they were in the bailey. "I wish we could go with her."

"Dartayous will watch over her," Conall said as he and Glenna came to stand beside them.

They watched as Moira with Dartayous ever by her side walked into the forest and the stone circle. After gathering provisions, they would begin their journey.

"Glenna, do you know what key Frang is speaking of?" Fiona asked.

"Nay. I didn't know one needed a key to get into the world of the Fae. I thought we weren't allowed."

Gregor and Conall nodded.

"Frang said that we had a journey to make," Fiona said. "Our journey was finding our mate."

"Then that must also be a part of Moira's," Glenna agreed.

"Dartayous," they said in unison.

# EPILOGUE

Fiona rode by Gregor's side as they entered the gates of MacLachlan castle. The people rushed toward them, but it was the woman racing down the castles steps that caught Gregor's attention.

With a smile on her face, Fiona watched Gregor jump down from Morgane and twirl his mother around in a fierce hug. She slid off her mount and soon found herself brought into their embrace. She finally had her family, and a home she could call her own.

"Mother, I would like you to meet my wife," Gregor said.

Helen smiled warmly. "I knew it," she said and kissed Fiona on the cheek. "Welcome to the family. Oh, I don't think I ever properly thanked you for saving Beathan."

"Then he is alive?" Gregor asked.

"Aye, son," Helen answered. "Come and see your father."

They had no sooner entered the castle and started up the stairs than Helen shoved Gregor down a hallway. "You know what you need to do," she told him and took Fiona's arm.

Fiona entered the chamber to find Beathan sitting up in the bed. He smiled at her.

"I knew you would return," he said. "Have you come back for good?"

"Aye, laird."

He waved away her words. "There'll be none of that. You are family."

Her heart nearly burst with joy. She was about to tell him that when Beathan's mouth fell open. She followed his gaze to the door and found Gregor standing there in the MacLachlan plaid.

She raised her brow and walked to him. After she kissed him she said, "I like you in a kilt."

He smiled and went to his father. She and Helen left the men alone. There would be time to celebrate later. Years, in fact.

Thank you for reading **HIGHLAND NIGHTS**.
Want to know what happens next in the series?
Order **HIGHLAND DAWN** right now!

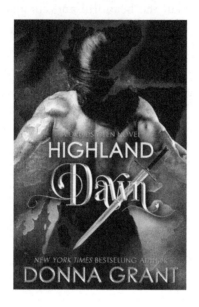

One prophecy to save the world. Two realms fighting for control. Three Druid sisters who hold the key to salvation and the hearts of the men who would love them. Join *New York Times* bestselling author Donna Grant as she transports you into the dark and dangerous world of the Druids.

**An immortal with unanswered questions...**

The immortal Dartayous, a powerful Druid Warrior, is given one mission–keep Moira alive to fulfill the prophecy. But with each passing day the burning desire he feels for her eats away at the wall surrounding his heart...

**A Druid priestess in search of a key...**

Moira Sinclair must find the key to enter the Realm of the Fae, but once she enters the sacred realm, secrets she has kept buried rise and force her to see herself for what she really is. Will the beautiful and commanding king of the Fae win her heart? Or will Dartayous finally claim her as his own?

**HIGHLAND DAWN IS NOW AVAILABLE!**

**Donna Grant**
www.DonnaGrant.com
www.MotherofDragonsBooks.com

NEVER MISS A NEW BOOK FROM
DONNA GRANT!

**Sign up for Donna's email newsletter at
www.DonnaGrant.com**

Be the first to get notified of new releases and be eligible for
special subscribers-only exclusive content and giveaways.
Sign up today!

## ABOUT THE AUTHOR

 *New York Times* and *USA Today* bestselling author Donna Grant has been praised for her "totally addictive" and "unique and sensual" stories. She's written more than one hundred novels spanning multiple genres of romance including the bestselling Dark King series that features a thrilling combination of Dragon Kings, Druids, Fae, and immortal Highlanders who are dark, dangerous, and irresistible. She lives in Texas with her dog and a cat.

**Connect with Donna online:**
www.DonnaGrant.com
www.MotherofDragonsBooks.com

facebook.com/AuthorDonnaGrant

instagram.com/dgauthor

bookbub.com/authors/donna-grant

goodreads.com/donna_grant

pinterest.com/donnagrant1